THE RESOLUTION
OF
RED TEARS

Janice,

Thanks for praying and supporting me!

Blessings,

Ayana Pozzolozzi

THE RESOLUTION
OF
RED TEARS

JAYNA PIROLOZZI

TATE PUBLISHING
AND ENTERPRISES, LLC

Published by Tate Publishing & Enterprises, LLC

127 E. Trade Center Terrace | Mustang, Oklahoma 73064 USA
1.888.361.9473 | www.tatepublishing.com

Tate Publishing is committed to excellence in the publishing industry. The company reflects the philosophy established by the founders, based on Psalm 68:11,

"The Lord gave the word and great was the company of those who published it."

Book design copyright © 2012 by Tate Publishing, LLC. All rights reserved.
Front Cover design by Jayna Pirolozzi
Front Cover edit by Rodrigo Adolfo
Back Cover design by Rodrigo Adolfo
Cover images credits Library of Congress Archives
Interior design by Ronnel Luspoc

Published in the United States of America

ISBN: 978-1-62147-324-4
1. FICTION / Cultural Heritage
2. FICTION / Christian / General
12.12.14

What would it look like and how would it sound should the United States of America follow the footsteps of Australia, Canada, and South Africa when its prime ministers stood before their parliaments and publicly offered an apology to the indigenous peoples of their land concerning past mistreatments? The Resolution of Red Tears will give us a peek that inspires hope that indeed such words spoken by our government will become a reality.

—Daphne Swilling, producer, "The Trail of Tears," the movie

The Resolution of Red Tears is an excellent book that shows the importance of The National Apology to Native Americans. God showed me that when President Obama signed this apology and looked to the east (Israel), God would bring healing to this land.

—Negiel Bigpond, Apostle and Senior Pastor of Morning Star Church of All Nations, president and co-founder of Two Rivers Native American Training Center, Founder of Native American Circle of Prayer. Named one of the most influential Christian leaders of 2006.

Acknowledgments

First, I will thank the Great Creator, His Son, Jesus, and His precious Holy Spirit, without whom I could not have written this book. Much that is written on these pages is not from me. I don't have the capacity to come up with such deep things. I did my best to listen and write. This is His burden, and I pray that it reaches those who can make the difference, make the apology.

I would also like to thank some very special people who helped me by praying and by being another pair of eyes, kind critics and editors. In no special order, they are Jim Chosa, who, in the Spirit, explained the Mt. Rushmore vision among other things in the book. Jean Steffenson and John Loren were also gracious to allow me to quote them. Senator Sam Brownback and the folks in his office, at the time of the writing, who advised me and helped me locate dialogue for the senate scene. Cheryl Bear, who has taken time from her busy schedule to read it and critique it.

Agnes, "B," and Michele, my foreign friends who read and critiqued the book as it was in process. My dear friend Peach, who spent many hours on Skype with me catching my mistakes and questioning things that didn't sound right. Terry, who also spent time on Skype and offered the same. Paula Michelson, author of the "Casa de Naomi series", who gave sound advice and much prayer, thank you dear friend. I want to thank Captain Toadlena from the Navajo Criminal Investigations Department for taking time on the phone with me to answer questions and confirm my details. I like to be accurate and he helped me do just that. Also, my writing coach, Cindy Coloma, who was a huge help in making the book just right. I did it, Cindy! I tried my best to take her advice, so don't blame her if you don't like it. But I'm pretty sure you will like it. Many thanks to my copyeditor, Nikki Jenkins, who readied me for publishing on Kindle. I would also like to thank everyone at Tate, especially Janey Hays, who chose my manuscript to publish and Hillary in editing, who made the process fun and encouraging. Also I want to mention Sterling Auto Repair in my town. They helped me so I am giving them a shout out. They are located at 11400 Hwy 49 in Jackson, CA. They are good people. Thanks.

The quotes from Oswald Chambers during the journey within this book are from *Still Higher For His Highest*, 1970, D.W. Lambert, Zondervan Publishing, Grand Rapids, MI.

Photo credits go to Manny Anecito at www.Na-haphotography.com.

INTRODUCTION

When I started writing this book in early 2009, I knew the burden for the First Nations People was in my heart. But as I continued to write and rely more on the Great Creator to lead the way, I realized it was all His. I am constantly astonished, honored, and humbled by the thought that the Great Creator desires to partner with us and work through the human vessel, if one is willing—and even sometimes when one is not willing.

This book is a message to all who read it. A message to repent, forgive, and reconcile. We try to make the world better by giving away money or standing for a cause, but do we actually let those actions change us? Usually not. It means nothing to do anything without a motive of pure love behind it. *Nothing*. Faytene Grasseschi said, "Social justice without truth is only good intention without transformation."

It is my prayer that the First Nations People would open their hearts to forgiveness. Some have, but some have not. I pray the American people not idolize those presidents of the past who may seem to have been perfect and yet did not see the First Nations People as worthy to share the land with. Pride runs rampant in America, and while certain pride is good, pride in our own opinions is a death sentence for a nation. The Great Creator founded this country and gave it to the First Nations People to care for. He gave them a revelation of Himself, and when we arrived, we were to join together in brotherhood under Him. Idealistic? Then God is idealistic.

I hope you let this word, this burden go deep into your hearts. Let it change and transform you. Let it bring you to repentance, forgiveness, and reconciliation with the Great Creator and with all whom He has made.

PROLOGUE

2003

A group of national spiritual leaders requested an audience with Kansas Senator Sam Brownback. At the time, he was the chairman of Indian Affairs. The subject on their hearts was an apology to the Native Americans on a national, public level. According to a book by John Dobson about reconciliation, the United States Government had offered apologies to African Americans and the Japanese for the atrocities done to them. No one, however, had made an apology to the First Nations People, the host people of the land. It had taken months to approve the idea and then present the written draft to the National Association of Tribal Chairmen. Some of the leaders could not understand, some would not understand, and those who did gave their blessing and authority to the draft.

The spiritual leaders bore no malice or ill will. It was not a demand, but the Great Creator had burned into their hearts a great need to forgive the "white fathers" of the American government for the atrocities that were experienced by their ancestors and even by current families. The main issues were broken covenants and defilement of the land. An apology to anyone is a spiritual issue.

What was supposed to be a fifteen-minute meeting with Senator Brownback to present the draft for the apology turned into a three-and-a half-hour meeting.

"Senator, we are here to give you something. This has to do with defilement of the land. When a land, America, is defiled with broken covenants, blood, murder, and extermination of a people group— in this case the host people of America—a curse is brought on the land. The spiritual state of America is obvious: abortion, murder, fatherlessness, greed, poverty." Jim Chosa, from the Crow Nation, stopped. He took a breath. "I could go on, but I believe you to be one who can see what America has become. It all started a little over four hundred years ago."

Senator Brownback gazed out his office window as he sat, letting the words penetrate his mind. He nodded.

"All the borders in the land are down, including spiritual borders. That means we are under attack from the enemy, spiritual and natural."

Senator Brownback looked at Jim. A light began to come on in his understanding.

"Senator, this is all about Homeland Security."

That did it for Senator Brownback. He understood now all that the last three hours had poured into him. "What do we do?"

"An apology will help not only begin the healing process spiritually but also it will help build cultural relationships between the ethnic people of the land, and it will help secure our borders."

All the other spiritual leaders nodded, pleased that Senator Brownback now understood the reality, meaning, and importance of an apology to the Native Americans.

Senator Brownback dropped to his knees. He asked the men for their prayers, and he issued words of repentance and confession. The chairmen gathered around the humbled man and asked the Great Creator to bless him. They asked for wisdom for him as he wrote the resolution to be presented to the senate and that the Great Creator would begin healing the nation of America. The apology was accepted from Senator Brownback and forgiveness held out to him. There was now a long road to a national public apology that would reach into the very heart of America.

It would require a willing president to make that apology so that forgiveness could be planted in the hearts of the rest of the First Nations People.

> "Now all things are of God, who has reconciled Himself to us through Jesus Christ, and has given us the ministry of reconciliation. That is, that God was in Christ reconciling the world to Himself, not imputing their trespasses to them, and has committed to us the word of reconciliation. Now then, we are ambassadors for Christ, as though God were pleading through us: we implore you on Christ's behalf, be reconciled to God."
>
> 2 Corinthians 5:18-20 (NKJ)

NOW ALL THINGS ARE OF
GOD, WHO HAS RECONCILED
HIMSELF TO US THROUGH JESUS
CHRIST, AND HAS GIVEN US THE
MINISTRY OF RECONCILIATION.

2 CORINTHIANS 5:18 (NKJ)

CHAPTER 1

Daniel Patterson, a man of Navajo blood, paced his room. Daniel was an undersheriff, a lieutenant in Stake Town, Arizona. Normally, being a law enforcement officer meant one was brave. Daniel was entirely so, but he was disturbed by a dream he'd just had—the same dream that kept waking him several times a week for the past two years, the dream of his wife's death in a car fire. This night had been slightly different in that he sensed an urgency as never before. He wasn't sure why.

Daniel walked into his bathroom. He flipped on the light and, leaning on the sink, looked himself in the eyes and sighed. "Great Creator, I need to get my daughter out of this town, but it is not in my nature to run. You created me to be a warrior. I have to protect my Jessica, but I am only one. I'm asking for your help."

He turned on the water and splashed his face. He heard a soft knock on his bedroom door, knowing it was Jessica. He dried his face and walked back into his bedroom to answer his door. "Jessica, why are you up?"

"I was checking on you. I heard you wake up," she explained. "Another dream?"

"Nightmare," he said. "I'm sorry I woke you." He pulled her into a hug.

"It's okay, *Shizhe'e* but I'm worried about you," she said, looking up at him.

He stroked her long black hair. She looked so much like her mother, a full-blooded Navajo. He smiled and walked her back to her room. "Don't worry about your old man," he encouraged. "I'm pretty tough, you know."

"I know, Dad. You're tough, and you're buff," she agreed, "and you're not old!" she scolded with a smile.

Daniel grinned at her and flexed his biceps. "Okay, flattery will get you everywhere. What do you want?" he asked as his daughter giggled at his display.

"Dad, why do you think I want something?"

"Nice try, sweetheart." He nodded. "Give." He gestured with his right hand.

Jessica sighed. "Well, Tommy wants me to go to the game with him and then take me for a burger afterward," she said in one quick breath.

"Who's chaperoning?"

"Dad!" she whined.

Daniel crossed his arms over his chest. "Jessica!" he mimicked back. "Tell you what. We'll talk about it at breakfast in"—he looked past her to her clock inside her bedroom; it was 1:30 a.m.—"four hours."

"Fine!" She let go a dramatic moan. "Good morning," she said, and then she kissed her dad on the cheek. She stepped into her room and closed the door with a slight wave and look of disappointment.

"Good morning," he answered through the door.

He heaved a heavy sigh. His daughter was growing up too fast. She was seventeen, and he wasn't sure he remembered how seventeen-year-old girls acted or, more importantly, what they needed. He felt that perhaps he was being overprotective since her mom had died. He had good reason to be. He believed his wife's death had been no accident. Trouble was, he couldn't prove it.

He got back into his bed and looked at a picture of his late wife on the far nightstand. "I'm trying, dear, but you know how it goes. Us men will never understand you women." He shrugged. He reached over, turned his lamp off, and closed his eyes, praying he'd be able to sleep the rest of the night. "Great Creator, I need your peace." He was silent for a moment. "Thanks."

It was 5:30 a.m. as Daniel prepared breakfast for himself and his daughter. He was in his uniform. It was May; summer was approaching, and the short-sleeved Khaki shirt was little help against the heat. The rest of the uniform consisted of forest green cargo pants and black Tek boots. His gun belt with his choice of weapon, a .45 caliber automatic, hung over his chair.

Jessica staggered into the kitchen, sleepily. "Hmm. Smells good, Dad."

Daniel turned to her, looking at her with amusement. "Are you awake?"

"My nose is." She yawned. "When can we have breakfast at a normal hour?"

Daniel turned back to the pan on the stove. "Soon, Jess," he promised.

The comment got her attention. She looked at him with a little more perk. "What do you mean by that?"

Daniel dished out some eggs and a bowl of fruit and placed it in front of his daughter. "I mean, we're getting out while the gettin's good. Maybe we'll go to the rez," he answered.

Jessica looked hard at him. "Give!" she demanded politely while she waited for her dad to get his breakfast together. He sat down with a smile and took her hand. They both bowed their heads to pray and then began to eat. "Come on, Dad, tell me."

Daniel stabbed some fruit and sat back, looking at her. "Jessica, this town has changed from when I was growing up," he began. "I can't do my job the way it was meant to be done because of the McKinleys." He put the fruit into his mouth and added, "And, with your mom gone—" He looked at Jessica for her response to the mention of her mother. He thought he saw a brief flash of sadness in her eyes. "We just need to leave," he finished, quietly. His gaze fell to his plate, focusing his attention there. Daniel knew she missed her mom and his work schedule was rough on her. Ultimately, moving away from the town would be the best course of action for both of them.

"So I guess what I want doesn't matter?" she asked. She cast her eyes to her plate.

Daniel chewed some toast, considering what she meant. "What you want does matter to me, but I want you to be safe." Daniel stopped abruptly.

"Safe from what? From Tommy?" she questioned. Tommy's dad was Tom McKinley Sr., Daniel's former high school classmate, a deputy sheriff in town, and an unashamed white supremacist. Tom Sr.'s brother, Bill McKinley, was the sheriff, and Daniel knew the two of them were building a small militia. "What about Tommy?" she reiterated.

"Jessica, you can go, okay?" He offered a weak smile, disliking the tension in the room. They had discussed her friendship with Tommy often, and Daniel trusted her judgment and discernment of Tommy.

"I don't mean that."

"What do you mean?"

"I mean I really like him and he likes me. I think he looks up to you, but he's scared of you. We can't leave now," she said.

"Jessica, you're young. You've got plenty of time to find the right guy," he said. He took hold of her hand with a gentleness he knew she loved. "Just trust me, okay?"

Jessica nodded but pulled her hand from his.

"It's only two hours away. Maybe he could visit." Daniel's offer was weak, but it was all he had at the moment.

They finished breakfast in silence. Daniel could tell she wasn't happy with him, but he was doing the best he could. He only hoped she knew that and that her best interests were in mind. He just wasn't ready to tell her everything about the McKinleys yet. Daniel cleared their plates, and both stood at the sink doing the dishes in the remaining time before leaving for the day. This was Jessica's last day of her junior year, and the big playoff game was that night.

"Are you okay?" he asked his daughter after a while.

"Yeah. I'm gonna get ready for school." She headed up the stairs.

Daniel followed upstairs shortly to brush his teeth. He returned downstairs and strapped on his holster. Jessica then came down, both of them hearing the honking of her friend's car.

"Shelly's here," he said. Jessica nodded. "Mind if I stop by the game?"

"Sure, Dad," she said, offering a half-hearted smile.

Daniel watched his daughter and waved at Shelly's mom as Jessica climbed in beside her friend. He shook his head, feeling slightly bewildered, and headed for the sheriff's office in town.

As Daniel finished some incident reports from the day before, preparing to put them on his secretary's desk, the sheriff's assistant entered Daniel's office with an air of sniveling arrogance.

"Boss wants to see you, Dan," Chuck said curtly.

"Good morning to you too, Chuck." Daniel smiled. He looked up at him, Chuck's back now turned to him. The weasel was scurrying off to his cubbyhole next to Bill McKinley's office. "Hey, where's my flak jacket?" Normally, he left it hanging in his office. He put it on when he left the office each day.

"We're all getting new ones. The old ones were turned in," Chuck answered. The distain in his voice, evident.

Daniel sighed. His rank was never respected by his subordinates, Chuck Smith and Tom McKinley.

"Now!" Chuck yelled from his desk, reveling in the power the sheriff had given him.

Daniel got up from his desk with his paperwork and headed for Bill's office, stopping at his assistant's desk. He handed it over to Jan. She offered an understanding smile.

He stopped at the sheriff's open door and rapped on the frame. "You wanted to see me, sir?"

"Come in, Daniel. Close the door."

Daniel stepped in, closing the door behind him and then took a seat.

"How's life treatin' you, Dan?"

"Oh, I can't complain," he answered with a content smile. "I'm blessed." Daniel shrugged.

Bill McKinley stiffened in his chair at the sentiment and cursed under his breath. "You seem distracted lately."

"No, I'm not distracted," Daniel answered with suspicious patience.

"How's Jessica?"

The hair on the back of Daniel's neck stood up. "Fine," he said with an edge of caution in his voice.

"That's good to hear," said the sheriff thoughtfully. "Listen, I've acquired permission from your pal, Captain Samson, for you to join him on the reservation. He wants you to be his senior criminal investigator. He's having trouble solving the disappearance of some of your people," he said, handing him a manila envelope. "I think you'll do better up there."

"I'm doing fine here, sir," Daniel said with certainty. "Jess has one more year of school," he added. Now that his decision to move had become a forced relocation, he understood how his daughter felt.

"Ever since Tom and I arrived, what, three years ago now, it seems you've become very discontented here. You don't fit in," McKinley suggested.

"I've served here for fourteen years. I belong here more than most," Daniel retorted.

The captain raised an eyebrow pointedly. "I know you don't like our recent procedural law enforcement techniques, Dan. Perhaps you'd like to be sheriff." The captain sat back.

"I'm not comfortable behind a desk."

"You'll do better with your own kind."

That was Bill McKinley. Direct and to the point, lacking all diplomacy. Daniel stood up, annoyance threatening to make him snap. "I'll take the transfer, okay?"

"Sit down, boy!" the sheriff snarled.

Daniel stared at the man in front of him as the order raked on his nerves. Slowly he took his seat again.

"Insubordination is a serious charge. You better watch yourself," he warned.

"I'm a clean sheriff. You couldn't make it stick," Daniel dared to counter.

"With the trauma of your wife's death, not being able to save her, and the little girl—"

Daniel turned his head away, squeezing his eyes shut for a brief moment. His enemy knew how to push his buttons. Daniel began a silent prayer. After a moment, he turned back to face the man across from him.

The sheriff continued, "Trying to deal with a violent career and raise a teenage daughter can drive any man to snap," he implied.

Daniel looked hard at the captain, but then a peaceful smile crossed his lips. "Whatever you say, sir," Daniel answered gently.

Unnerved, the sheriff barked, "Dismissed!"

Daniel rose from his chair and left the office.

The sheriff, his blood boiling, watched Daniel walk back to his office to retrieve his beat sheet and then leave the building. McKinley snatched up his phone.

"Jeff!" he said. "I've got something for you. Meet your dad at the warehouse tonight. He'll give you the details."

CHAPTER 2

The town's ball field was filled to capacity with most of its population there to cheer their team to a season victory and a shot at the regional title. Daniel stood covertly beside the home team bleachers, not wanting Jessica to feel uncomfortable with him there. He scanned the crowd for her and smiled in relief when he spotted her. She was, of course, sitting with Tommy McKinley, obviously enjoying herself and his company.

Daniel checked his watch; the game had another hour to go, and he didn't want to put a damper on her evening. He stood there for a moment, watching the pitcher, and smiled as he reminisced about his stint as the team's champion pitcher in high school. Back then, as long as he was leading the team to victory, he was welcomed and accepted.

Daniel pulled himself out of his reverie when a cheer went up for a homerun hit by one of the players. As he walked back to his SUV, a call came through on his walkie-talkie.

"Lieutenant, we need a hand. We've got a robbery suspect on foot at Fifth and Warren."

"On my way," he responded into the mic on his shoulder.

Daniel drove quickly to the location. It was an old, abandoned textile factory on the outskirts of the town. It was a known drug-dealing hot spot and sanctuary for local and visiting criminals. He pulled up quietly, lights off, and parked near the side of the building. Deputy Tom McKinley and Chuck Smith met him and filled him in on the information they had.

"Looks like the two nig—ah, perps are probably from out of town. But they knew we had the game tonight because they robbed Harold's," Tom said. "Figured we'd all be occupied."

Daniel ignored Tom's slip of the tongue and stared at the building.

"They're inside," Chuck said.

"Great," Daniel mumbled. He was not looking forward to having to step into the bowels of the beast. "Okay, I'll go around the back, and you two each cover a side. We'll meet in the middle," he directed.

Daniel pulled his weapon as the three split up. He walked down the dirt road alongside the building where pallets and old tin garbage cans had remained undisturbed for years. A feral cat was spooked by his presence and scooted across his path. Its movement disturbed a pile of bottles and garbage, sending the relics scattering. Daniel jumped slightly at the commotion but continued on to the back. Rounding the building, he stepped through the dilapidated doorway. The iron door had long been scavenged by metal collectors. He stopped.

"Keep me safe, Lord," he whispered as he wiped the sweat dripping from his temple.

The inside of the building reeked of animal and human feces, enhanced by the weather. Daniel pulled his flashlight and held it over the barrel of his .45 as he scanned the ground floor. There was a basement and a second level, consisting of catwalks. He spoke into his mic. "Tom, Chuck, what's your twenty?"

The radio crackled with static, but no one answered. He breathed out, annoyed. A pipe clattered above him, and he shot his beam upward at a catwalk. He couldn't see anyone, so continued his ground-floor search. He felt like he was being watched.

He neared the stairs to the basement and was struck by a jolt of electricity, shaking him violently to the ground and leaving him stunned and gasping for breath. He'd lost his grip on his gun and flashlight, which clattered away out of reach.

He searched through his slowly clearing vision for his gun. He saw it and reached for it, but a familiar pair of boots kicked it farther out of his reach. The boots rammed him in the ribs. Daniel's mind reeled for a moment at what was happening. Tom McKinley had used a *taser* on him. He felt the tines being ripped from his skin. He was betting the McKinnleys made sure he didn't have his flak jacket for this very reason.

Daniel tried to get to his feet, but he was kicked again and he rolled to his back, coughing. Tom backed away from Daniel as three shadowy figures stepped out from behind a stack of crates. With a nod of his head, Jeff McKinley and two of his buddies began their assault on Daniel.

"Think he'll get the message?"

Through a haze of pain, Daniel could just hear the voice. It wasn't Tom's; it was Chuck's. Daniel had been set up, and he realized this as he caught Tom's answer.

"For his daughter's sake, he'd better."

Daniel couldn't believe what he was hearing and experiencing at the hands of his own law enforcement team. As Daniel was roughly hoisted to his feet and slammed up against a wooden post, he caught a glimpse of Tom spitting and then turn to leave with Chuck. Daniel could hardly get his lungs to take in air when he recognized Jeff, McKinley's older son. He also recognized Jeff's friends, Snake and Sam. Jeff ripped the mic from Daniel's shoulder and yanked it from its plug on his radio. He threw it aside, along with Daniel's utility belt. While the other two held him, Jeff slammed a right fist across Daniel's face. The blow snapped Daniel's head to the right, causing a gash to open up on his cheek. Blood sprayed the thug, Snake, on Daniel's right.

"Don't you bleed on me, you stinkin' half-breed!" he snarled, twisting Daniel's right arm painfully behind him.

Jeff then backhanded the dazed undersheriff. Daniel mustered his remaining strength. He pulled the thug on his left, Sam, with his arm and threw the lackey into Jeff, knocking them back and down to the ground. Daniel was able to maneuver his right arm free. He got it loose and slammed his fist into Snake's face, breaking his nose. The skinhead staggered backward, screaming, as Daniel dove for his gun. Snake quickly recovered and grabbed a nearby pipe. He struck Daniel across the ribs. Daniel rolled to his back and shot Snake. Jeff had managed to untangle himself from his friend and kicked the gun out of Daniel's hands.

Jeff landed several vicious kicks to Daniel's ribs. Jeff and Sam pulled Daniel to his feet again, pinning him to the pillar. Jeff delivered punches until all the fight left Daniel.

Jeff gave a nod, and Sam released Daniel, letting him crash to the ground, nearly unconscious. The two brutes pulled him over to the basement stairs and threw him down.

"Gotta be careful around here, Danny boy! One misstep and oops!" Jeff cackled.

Daniel was too weak to catch himself and tumbled painfully to the bottom of the steps. He lay on the dirt floor. As his brain tried to stay conscious, he saw a demonic face laughing at him, and then all went black.

The two boys shared a laugh over their work on Daniel. They sobered quickly when they found Snake was dead.

"Oh, he's gonna die now!" Sam said. He spat in the dirt and turned back toward the stairs.

Jeff caught him by the arm. "I'm just as ticked as you, Sam, but Dad said we can't. This was a warning only!"

"Why can't we? What's the difference?"

"We have to stick with the plan. We get to kill him once he's on the reservation. That way, no FBI'll snoop around." Jeff released Sam's arm. Sam kicked the dirt in frustration. They picked up their friend and disappeared into the night.

The game ended with a rousing victory for the home team. The crowd broke off into various groups of friends and family, all planning to gather at the hometown diner to celebrate. Tommy and Jessica checked the number in their party and headed for the diner to save seats.

"Is your dad going to come by?" Tommy asked Jessica.

"I think so. He said he wanted to."

"Good. I want to ask him about the wrestling program at the college."

Jessica looked at him, surprised.

"Maybe he'll tell me about his glory days as a baseball star too." He shrugged with a smile.

"You really like my dad?"

"Yeah, why wouldn't I?" he asked.

Jessica was quiet for a moment, knowing his family was all bigots. She and Tommy had talked about his family. All the Navajo kids at the school liked him, and he liked her. She was comfortable with him, knowing he'd never hurt her or let her be hurt.

Tommy spoke up. "Look, Jess, I know you're still struggling with this. I don't know how to prove myself any more than I already have. My family's way of thinking is archaic and wrong. At least my mom raised me right. She never went along with dad either."

"I'm sorry about your mom. She died last year, right?"

Tommy nodded. "At least dad can't mistreat her anymore." He looked away.

Jessica looked at him, feeling his pain. She wanted to change the subject. "Why are they letting you see me?"

"I think they think it's just a phase. They're tolerating my behavior. They believe I'll discover the truth."

"What's the truth?"

"We all have red blood, right?"

Jessica smiled at his reasoning. "Right," she agreed, and she hugged his arm. "You articulate yourself very convincingly."

"They say I'm not your typical high-school jock," he teased, pulling a giggle from Jessica.

Ten miles outside of the town, Jeff and Sam buried their fallen comrade, eager for revenge. Bill McKinley leaned on the hood of his car with the headlights shining so they could see.

"Make it deep, boys," he said, chewing on a toothpick.

"If he thinks he's hurtin' now, just wait!" snarled Jeff.

"We're in a war, Jeff. We're going to have some casualties," Sheriff McKinley said with a shrug.

Jeff glared at his uncle for a moment and then took his anger out on the dirt. "That half-breed's gonna be one of 'em!" he vowed.

McKinley stood up and threw his toothpick aside. "You'll have your chance, Jeff. Don't worry, but you better grow up. You can't win a war on adrenaline and vengeance," he said, getting into his car. "Just play it cool and play it smart. Got it? Sam, you too."

Jeff and Sam nodded.

"I want you to find Johnny Smith."

"The brother of the girl who died with Patterson's wife?" Jeff said.

"Yep. Offer him some cash, and tell him he can get his revenge."

Jeff smiled at the idea.

"Once Patterson gets up there, we can grab his whole clan."

"Nothin' like the slave trade," Jeff snickered.

Jeff's uncle pulled away and disappeared into the darkness, leaving the boys to finish burying Snake.

As Tommy pulled his car into Jessica's driveway, she noted the dark house. Worry crossed Jessica's face.

"He probably had a call and had to stay late to do the paperwork," he tried to encourage her.

"He always calls when he's going to be late."

Tommy turned the engine off. "Let's go inside and call the station," Tommy suggested. He got out of the car and hurried to the other side to open the door for Jessica. They went inside and Jessica made a beeline for the phone.

"Hi, Deputy McKinley, this is Jessica Patterson. Is my dad there?"

"No, Jessica, I haven't seen him all day. He was in this morning but hasn't been back. He's probably on his way home."

"Well, he always calls me if he's going to be late."

"I wouldn't worry. He's probably busy on a call and lost track of time," McKinley offered.

"Okay, thanks." Jessica hung up, worry still etched across her face.

"Do you want me to go?" Tommy asked her.

"No! Please stay until my dad gets home," she pleaded.

"Okay," he said, pulling out a chair. "Do you have any cards?"

"Sure." She smiled weakly and then went to a drawer and pulled out a deck of cards.

She placed them on the table and then went to the refrigerator to get them some orange juice. She paused and stared at the picture of her mom, dad, and herself at her fifteenth birthday party. They were a happy family, and that day had been one of her favorites. She and her dad had grown very close since her mom had been killed, but looking at the picture made her miss her mom even more.

With her dad heavy on her mind, she breathed a prayer for him. She opened the door and pulled out a carton of orange juice. She sat down, and Tommy poured the OJ.

"Hey." Tommy took her chin with his fingers. "He's all right," he said, trying to remove the stress from her young, beautiful face.

Jessica offered a cautious smile.

Daniel's body jerked as he regained consciousness on the floor of the dark basement. He let out a low groan as he hugged his injured ribs. Pain wracked his body with every breath he took. He didn't know if his ribs were cracked, but he knew the pain was beyond what he'd ever felt before. He slowly opened his eyes, grimacing as he tried to orient himself. The moon's light poured through the warehouse's collapsed roof. He saw the stairs and vaguely remembered being "helped" down them by his attackers. Carefully, he managed to sit upright against a support beam and rested there.

His face was stinging as he lifted his hand to his left cheek, wincing when his fingers brushed the open gash. His fingers were covered in blood, and he assumed as much about that side of his face. As he became more aware, he also tasted blood and felt his lips. There was a cut on the left side of both lips. He spit out some blood and then rested his head back against the pillar. He looked up the stairs and was reluctant to have to climb them. Once again, he calculated his moves and got to his feet.

One by one, he made the agonizing ascent to the ground level of the factory. After what seemed like a lifetime of painful and brutal steps, he came to the landing and collapsed there. Overwhelmed by pain and exhaustion, he passed out.

It was 11:00 p.m. Daniel's shift ended at nine. Jessica looked hard at the kitchen clock as if willing it to turn back two hours so she wouldn't have to worry. When that didn't work, she prayed she was dreaming, but Tommy touched her arm. She looked at him and then looked at the clock again.

"Do you want to go look for him?" he suggested.

"No, he might come home, and then he'd be the one to have to worry."

Daniel again regained consciousness. He squeezed his eyes shut as a wave of nausea reminded his ribs of their condition. "Please, God. I could use a hand here." He opened his eyes, and a wrinkled old hand reached down to him. Daniel looked up and saw his sicheii, smiling at him. Daniel was confused, causing him to hesitate. He hadn't seen his sicheii since after Sarah's funeral. It had been too painful for Daniel after the funeral to see Sarah's parents. He'd asked them not to visit until he was ready, and being so busy with his job and being a single parent, he never found the time to go back to the rez.

"Sicheii?" Daniel reached out and took hold of his hand and got to his feet almost effortlessly, but then the pain hit him again. He leaned against a wall, hugging his ribs. He closed his eyes tightly. When he opened them again, the old man was gone, but there at his feet were his gun, flashlight, and belt. He knelt on one knee and gingerly gathered them up. He staggered out of the building and almost fell again but caught himself on his SUV. He got the door opened and climbed in. He leaned his head on the steering wheel. The pain made him want to vomit. Trying to stay conscious, he turned the key.

Jessica and Tommy were finishing their fifth game of cards when they heard a vehicle pull into the driveway. Jessica bolted from her chair and went to the door.

"Dad?" she called out to the SUV. The engine was still running, and the lights remained on, but her dad didn't emerge. "Dad?" she called again, and she began to walk to the vehicle. As she approached the SUV, she could see Daniel slumped against the steering wheel. "Oh my God!" she yelped. "Tommy!"

Tommy ran outside and found Jessica crying as she looked at her dad in the driver's seat. Tommy gently moved Jessica aside and opened the door, catching Daniel as he fell out of the vehicle.

"Mr. Patterson!"

"Jess," Daniel said, barely audible as Tommy helped him stand up. Tommy placed Daniel's arm over his shoulder and then put his arm around his waist. Daniel let out a yelp of pain as Tommy assisted him inside and laid him on the couch.

"Call an ambulance!" Tommy ordered as he placed a pillow behind Daniel's head. He opened his blood-soaked shirt and lifted his T-shirt to find blue and yellow bruises covering his ribs and chest.

"No!" Daniel sputtered. "Call Doc Thompson," he told his daughter.

Jessica ran to the phone and made the call.

"Sir, you're hurt really bad. You need a hospital," Tommy tried to reason.

"No," was Daniel's weak response.

"Jess, grab a wet towel while you're in there!" Tommy called as he looked at the cuts on Daniel's face.

Jess returned with the wet towel, and Tommy got up, allowing her to kneel next to her dad. With gentleness, she wiped his face as she forced back her emotions. Her attempt to show bravery faltered. "Daddy, what happened?" Her voice cracked.

Daniel had to wait as a wave of pain made him groan. Tommy winced in sympathy. Daniel looked back and up at Tommy and then at Jessica and then closed his eyes again. Jessica realized her dad didn't want Tommy to hear what he was going to say. Jessica calmed herself and looked up at Tommy.

"I'll need a fresh towel and a bowl of ice," she told him. Tommy nodded and left the room.

"Doctor Thompson is on the way," she told her dad. "Who did this?"

"Who won the game?" he rasped.

Jessica gently turned his bloody face to look at her. "Dad, who did this?" she asked him with quiet determination.

"Tom Sr., Jeff," he whispered.

Jessica clapped her hand to her mouth. Tommy came in then with the towels and ice.

"Thanks," Jessica said, regaining her composure as she took the items. She wrapped a small amount of ice into a wet towel and took her dad's left hand and helped him hold it to his mouth.

"Anything else I can do? Who did this, Mr. Patterson? Shall I call my dad?" Tommy asked with genuine concern.

"Go home, Tom. Thanks," Daniel said.

There was a knock on the door, and Tommy hurried to answer it. He ushered the doctor in and indicated the living room. Jessica got up, having made sure her dad could hold the pack himself. She greeted the doctor and then saw Tommy out.

Tommy stopped on the porch and turned to Jessica. "Did he say anything?"

Jessica bit her lip but shook her head. She knew if she told Tommy who had beaten her dad, he'd have it out with his brother Jeff and Tom Sr. That could lead to serious repercussions for everyone involved.

Tommy hugged her. "I'm so sorry, Jessica."

Jessica hugged Tommy tightly, grateful for his friendship and care. "Thanks," she said quietly.

After another reluctant moment, Tommy left and Jessica went back into the house.

Jessica took a seat in a nearby chair, worry etched on her young face. She watched stoically as Doctor Thompson examined Daniel's face, checked his torso for internal bleeding, and then arduously stitched the gash in Daniel's cheek. "Doesn't that hurt him?" She cringed.

The doctor didn't look at her as he concentrated on his work, but he answered, "He's out. And I used an anesthetic." Doctor Thompson had been the family doctor ever since Daniel was born and had even delivered Jessica. He lived just two houses down. "This must be rough on you, Jess. Why not go upstairs?" He tried to ease her mind. "He'll be okay, but he should get to a hospital for X-rays. I can't say for certain if his ribs are cracked or not," he told her.

"He won't go," she said. "Too proud."

"Or stupid."

Jessica didn't like the comment, but she had to agree. She really wasn't sure why Daniel refused to go to the hospital.

"Will you be all right here tonight with him?"

"Yeah, I'll sleep on the other couch," she indicated with a nod of her head.

"I'll be back in the morning to wrap him up. Don't let him move," he instructed her. He pulled out a bottle. "This is for pain. Give him one every four hours as needed."

Jessica stood with the doctor after he finished his repair work on Daniel's face, and he gave her a hug.

"You call me if you need to. I don't care what time it is," he ordered her.

Once Doctor Thompson left, Jessica got a glass of water and helped her dad swallow a pill. He was immediately out again as she picked up his blood soaked uniform shirt and the t-shirt that had been cut off him by the doctor and trudged upstairs with them. She got ready for bed and returned to the living room with her pillow and two Pendleton blankets, covering her dad with one of them. As she lay in the dark of the room, the moon bathing the front room in a soft light, Jessica felt herself shaking with anger. In the excitement from earlier, she hadn't noticed it. Now, she felt ashamed as she thought of the vengeance in her heart. A tear streamed down her face at the thought that entered her mind. She wanted Tommy's dad and brother to pay for what they'd done to her dad.

She knew it was wrong to carry these thoughts, so she offered it up to the Great Creator and hoped his actions would be swift and merciful.

CHAPTER 3

Jessica awoke at four in the morning to the sound of someone talking. She sat up in her makeshift bed and bent her ear to hear in the darkened room. The more she listened, the more she realized it was her dad talking. He was mumbling something in a dream. She threw her blanket aside and quietly made her way over to him. She pushed her long black hair over her shoulder and gently knelt beside the couch and listened as he spoke in Navajo. He was trembling through an obvious nightmare. She never knew he could speak Navajo. She'd heard her mom speak it, and she had been given a Navajo name and its meaning, but she'd never heard her dad actually speak the language beyond a word or two.

Daniel was desperately trying to get to a burning car, calling out for his wife who was still inside. Tom McKinley and two other deputies were holding him back as he fought to get past them.

Suddenly, Daniel was walking around a smoldering ash heap all alone and mumbling his wife's name in Navajo. Her name, Yanaba, meaning "brave," was what her mother had named her. It fit her well as she died bravely in the fire while she tried to push a little girl from the flaming wreckage.

Her body, and that of the little girl, had long since been removed. Daniel stopped, catching a glint of something in the ashes. He squatted down, sifted the debris with his fingers, and discovered the carved stone pendant depicting a dove he'd given his wife on their wedding day. He dropped to his knees and began to weep.

Jessica touched her sleeping father's face, wiping the tears away. She had a feeling she knew what the dream was about.

Slowly, Daniel opened his eyes as he felt his daughter's gentle hand on his face. "Did I wake you?" he asked, groggy from pain.

"No, Dad. Are you feeling okay?"

"You mean aside from feeling like I've been trampled on by a herd of wild horses?"

She gave him a stern look that warned him to stop joking.

"Now that I know that you're okay, I'm fine." He attempted a smile.

"I didn't know you could speak Navajo," Jessica said.

Daniel looked at her for a moment and then put his left hand to his brow, squeezing his eyes shut. "I don't," he told her.

Jessica smiled at her dad's modesty. "Dad, please. I heard you."

Daniel looked again at Jessica with confusion. "When?"

"Just a moment ago. In your dream." She grinned.

Daniel was silent, and she knew he was trying to remember the dream. Jessica noticed that he seemed disturbed by what she'd said. "Don't worry. I'm sure it'll come back to you."

He only nodded. After a moment, he looked at her. "Why don't you go upstairs to bed? I'll be fine."

"I'm staying here," she informed him in no uncertain terms. "It's four fifteen, and I'm wide awake. I'm here if you need anything."

"Will you help me get ready for work?"

"Nope," was her quick reply, knowing he was testing her resolve.

"I didn't think so," he said.

Jessica patted his right hand, adjusted his blanket, and then got up and went back over to the love seat. She pulled the blanket over herself and made herself comfortable for the remainder of her vigil.

Father and daughter slept in. Jessica was out of school for the summer, and Daniel was in no shape to return to work. At 8:00 a.m., she heard noises in the kitchen. She looked to the couch where her dad was supposed to be sleeping and found it empty. She got up to scold his machismo. She stopped at the doorway to the kitchen and looked at him.

"Dad, what do you think you're doing?"

He was leaning on the sink, wracked with a spasm of pain. He slowly turned to her, trying to mask it, but she could see it in his eyes and pale expression.

"Fixing breakfast?" he offered.

She walked up to him, ready to offer a reprimand, but noticed his body trembling. She caught him just as his legs gave out. He threw his arm over her shoulder to catch himself, and she helped him to a chair at the table in the breakfast nook.

"I'll do the fixing around here for now," she said with authority.

"You sound like your mom." He groaned.

"Good. Then maybe you'll listen."

"Ouch! Point well taken," he said.

Jessica retrieved the pain medication from the living room and put a pill in front of her dad with a glass of water; both glanced at the clock before he popped it into his mouth. Jessica then went to work on breakfast.

As they sat at their morning meal together, Jessica thought about the previous evening. She was afraid to broach the subject, and she knew her dad would hesitate to answer her questions. There was an unspoken understanding about the McKinleys' power in Stake Town and why they had come in the first place three years earlier. She started with a less painful subject. "You don't like Tommy, do you?"

Daniel took a sip of orange juice and considered his daughter's question. "It's not that I don't like him—"

"Then what?"

"If you'll slow down, I'll tell you, sweetheart," he said as he reached for the saltshaker, groaning in pain.

Jessica scrunched her face in sympathy and put the salt next to his plate for him. "Sorry," she said in a quiet voice.

Daniel let out a careful sigh. "Jessica, you know his dad and uncle are—"

"I know the history, Dad, and we've talked about this before. But Tommy told me last night that he thinks their way of thinking is archaic and wrong," she explained. "I didn't tell him who did this because I knew he'd get into it with his dad and Jeff." She chomped on her toast for emphasis. "If you don't trust him, why'd you let me go out with him?"

"Because I trust *your* judgment."

"So you're leaving me to do all the work of discerning for myself? I thought you were supposed to protect me."

"And I thought you wanted to be treated as an adult."

"You're avoiding the question." She raised her eyebrow at him.

Daniel looked at her for a moment. She could tell he was digesting what she'd said.

"Besides, would Tommy have gotten your filthy 'half-breed' blood"—she wiggled her fingers in quotation marks—"on him if he was like them?" Her eyes pleaded with him to believe her.

As he chewed his food and swallowed, he answered, "Okay, okay. It is possible that he thinks for himself," he confirmed. "He sounds pretty articulate."

"Thank you," Jessica said.

"For a jock," he finished.

"Dad! You were a jock once upon a time!" she said, punching his arm.

"Ow, ow, ow!" he cried for sympathy.

"Sorry! I'm sorry." She felt sorry for her dad and mad at herself for contributing to the pain he was already in.

"Psych!" He grinned and so received another punch.

"Ow!" he said seriously.

Jessica stood with her empty plate. "You deserved that!" She walked to the sink with both of their plates.

"Can you help me upstairs? I need a shower."

"Yes. But you're not going anywhere today. Doctor's orders."

"I don't remember him saying that," Daniel retorted.

Jessica turned from the dishes. "You were unconscious," she told him. "He said a lot of stuff that you didn't hear."

"For instance?" he challenged.

"No work for at least two weeks, and you have to let me help you."

Daniel grunted. "At least I'll have time to get the house on the market."

"What?"

"I told you yesterday morning," he said.

"No, we were supposed to talk about it but never did," she argued. "Why are we moving?"

"Sheriff McKinley is sending me to the rez. Special assignment," he told her.

"Can he do that?"

"Sort of. Besides, Ben requested my help."

"Why?" she prodded. Now that he'd opened the door to the subject, she was determined to get some answers.

Daniel sat back slowly, hugging his ribs. His action reminded her of something. "Oh yeah. Dr. Thompson said he'd be here at nine to bandage your ribs."

"Then I need to get upstairs," he said, preparing to get up. "Subject closed," he mumbled under his breath.

She put a hand on his arm as he tried to push away from the table. "Give," she said with a determined look in her eyes.

"Jess." He sighed. "It's complicated."

"I'm not a baby."

"I know, but you don't need this on your shoulders right now. I want you to enjoy your summer."

"Yeah, I'll have fun packing the house for reasons unknown while I worry about you anyway." Her protest was sarcastic.

Daniel gave in. "Help me upstairs, and I'll tell you."

Jessica agreed to the compromise, and the two of them headed for the stairs.

After a long, painful climb, she left her father standing by the bathroom door of his bedroom and pulled a fresh shirt, a pair of boxers, and pair of jeans from his dresser. Leaving the shirt on his bed, she handed him the rest of his clothes and then waited for him to explain.

He hesitated for a moment. "The climate of the town has changed. Like I told you, I can't do my job the way it's supposed to be done, and they're looking for any excuse to nail me."

"Why? They've never caused you trouble before."

Daniel guffawed at that. "Sweetheart, they've never liked me. They only tolerate me because they have to." He paused, preparing to dive in. "Jessica, I uncovered something two years ago," he inferred.

"I think they want me on the rez to make it easier to get rid of me," he said.

Jessica searched her dad's eyes. She was stunned. "What do you mean?" she asked pensively.

Daniel looked down with a small sigh and then looked into his bedroom. "This beating was a reminder to keep quiet."

Jessica fought tears as she went over what he'd just told her. Now, she wasn't so sure she wanted the whole picture. Everyone knew they were bigots. What more could there be?

"I need you to trust me, okay? We need to go up to the rez so I can help Ben with an investigation."

Jessica looked into his eyes, realizing the weight of the matter, and softly nodded her head. "Okay," she whispered.

"I love you, sweetheart," Daniel said, giving her a careful hug.

"I love you too, Dad."

Jessica returned to the kitchen to clean up before the doctor arrived and then hurried upstairs for her own shower and change of clothes. She had just finished drying her hair when there was a knock on the door. As she headed for the stairs to answer it, she noticed her dad sitting on the side of his bed in his jeans, staring at the floor. His body language revealed the turmoil boiling inside of him. She rapped on the doorframe. "I'll send him up," she told him.

He looked up. "Thanks, Jess."

Jessica bounded down the stairs and opened the door to a chipper Doctor Thompson.

"Good morning, Jessica! How's the patient?"

"Impatient!" She smiled. "He's upstairs."

Doctor Thompson stepped into the house, glancing around at the orderly home. "Like nothing ever happened," he mumbled. "Did you end up sleeping upstairs?"

"No, we both used the couches. I helped him upstairs this morning. He wanted a shower before you came."

"Did either of you sleep well?"

"I did, but I don't think Dad did, for obvious reasons, but he also had another nightmare."

"He's having a lot more lately." he said.

She nodded as a shadow dimmed her beautiful Navajo features. She thought about the first seven months after her mom had died. Her dad had blamed himself for not being there. She went over that fateful day again.

Daniel was to have met her and her mom for lunch but a call came through, and he had been forced to postpone it for an hour or two. Sarah and Jessica decided to go back to the youth center where they were volunteers and wait for Daniel's call. One of the little girl's parents called and couldn't pick the child up, so Sarah offered to drive the child home while Jessica stayed behind.

On the way to the child's home, on a deserted stretch of highway, Sarah's car mysteriously went off the road and crashed in a small ravine, bursting into flames. Sarah was too injured and the little girl was already dead, but Sarah still tried to get the girl out. Daniel received the call and sped to the scene. Bill and Tom McKinley were there already, standing above the accident. Daniel hurried into the ravine and tried to get to Sarah and the girl, but the car exploded. The girl's brother arrived just after the car was extinguished and railed at Daniel for not having saved his little sister.

Doctor Thompson patted Jessica's back and started for the stairs, not having any comforting words to offer her. "I'll see to him then," he replied. The doctor reached the top of the landing and headed straight for Daniel's room. The door was open, and Daniel waved him in.

"Daniel!" the doctor greeted.

"Hey, Doc," Daniel said with a raspy voice.

"Let's get you wrapped so things will be a little easier for you." He smiled.

"Yeah, you can smile," Daniel snapped sarcastically. "Want to trade?"

"No, thank you," he assured as he pulled a large roll of gauze and some Elasticon from his medical bag.

Daniel eyed the six-inch-wide self-adhesive. "Isn't that for horses?" he asked with concern.

"Sure is, but I have found it does wonders stabilizing the ribcage," Thompson enthused.

"You get a lot of calls for injured ribs, do ya?"

"No, I'm just experimenting." He grinned, opening the gauze roll and measuring it out. "You're my first." There was mischief in his voice. "Stand up and raise your arms if you can."

Daniel looked at him with a raised eyebrow and stood slowly with a breath of pain. Thompson wrapped his ribcage with the gauze as tightly as he could, eliciting several groans from his patient.

"Oh, quit it! You sound like a girl," Thompson scolded.

"Yeah, well, your bedside manner is getting—"

Thompson gave an extra squeeze as he applied the Elasticon, causing Daniel to yelp.

"Rusty!" Daniel's voice broke.

After twenty minutes, the doctor announced the completion of his task. "All done!" Thompson handed Daniel his shirt and began to put his supplies away. "Sit down, Dan," he invited.

Daniel complied. He had no choice, he was exhausted.

"Jessica said you've been having nightmares again."

"I'm all right." Daniel waved his concern off.

"What's going on?" Thompson asked him with a voice that told Daniel he'd better tell him.

"The fewer who know, the better," was his reply.

"Daniel Patterson, I've been your doctor all of your life. Hell, I delivered you, son! We're family," Thompson reminded him.

"I agree with the whole family thing, Doc," Daniel started as he rubbed his ribs, "but as I indicated, I'm trying to protect my family." He looked at Thompson with an expression that told him it was a serious matter. "Trust me, okay? All I can tell you is that Bill McKinley assigned me to the rez."

Thompson cast a considerate look at Daniel and then slapped his knee. "Understood."

Daniel sighed in relief, knowing he wouldn't ask any more questions. Everybody in town knew that asking too many questions often got one in trouble, especially if the McKinleys were the topic.

CHAPTER 4

Daniel was rattled about what Jessica had told him regarding his having spoken Navajo. He had remained upstairs after the doctor had taken his leave and felt drawn to the hope chest that resided in the back of the large walk-in closet off the bathroom. Sarah, his wife, had always felt spoiled by the large house they lived in. All in all, it really was an average-sized home for the area. It was nice, but compared to the hogan Sarah had grown up in, this was a mansion.

He walked to the closet slowly as if exploring the realm beyond the hangers for the first time. The only thing hanging on that side of the closet that had held Sarah's clothes was the wedding dress her mother had made for her. He touched the white leather dress, admiring the beading and crafting of the garment. He saw Sarah in it for a moment and smiled, but then she faded.

He gently pushed the dress aside to reveal the hope chest. Daniel's mother had prepared it for Sarah as a wedding gift. Unfortunately, Daniel's mom and dad died in a car crash the night of his high school graduation. He had never looked inside of the chest even though Sarah had asked him to. He was a guy, and the thought of having to pretend to be interested in the family heirlooms that only his wife could appreciate, at the time, made him want to run for the mesas and do warrior stuff. He was never rude to her about it, but after asking him once, she never bothered him about it again. Tears brimmed in his eyes as he now realized he'd missed out on something special with his bride.

His dad and sicheii had built the oak chest to his mom's specifications and lined it with cedar. Daniel placed his hand on the lid of the chest, feeling the smooth wood. The craftsmanship was exquisite. He expected it to feel cold and concealing, but as his hand stroked the smooth wood and carved images on the lid, he felt warmth and life there.

Daniel knelt on one knee in front of the chest. Slowly, cautiously, with a shaky breath, he opened the lid. Inside was a main compartment with a cedar drawer above it. In the drawer was a large hand woven white woolen blanket. Subtly accented, it was flecked with blues, reds, purples, greens, and yellows along the four edges. Daniel remembered seeing his mother and some of the other women of his clan working on the blanket when he was a child. They had told him they were making it for the wife the Great Creator had chosen for him. He smiled with a quick but sad chuckle at the memory.

He stroked the blanket's soft texture for a moment, wondering why Sarah had kept it in the chest instead of putting it on the bed. He pulled the drawer out and set it aside, his ribs reminding him just how sore they were. In the main compartment was a smaller wooden box. He pulled it out and stood, taking it to the bedroom. He sat on the side of his bed and opened the lid. He smiled again, seeing a stack of color and black-and-white photos inside. There was a picture of him with his mom and dad the day of his graduation. A tear escaped the boundaries of his right eye and slipped down his cheek. He wiped it on his shoulder and cleared his throat.

Next he found some pictures of his shimasani (grandmother) and sicheii on the reservation and smiled at the typical old-school scowl of early 1900s photography. Then he found pictures of his marriage to Sarah on the reservation, along with a leather-bound baby book of Jessica, containing pictures of her many birthdays over the years. There was one last photo caught under the inside edge of the box. He gently freed it and turned it over. He froze as a painful memory came flooding back.

It was a black-and-white photo of him from 1960 when he was four. He was atop a mustang pony his sicheii had taken from off the Arizona plains and given to him for his birthday that year. Daniel was in buckskin breeches and shirtless with a bow and quiver slung over one shoulder and a long spear lying across his lap. A feather hung from his long black hair and rested over his shoulder. He stared at the pouch around his neck. He looked inside the box again and discovered that same leather pouch. He took it out and looked at the picture again.

The last time he'd seen the pouch, he and his mom had had an argument over it. He'd worn it from the time he was four until he was about fifteen. His mom had given it to him for his birthday and told him when the time was right, the Great Creator would tell him what the symbols inside meant. They had moved off the reservation to Stake Town so Daniel could attend high school, and after a year of harassment by Bill and Tom McKinley, he refused to wear the pouch any longer because it drew attention to him. But his mother had insisted that he continue to wear it to remind him of his heritage.

The day of the argument, he had yelled at his mom, pulled the pouch from around his neck, thrown it on the table, and stormed out of the house. Daniel closed his eyes tightly, trying to remember what he and his mom had said so long ago but after several moments, he gave up. All he could remember was how angry he had been and the heartbroken look on his mother's face when he'd left. Daniel squeezed his eyes closed tightly, trying to maintain composure. He pinched the bridge of his nose with his left hand while squeezing the pouch intently with his right hand. He understood now how important heritage was.

"Oh, Mom. I'm sorry." Daniel sniffed, looking up at the ceiling. Finally, he took a deep breath and opened the pouch. He shook the contents out into his left hand. There were three small carved stones and a tiny scroll. One shiny black stone had a red tear carved into it. It represented his Navajo name, Red Tears, which he'd almost forgotten until that moment. Another stone, a blood stone, had a small hand with a spiral design in it representing healing and on the other side a heart with a break through it.

There was another shiny stone—white with a golden eagle carved into it. He wasn't sure what it meant except that to the Native Americans, it represented the divine Spirit of the Creator and oneness with his Spirit. And then he looked at the scroll. Carefully he untied the leather string and unrolled it, revealing one word: *Res*. The word wasn't the *rez* word the natives used when speaking of the reservation. It was another word for which he didn't understand the meaning.

"*Resolution,*" a voice said.

Daniel asked the Great Creator, "What does that mean?"

"*My word is my resolution. My resolution is my word, and it is what you carry in your heart. I put it there, my son. It is repentance, forgiveness, and reconciliation. It is a resolution in the Senate—a cry for peace and truth. Fourteen.*"

Daniel digested what he'd heard and understood that there was more to come. More for him to do. "*You will know more when you are ready,*" the Great Creator told him.

Daniel sighed and gave a nod. He stared at the scroll for a long time and the rest of the contents of the pouch with a strange feeling of familiarity, as if he should know what all of these things meant, but it wasn't clear to him yet. He put the symbols back into his pouch. One thing he did understand and knew for sure. He was to wear the pouch. He slipped the leather strap over his head and let it rest against his shirt. The movement caused his ribs to scream. He embraced the pain. He touched the pouch. It seemed that pain and the pouch were to go hand in hand.

Jessica came up the stairs and saw her dad sitting on his bed in deep thought. She knocked on his door. "Dad?" she said, careful not to invade.

"Jessica," he replied.

"What are those pictures?" she asked with a casual gesture toward the scattered photos on the bed and the box next to them.

"Memories, mostly." He forced a smile and picked them up like cards.

Jessica joined him on the bed beside the box and reached for the photos. He handed them over so she could look at them. She smiled and cooed at many of the pictures and then held one out to him. "Is that you?" she asked of the boy on his pony.

He nodded. "That's this pouch," he said, tapping the leather around his neck.

Jessica hadn't noticed the pouch around his neck until he pointed it out to her. "What's it for?"

"I just found it with these pictures," he told her. "I used to wear it all the time as a kid."

"Why'd you stop?" Jessica asked, tucking her legs under her, ready for a story.

Daniel shrugged. "As I got older, in high school, it got me into a lot of trouble with the McKinleys. It was a symbol of my heritage, and I didn't want anyone to hassle me about it anymore," he said.

Jessica took hold of his hand with an understanding smile.

"It broke Mom's heart." His words were almost inaudible.

Jessica gave her dad a hug. "I'm glad you found it, and I'm sure your mom would be, too." She looked at her dad, holding his gaze. "Tell me about Shimasani and Sicheii."

"Well." Daniel took a deep breath. "They were beautiful people. Mom was full-blooded Navajo, and Dad was a white missionary. He fell in love with Mom, and they married. Some of the other clans didn't like the mix, but love prevailed. They were deeply spiritual. Committed to the Great High Chief."

"I wish I could have met them. How did they die?"

"There was a drunk who hit them head-on when they were going home from my graduation."

"Oh no!" she whispered. Tears welled in her eyes. She felt what she thought her dad was feeling at the moment.

She squeezed his hand. "God wanted you to find this, Dad," she whispered.

Daniel smiled at his daughter's wisdom.

"So what's in the pouch?" she asked, throwing her long black hair over her shoulders.

"Stones with symbols on them and a scroll. Mom told me when the time was right, I'd understand their meanings."

"See!" Jessica said excitedly.

"Yes, I see." Daniel smiled at her enthusiasm. "But don't push me for answers I don't have yet. I need you to do some research for me though. About a resolution in the senate called Resolution 14."

"I won't push, and yes, I'll look it up for you," she assured, getting quiet. A picture in the stack she was holding slipped out and fluttered to the floor. Jessica retrieved it. It was a picture of four children, their arms around each other as they stood in a line with joyous smiles on their faces. One she recognized as her dad, another her mom, but the other two she didn't recognize. "Who are these kids?" She held the photo out to her dad.

Daniel traced the picture's images with his fingertip, a soft smile on his lips. And yet, Jessica saw a sadness in his eyes. "This is Ben"—he pointed to one of the boys—"your uncle." He paused for a moment. A shadow dimmed his features as he stared at the other boy. "This one is Hawkeye." He tossed the photo in the box.

"Whoa, what's the matter? Who's Hawkeye?" Jessica rescued the discarded photo and looked at it again. She watched her dad tuck the pouch inside of his shirt with a wince and then wipe his face. They both sat quietly for a moment as they put the pictures back in the box.

"Dad?"

"Hmm?"

"Who's the other little boy?"

Daniel sighed. "He's your true uncle. Your mom's half brother."

"You guys never mentioned him before. Why not?"

"Later, Jess, okay? I'm tired."

Jessica nodded.

He showed Jessica the chest, and after closing it, he spoke up. "This will be yours one day. My mom had it made for your mom as a wedding gift," he told her. "My sicheii, your great sicheii," he clarified, "and my dad actually built it."

"Dad, it's beautiful."

Daniel nodded in agreement. "I need you to drive me to the real estate office today."

Jessica stood up from the chest. "What's the hurry?' she asked.

"Last night was a warning, Jess. Sheriff McKinley gave me the paperwork for my new assignment." He nodded toward his dresser. "He wants me out."

"Why?" Jessica insisted. "Why do people with power always push us around?"

"Because they think they can," he answered, turning back into his bedroom.

"You mean because we let them?" Jessica retorted, following him.

Daniel stopped at his doorway, turned, and looked at her. "I suppose I deserved that, but I'm not *entirely* sure I did. Turn the other cheek," he reminded her.

"But are we supposed to let them use us as doormats or…" she hesitated, "punching bags?" she finished with a reserved irritation in her voice.

"I fought back, Jessica. It was five to one," he said with exasperation. "McKinley even used a *taser* on me, okay?"

"Ouch. Sorry," she apologized with slight embarrassment.

Daniel softened. "It's fine," he turned from her for a moment. "Now, will you take me?"

"Sure."

The real estate office was the typical small-town storefront. A one-room office with a kitchen/bathroom sat in the back. Maria Tannin was the only agent there. She saw Daniel's injuries. "I'm sorry about last night, Daniel. Fighting crime is a dangerous job, I guess."

"I guess."

The well wishing had sunk like a lead ball. It filled the room with a discomfort everyone felt. Marie went back to the topic at hand. "Everything looks good. I'll be by tomorrow to put the sign up and take pictures, and they'll be on the net in the next few days." She smiled at father and daughter and then put the papers in a manila envelope.

Daniel stood, but before he departed, he asked a final question. "Maria, why do you stay here?"

Maria gazed out the storefront window for a moment. "It's home," she finally said with a smile of contentment.

Daniel gave her a nod of understanding. "Thanks," he said, shaking her hand. "We'll have the house cleaned and ready for you by morning."

"Take it easy, Daniel. Don't hurt yourself. I know how Jessica keeps the house. I'm not worried."

As Daniel and Jessica stepped outside to their SUV, Daniel looked across the street and noticed Tommy, Jr., in the café. "How about lunch?" he suggested.

Jessica was about to open the driver's side door but looked at him with shock. He hated eating at the café. He usually made his way home for lunch, claiming health code violations and any other reason he could think of. He loved Marge, the owner, and used to eat there until the McKinleys moved in.

"Are you sure?"

"Why not?" He shrugged, walking around the vehicle. "We'll have a chance to say good-bye to Marge."

Jessica gave him a look of suspicion as they crossed the street and then grinned when she saw Tommy inside. "Thanks, Dad." She nudged him affectionately.

"For what? You're buying." He grinned back. He opened the door for her and stepped in out of the midday heat. Unfortunately, what he hadn't been able to see from across the street was Tommy's brother, Jeff, with his assistant goon, Sam, sitting at the back of the diner. Daniel stopped for a brief moment, surprised by the fear that threatened to rise up in him. Tommy stepped into his line of sight.

"Mr. Patterson, Jessica!" Tommy sounded thrilled and offered his hand. Daniel shook it gratefully. "You're welcome to join me," he invited.

"Thanks, Tommy, I think we will," Daniel said, and he sat down across from Tommy as he watched the young man seat his daughter, raising his opinion of him a few notches. Marge came by soon after to take their order.

"Well, if the world don't stand still and go flat!" she exclaimed at her unexpected guest. "Finally trying the best of the local cuisine after all these years?"

"You mean the only cuisine?" Daniel retorted.

She ignored him by snapping her gum and chewing it more fervently than before. And therein lay the reason for Daniel's aversion to eating at Marge's diner.

"I hear you're moving," she said, pulling a pencil from her tightly bunned hair.

"It never ceases to amaze me how quickly news travels in small towns," Daniel said, looking at Jessica and Tommy. Tommy snuck a look of surprise at Jessica, who looked down at the reminder. Daniel gave a patient smile and looked at Marge.

"You're still the local hero. Gotta gossip about something," she said, waiting for his order. "What'll you have?" Daniel and Jessica gave her their order, and then she walked away.

"You're moving?" Tommy was taken aback.

"I'm sorry. I didn't have a chance to tell you. It was sort of sudden," Jessica said.

"Gee, I wonder why," Daniel muttered.

The comment was lost on Tommy, but Jessica shot her dad a warning look.

"I don't listen to local gossip. I like to hear it straight from the source if they're inclined to tell me."

"What about your dad?" Daniel asked.

"We don't talk much. We don't see eye to eye on a lot of things," Tommy said, popping some fries into his mouth as a shade of sadness crossed his face. He looked up. "I'm glad to see you doing so well."

Daniel smiled politely. "I want you to know I'm grateful for your help last night," Daniel said with sincerity.

Tommy waved it off. "I just hope they get the guys who did this to you."

"It's not likely," Daniel mumbled. He found it difficult to believe that Tommy really didn't know what his dad was up to and who had attacked him. "I guess you and your brother don't talk much either, huh?"

"No, sir. They're not too happy that I like Jessica. They're expecting me to grow out of it." He smiled at Jessica. "I think they're wrong."

"When did you change?" Daniel asked.

Tommy looked at him, confusion on his face. But he ventured an answer. "I've never agreed with them, Mr. Patterson," Tommy said, taking another bunch of fries.

Marge brought out Daniel and Jessica's orders and set them down. They both thanked Marge, and then Tommy continued. "I always knew in my heart that they were wrong. Hatred of any kind is wrong. It isn't a secret that Dad and Jeff hate you." Tommy held Daniel's gaze for a moment. "I don't hate you, Mr. Patterson. You're a man like any other. Your blood is red, just like mine."

"You have a good heart, Tommy," Daniel said.

Daniel took his daughter's hand and bowed his head. Tommy looked uncomfortable until Jessica took his hand as well. He smiled and bowed his head with them as silent thanks went up to the Great Creator. When Daniel finished and raised his head up, he saw Jeff and Sam sauntering toward their table. They were snickering when Jeff pushed Sam into Daniel, nearly knocking him out of his seat. Daniel winced, holding his ribs at the intrusion. He stood up with a warning look to Jeff.

"Grow up, Jeff!" Tommy snarled in disgust.

"Chill, little bro. Sam here said somethin' funny, and I just had to respond," he feigned innocence.

Sam ended up on the floor and purposely pulled Daniel's plate off the table in his attempt to get up.

"Hey, sweet thing," Jeff said, reaching for Jessica.

Daniel's hand shot out and grabbed Jeff's wrist with a vice-like grip. Jeff's eyes registered surprise at Daniel's strength as he tried to free himself from the father's hold.

"Don't ever touch my daughter," Daniel warned, his eyes flickering with fire. He released Jeff, who staggered back a couple of steps, rubbing his wrist with a scowl.

"Heard you had a rough time last night, Patterson," Sam taunted, trying to take Daniel's attention off Jeff.

"Just some cowards trying to prove their manhood. They failed miserably at it," Daniel jibed in return. His stare backed the boys toward the door.

"Hey, you two, get out of my diner! I've told you before to quit causing trouble!" Marge shouted, marching into the main room.

Jeff and Sam scurried out. "I'll be talkin' to you when you get home, little brother!" Jeff jabbed a finger in Tommy's direction as he pushed through the door.

Daniel relaxed when they left, but Tommy remained standing, watching to make sure his brother wouldn't cause any more trouble. After a moment, he sat down again. A busboy came by with a broom and bus tub to clean up the mess on the floor. After he left, Marge came by with a new plate of food for Daniel.

"Thanks, Marge." Daniel smiled.

"On the house, baby. Sorry for the trouble," she told him.

"It wasn't your fault. I'll pay," he reasoned.

"Are you hungry?" she shot back at him like a mother. "You better eat what's in front of you, or you'll be doing the dishes," she warned. "I ain't in the mood for arguing."

"Yes, ma'am," Daniel submitted to the matron of the house. As Marge walked away, Daniel leaned toward the two kids in front of him, loving to tease Marge. "Can you believe her?" He said it just loud enough for her to hear.

"I heard that!"

"Yes, ma'am, looks great! Thanks!" Daniel said, sitting up and putting his napkin in his lap. "Argh!" he yelped, rubbing his ribs.

"Serves you right!" she shouted over her shoulder, disappearing into the kitchen.

Tommy and Jessica burst out laughing, grateful for the comic relief. With the tension dissipated, Tommy then launched into his questions about the local college and about Daniel's glory days. Daniel spoke humbly, not seeing his championship days as anything special. His biggest memory was the stress and pain it caused him. The better he played, the less harassment he got. In the end, he felt used and cheap for going along with it to stay in favor with the enemy.

As Daniel told him the stories, Tommy dropped his head silently as Daniel finished.

"You okay?" Daniel asked him.

Jessica looked at Tommy with concern. "Tommy?" She touched his arm.

"I'm so sorry," Tommy whispered, not looking at Daniel and trying to keep his composure. "It was my dad and Jeff, wasn't it?" When Tommy finally met Daniel's eyes, Daniel looked away with a nod of his head.

When Daniel looked back at him, he could see in Tommy's eyes that he really had no idea what his dad had done over the years and most likely wasn't aware of his current activities with the Aryans in the town. He wasn't going to tell him. It wasn't time yet.

"Jess, we better get home. We need to get the house ready." Daniel stood up slowly as Jessica patted Tommy's arm and rose to leave with her dad.

Tommy sat back, still taking in the gravity of the situation. He watched them as they headed for the door. He got up quickly and followed them out.

"Mind if I come along?"

Daniel and Jessica turned. Daniel's look was questioning.

"I'm sure you're not supposed to be moving around too much. I can clean a house as good as the next guy."

"That's not saying much," Jessica mumbled.

Daniel smirked at the comment. "Come on," Daniel invited, eliciting a grin from Jessica.

"I'll follow behind." Tommy indicated his car.

At the Patterson's house, Tommy helped to vacuum and dust while Jessica cleaned the kitchen and bathrooms. Daniel sat at the kitchen table, feeling completely useless. When Jessica entered the kitchen after cleaning the upstairs, Daniel turned to her with a thoughtful glint in his eyes.

"You're right, Jess."

"About what, Dad?"

"Tommy. He'd make a great wife." He laughed at his joke and then winced gingerly, touching his split lip.

"You're just full of humor today," Jessica said, rolling her eyes.

Daniel pulled his hand down and found blood on his fingers. Jessica went to the sink and wet a clean towel for him.

"Maybe you should save it until you get better," she suggested with a smirk, handing him the towel.

He gave a nod of agreement.

CHAPTER 5

The next morning, Jessica drove Daniel to the sheriff's office. His nerves caused butterflies in his stomach. He'd gone into dangerous situations without so much as breaking a sweat from nerves, but here, he felt as if he were going into the lion's den. He'd rather confront a thousand masked murderers than have to face the McKinleys after the beating he received. Two thoughts occurred to him as he began to pray. The obvious thought was trusting the Lord, and the next one was that he was going in victorious, showing the enemy he couldn't be kept down. That wasn't his intention, of course, but it helped ease his nerves.

Jessica pulled up in front of the old adobe building in her dad's SUV so her dad could clear out his belongings. "I don't want to go in, Dad," she told him.

He looked at her. "Why not?" He could have used some moral support.

"Because I might tell Deputy McKinley off. He told me he hadn't seen you all day when I called to check on you the other night."

Daniel gave her an understanding nod and gentle smile. "I won't be long," he assured her. Daniel walked into the station as if it were a workday and found a box on top of his desk, the walls and bookcases of his office bare. His personal belongings had been thrown into the box for him. He'd almost expected it. He was going in to get his things anyway. At least they packed for him.

"Up and around so soon?" Tom McKinley asked with annoyance and surprise.

Daniel gave him a wry smile. "Sorry to disappoint you, Tom. I'm kind of hard to keep down," Daniel said while looking through his belongings. "Maybe you should do your own dirty work." He turned to Tom, who was obviously about to blow a gasket. "Hey, thanks for packing my stuff for me."

Daniel's sincerity caused the bigots to bristle even more. He knew they weren't expecting such a response. He tested the weight of the box and then began to carefully maneuver it to the side of his desk to lift it. Picking up the box was going to hurt no matter how light it might have been, and, of course, no one offered to help him. Just then Jessica was behind him.

"I'll get that, Dad." She smiled as Daniel turned to her in surprise.

"Thanks, sweetheart." He smiled back. Together they walked through the station with their heads held high.

Daniel's secretary followed them out and stopped them just outside the door of the building. "Daniel," she called.

Daniel and Jessica turned to her.

"I'm sorry about your belongings. I was packing them, but someone thought I was moving too slowly and took over for me." She snuck a glance at the building.

Daniel could tell she was nervous. "I understand. Thanks, Jan."

"I'll miss you, Daniel. You were a pleasure to work for and the only really nice guy in there."

Daniel chuckled at that. "Well, you were the best assistant anyone could ask for."

"You may have just given me an excuse to retire." She smiled brightly.

"I'm sorry," Daniel said. He had never intended to put anyone out of work.

"Oh, no, no, no! I've wanted an excuse for quite some time, but as long as you were there, I was going to stick it out with you."

"That means a lot, Jan. Enjoy your retirement." He smiled. Jan carefully hugged him and then went back into the station, looking determined.

Daniel and Jessica got into the SUV and were just about to pull away when the sheriff stormed out of the building toward the vehicle.

"What the hell do you think you're doing, Patterson?" he shouted.

Jessica stepped on the brakes as the sheriff put his hands on the doorframe next to Daniel's arm.

"What do you mean?" Daniel asked, not having a clue why he was ranting at him.

"Jan just quit!"

"Well, good for her. It's a free county, isn't it?" Daniel asked.

"You put that idea into her head!" he continued to yell.

"Sorry, sir. She's an adult. She came up with the idea all on her own." Daniel shifted to avoid the sheriff's saliva spray.

"You're just trying to get back at me!"

"Actually, the best revenge is forgiveness. I forgive you for sending your dogs after me."

"What?" McKinley roared.

"And for trying to get rid of me." Daniel smiled like an angel.

"Now you're accusing me!"

Daniel simply looked at Jessica and motioned for her to drive away.

"You hold on there, boy!" he shouted as Jessica pulled the vehicle away from the curb. "I'm not finished with you!"

Daniel gave a casual wave, watching the man, in his side view mirror kicking invisible dirt like an angry coach at an umpire.

His heart was pounding from the confrontation, and as his daughter drove, he sat back in his seat and searched his heart. He hated such encounters and always felt it necessary to ask the Great Creator to check him to see if he may have handled it with the wrong attitude.

Jessica noticed the pensive look on her dad's face. "Dad? Are you okay?"

Daniel exhaled slowly and then opened his eyes. "Yeah, I'm fine. Let's go up to the rez this weekend. I think we need to move things up a little bit," he told her as he looked out his window at the Arizona landscape.

Jessica nodded. "Okay," she said, her heart now pounding.

Daniel noticed the worried look on her face. "I'm sorry if I'm scaring you. I just want to get a lay of the land, hook up with Sicheii and Ben, and be one step ahead," he explained.

"Ahead of what?"

"The enemy," he muttered.

"Okay. Now you're scaring me," she confessed. "Dad, I'm not a child. Tell me what's going on."

Daniel sighed. "You look so much like your mom. She was confident, strong, and sometimes demanding."

Jessica shot him a look.

"All right." Daniel rubbed his face in exasperation. "I found out about three years ago that the McKinleys were working to form a militant Aryan group. They're putting together an arsenal. I just don't know where. Since they run the sheriff's office, they have free reign. They came to this town for a reason, Jess."

"That's what you were talking about when you said you uncovered something?"

He nodded and glanced at her a couple of times, not ready to look her in the eye. "Jessica, they were the ones behind your mom's death," he said.

Jessica slammed on the brakes in shock. The seatbelt bit into Daniel's ribs, causing him to groan. Jessica trembled as tears streaked down her face. "Are you sure?"

Daniel regained his breath and nodded to her. "I went over the crash site again and again. There was an extra set of skid marks. I looked at Tom's cruiser and found paint flecks from mom's car on it after they'd repainted it. I was too afraid to say anything, but they know that I know. There's just no proof of what they did. They would deny it, and you'd be in danger."

"I don't understand."

"Killing your mom was a warning to keep me quiet about their activities. I had to go along with it or they'd—" He stopped, turning his face from her. He took a deep, careful breath. "They might have hurt you next."

Jessica touched her dad's arm.

"Leaving too soon would have made them think I was trying to report them," he added.

Jessica wiped her eyes and then put the SUV into motion again. She remained silent for the rest of the drive home.

Arriving home, Daniel immediately headed for the stairs as fast as his aching body would allow him to climb. Once in his room, he pulled his .45 automatic pistol from the nightstand and checked the clip. He then went to his gun safe inside the closet and retrieved a couple of his rifles and ammo for all three weapons. He placed the rifles and ammunition into a gun bag.

"Jessica!" he called to her.

Jessica ran up the stairs to his room. "Yeah, Dad?"

"I want you to pack everything you want to take with you," he told her with a new urgency in his voice.

"What are you not telling me?" she said, stepping up to the bag of guns.

He zipped it closed quickly and clipped his handgun to his belt. "You'll be staying at the rez," he told her.

She looked at him with a flash of protest in her eyes. "Dad, what about my friends? Don't I get to say good-bye?"

With a weak reply, he kept packing his clothes. "Sorry."

"Dad!"

"Jessica, please, you'll be safe on the rez."

"I'm in danger? I thought as long as you kept quiet, everything would be all right."

"I think I really stirred them up back there. I'm not going to let anything happen to you."

She stared at her dad. Daniel knew he was moving too fast for Jessica. Better too fast than risk her life. As she was driving them home, he'd realized just how angry he'd made his enemy, like stirring up a hornet's nest. He wanted Jessica far from harm, and Ben could keep her safe on the rez.

"Let me do this, please." He walked up to her and hugged her. "I'll tell Tommy everything. I promise." He kissed her forehead.

"I'll get packed." She turned and left the room. Daniel could see the confusion in her eyes, and yet her quick submission was what hurt more. He didn't know if she was giving up or preparing for a fight. He hoped the latter.

Jessica's emotions were running high. Her dad was in an even greater hurry than before, and she was upset that he hadn't told her until driving home how urgent the situation really was. She gave him the benefit of the doubt that as they drove home, he had been mulling it over in his mind. The sheriff had truly threatened them. She thought her dad must have realized it wasn't safe to let her stay until the house sold. She sighed, knowing she couldn't stay angry with him. He was doing the best he could; of that, she was sure.

Jessica sat at her desk and looked at her laptop and the various pictures of friends from school as well as some of family taped on and around the desk unit. She pulled them down one by one, removing the tape from the backs of them and then placing them into a shoebox. She couldn't help but think how odd it was that all the family pictures seemed to end up in boxes as if preparing for a funeral. She couldn't be sure if her box of memories she was packing would ever be emptied or if it would remain, sitting in some corner collecting dust and living an uncertain future.

She put her laptop into her backpack, slid the shoebox in with it, and then set it aside. She then went to her closet and packed the clothes she wore most. In no time, she was nearly finished. She looked at her dresser. She had few favorite keepsakes. There was a one-inch rose quartz horse and a Navajo baby doll her mom had given her when she was a very young girl. She smiled as she looked at the doll. She was eager to get back to the rez even though she'd only been there once as a small child. She didn't know why, but her great-grandmother and great-grandfather would always come down from the rez and visit them. After her mom died, her dad had asked them to stop coming because it was too painful for him. She missed them. Her great-grandmother had died a year ago, and she hadn't been able to go to the funeral. At least now she would be able to see her great-grandfather again.

She put her doll into the backpack, finding that it would be the last item to fit into the now-stuffed bag. Suddenly, her last year of high school didn't seem so important after all. She wouldn't be that far from Tommy, and he could visit, she reasoned to herself.

Daniel had been up and down the stairs several times and was exhausted and in more pain than he cared to be in as he climbed the stairs for the last time, dragging a hand truck with him. "Jess!" he called.

Jessica hurried to him.

"Can I get a hand with the trunk?"

She applauded wildly as she followed him into his room.

"I would take a bow, but I'm a little sore." He offered a congenial smile.

"Just trying to lighten the mood."

"I appreciate what you're trying to do, sweetheart."

"Is the trunk heavy?" she asked, looking at the item in the back of the closet.

"Not really, but it's awkward, so I need some help."

"But normally you wouldn't, right?" she said, winking and gently jabbed his arm.

"Absolutely!" He grinned.

Jessica grabbed one of the leather handles and proceeded to drag it out of its hiding place.

"Hold on. Let me get this," he said. He took the wedding dress off the rack and held it up to her. "Beautiful!"

Jessica opened the lid of the trunk. "Do you know something I don't?"

Daniel shrugged but didn't answer. She carefully placed the dress inside of the trunk and then closed the lid. Jessica helped him load it onto the dolly and together they got it down the stairs and into the SUV.

"Are you about ready to go?" he said.

She nodded. "Can I come back when it's safe and say good-bye to my friends?"

He helped her bring her suitcases and belongings down and loaded them. "Of course." He looked at her. He now understood how she felt. She was being ripped from her home, the only home she'd known. It was like the forced relocation of the First Nations People. It wasn't right.

With the tailgate up, Jessica turned to face the adobe-style home she'd grown up in, the For Sale sign making the finality starkly real. Daniel stepped up beside her, putting his arm around her. "Remember your name, Yanaba," he whispered.

"I don't feel brave at the moment, Dad. Maybe I'll grow into it," she said.

Daniel gave her a gentle squeeze. "You are the bravest woman I know."

"Yeah," she said.

Daniel handed her the keys, and before they pulled out, they said a prayer for their safety and for Tommy's.

CHAPTER 6

The drive was a long but beautiful two hours. Daniel was asleep in the passenger seat. He had reluctantly taken a pain pill at Jessica's request, resulting in his impromptu nap. As she drove, Jessica felt her heart being drawn to the landscape and the reservation. She felt her emotions stir and a strange urgency in her heart that she didn't quite understand.

"Lord, what is this?" she whispered.

She heard a voice in her heart and seemingly on the wind.

"Heritage," the voice echoed.

Daniel suddenly awoke and sat up. "Stop!"

"What?"

"Pull over here! Here!" He motioned to the right side of the highway.

Jessica complied, pulling the SUV to the side of the road. Daniel climbed out, walked several yards into the scrub, and then froze.

"Dad, what is it?" She followed him.

Without looking at her, Daniel motioned for her to stop. She obliged and watched as her dad stretched his arms out to his sides and tilted his head skyward, his eyes closed. High above, in the cloudless sky, a golden eagle circled and gave a shrill cry. Jessica squinted upward and watched as her dad and the eagle somehow communicated. Suddenly, Daniel dropped to his knees as a Navajo song began to emanate from his being.

She didn't understand what he was singing, but was touched deeply as she watched her dad commune with God. She'd never seen him do that before. They prayed together all the time, and she'd seen and heard her parents praying together, but this was altogether different. This was deeper. Tears glinted in the sun off her dad's face as the song eventually faded. Daniel sat back, remaining on his knees, his hands resting on his thighs. His shoulders shuddered as his crying turned into sobs. Jessica slowly made her way to her dad and knelt down beside him.

She wanted to know what he was feeling. She needed to know what he was feeling, and she wondered if it was the same thing that had grabbed her heart earlier. Daniel drew in a deep breath and then slowly let it out. He opened his eyes and looked up into the sky at the eagle. It let out a farewell cry, and Daniel gave a wave. He was smiling as he turned to Jessica.

"What was that?" she said.

"I'm not sure," he answered with a reassuring smile, "but it was good."

Jessica returned his smile with one of her own. Daniel then reached out for her hand, and she helped him to his feet. He headed for the driver's side and stopped again. "We're here," he announced.

"The rez?" Jessica asked.

Daniel pointed to a dirt road across the highway. Jessica had only been to the rez once as a small child for her dedication ceremony to the Great Creator, so she really didn't remember much.

"Down that road," Daniel said, carefully climbing into the SUV.

"How does it make you feel?"

"What?" Daniel started the SUV.

"Returning to the reservation. Are they good or bad memories?" she clarified.

"Anxious. Maybe afraid?"

"Afraid of what? Aren't you a warrior?"

Daniel smiled. "I am at that. But I'm walking into dangerous territory. A little fear keeps one on guard."

"From the fry pan to the fire, eh?"

Daniel snorted. "Something like that."

Jessica gave a thoughtful nod, got in, and rolled up her window for the final dusty ride to the village where her dad had grown up. As they drove, Jessica took in the distant mesas and wondered what they would look like as the sun rose and set on them. She imagined vibrant hues of blues, purples, and reds, and smiled at the imagination of the Great Creator. What she saw in her mind's eye was in sharp contrast to the abundance of tumbleweeds on the flat dry landscape they were traversing.

After half an hour, still being just outside the borders of the actual reservation, they pulled into a small service station and trading post. It was everything depicted in old westerns of ghost towns, complete with the rickety sign flapping in the desert wind, and not a soul to be found. The only testimony to its actual era was the set of gas pumps, and even they predated Daniel. Daniel and Jessica got out of the vehicle. Daniel filled the gas tank while Jessica took in the surreal scene.

"Come on, Jess. It's probably a whopping two degrees cooler inside." Daniel nodded in the direction of the store as he replaced the nozzle on its hook.

Jessica chuckled at the remark and joined her dad as they stepped inside the building. Time warp came to Jessica's mind as she looked at the worn wooden floors and wooden shelves that lined the aisles and walls. The main room was stocked with all of life's essentials from cloth of various prints, textures, and colors to canned food and loaves of bread.

Off to the left was a half room with a fry counter where one could order hamburgers and hotdogs, fry bread, and any other grease-laden fast-food offerings imaginable. The room was occupied by two skinheads and in the corner an angry-looking Navajo whom Daniel steered Jessica's attention from with a gentle hand to her back.

"Three degrees," Jessica commented to her dad as he stepped up to the Navajo man behind the counter.

Daniel pulled out his wallet to pay for the gas. "Are Ben Samson and Lukas White Wolf still around?" he asked.

The clerk looked at Daniel and then at Jessica. "Family?"

Daniel gave a nod.

"Another five miles down on the right." The clerk pointed. "Your money's no good here," he said, looking at Daniel's cash. Just then the Indian from the other room staggered up to the counter with a beer bottle in hand.

"Yeah, we don't want your money. It ain't as green as ours," the Indian said, shaking Daniel's cash in his face.

The clerk stepped back, slightly annoyed at the intrusion. Jessica also took a step back, appalled at the stranger's brazen behavior. Daniel took his cash from the drunk and then put it back on the counter for the clerk.

The clerk eyed him for a long moment. "I know you. You're Red Tears. You're my brother. I won't take your money," the clerk told him.

The drunk Navajo rolled his eyes and guffawed at the sentiment. "*I'm your bro*, bro, but you still take *my* money!"

The clerk and Daniel both ignored him.

"You can't tell me your whole business is supported by him and those skinheads back there," Daniel said. "What are they doing here anyway?"

The clerk put his head down. He shook his head, regret visible on his face. The drunk even gave a look of compassion and then looked over his shoulder at the two young men.

"They just stopped in a while ago. Thirsty is all. Keepin' de peace. Gotta trust the Great Creator," he admitted. Again, this elicited a roll of the eyes from the drunk.

"So use the wisdom he gives you and let me pay," Daniel insisted. "Have there been any more?"

The clerk finally consented, taking the money and putting it in the register. He shook his head. "They're the first."

During this exchange, the Indian began to take notice of Jessica and walked to the other side of Daniel. He stared at her as if he knew her somehow. "Yanaba?" he said uncertainly. Jessica was not happy with this man staring at her. Daniel put a protective arm around her and guided her out of the store.

The Indian was offended. "Hey, Danny boy, aren't you going to introduce me?" he called after them.

Jessica looked over her shoulder with worry at the man following them and then quickly climbed into the SUV, slamming her door and locking it.

"Do you know him?" she asked her dad as he got in and closed his door.

The Indian put his free hand on the window frame of Daniel's door and took a swig of beer, waiting for an answer.

Daniel sighed. "Jessica, this is your uncle, Bannin Hawkeye. Hawk, this is Jessica."

Her eyes went wide as her jaw dropped. Her mom's brother.

"Hey, Niece, pleasure to meet you. Nice to see ya all grown up. It's been a *really* long time," Hawk said with a look at Daniel. "I see you can't take a beating. That'll make it easier."

Jessica was in shock and turned her head away and stared out the windshield.

Daniel started the vehicle. "We're going, Hawk. I'd move if you want to keep your toes." Daniel was cordial, putting the SUV in drive and pulling out.

"Nice way to greet family! I'll keep that promise!" Hawk yelled at him. "You damn half-breed!" He staggered backward, landing on his butt.

Daniel stopped to make sure he was all right.

The move angered Hawk even more. "Don't even pretend to care!" he raged, getting himself off the ground. "Get the hell out of here!" Hawk threw his beer bottle at Daniel. It missed him but dented the SUV.

Daniel shook his head and looked at Jessica. "Sorry." He pulled back onto the road.

Jessica nodded quietly. "What was that all about?" she asked.

"He hates me." Daniel shrugged.

"Why?"

"He didn't want a half-breed to marry his sister," he began. "I guess after your mom died, he started drinking. I haven't seen him in a while, but I know he wasn't drinking the last time I saw him. I guess he blames me for her death, too." He glanced in the rearview mirror at his brother-in-law staggering back into the trading post, no doubt for another beer.

"When's the last time you saw him?"

"About seventeen years ago at your dedication. He wouldn't talk to us, so he only saw you from a distance," Daniel told her. "I saw him two months before your mom and I got married. He refused to come to the wedding, and Sarah wanted me to try to mend things between us."

"Why does he hate you so much?"

"I don't know, Jess. Me, your mom, him, and Ben, who you'll meet, were inseparable when we were kids."

"I guess I'd start drinking if I chose to hate someone for so long," Jessica said, sadness evident in her voice.

"There's too much hate, Jessica. If we can't even love our own family, then we aren't much better than those skinheads back there."

"He said something about a promise?"

"He said he'd kill me if I ever returned to the rez."

"Is that why Shimasani and Sicheii always came to visit us and we never went to the rez?"

"I'm afraid so."

Jessica nodded, taking in the many facets of her family as she watched the Arizona desert rush by her. She suddenly changed the subject. "Why did Sheriff McKinley really send you up here?"

Daniel glanced at his beautiful daughter and then back at the road in front of him. "Some tribal members disappeared from the rez, and I'm supposed to help Criminal Investigations up here figure out what's going on. But that's probably not the real reason."

"Captain McKinley hates you. Why would he even want you to help your own people?"

"To get rid of me," Daniel told her straight out. "He's probably setting me up. You know, so they can say I died in the line of duty."

"Dad, you're scaring me again."

"I'm sorry, Jess, but you said you wanted to know everything. I'm telling you so you can be prepared for what might come."

"What might come?" she asked him.

"A war," he said, glancing at her. "Hey, we don't need to be afraid, eh? We have the Great Creator behind us," he reminded her.

"Does anyone else here trust him like we do?" she asked, hoping they weren't the only ones on the rez who knew God personally.

"Yep. Ben and Sicheii."

"I can't wait to see him again. Two years is a long time. I wish we could have gone to Shimasani's burial."

Daniel glanced at Jessica noting the sadness in her eyes.

"I don't think I know Sicheii's history. I never thought to ask. Tell me about him. Was he forced into a boarding school?"

"Yeah. He was five years old when they took him. Although at that time in the thirties, Congress was beginning to make changes about forced removal. The process was slow, of course, as anything the government does regarding our people."

"What changes?"

"Well, the Secretary of the Interior had to start contracting with the states and territories to provide health care and education. That doesn't mean they regulated the humane treatment of the children."

"So was Sicheii mistreated?"

"Unfortunately, yes. But the Navajo don't like to speak of such things. All I know is that Sicheii made a choice to take the good from it."

"What possible good could have come out of any boarding school?" Jessica adjusted herself in her seat so she could look at her dad. Any signs of human activity were still an hour out.

"Well, some wouldn't agree with me, like Hawk, but Sicheii would say, what you determine to take with you will mold you. Some missionaries had visited the school when he was there, and they were different from the supposed Christian that ran the school. They knew that the children would be punished if caught with a Bible, and Sicheii said that they tried to give them out with the permission of the school, but the school said no."

"Figures."

"One of the missionaries talked with Sicheii because he'd been assigned to show them around and lie for the school about the wonderful care the children received there."

"Sicheii's not a liar, right?"

"Right. So when the missionaries left, they snuck a small handwritten portion of the Bible to him. He devoured it, and he met the Great Creator personally. That's how he got saved. So he left the school with knowledge of the real truth and of man's truth."

"Lies is more like it."

"You sound bitter, and you've never been to a boarding school. That's dangerous, Jessica. Don't take the pain of your ancestors and allow it to be a chip on your shoulder. There are too many of us who do that. We need to repent as much as the white man."

Jessica was silent. She looked out the window, considering her dad's words. The tumbleweeds and scrubs seemed to go on forever, but to the east were the Chuska Mountains. Cottonwood was their destination, near Chinle. She would ask Sicheii to take her to the mountains sometime. When it was safe.

"You know the Great Creator and the Great Chief. You know forgiveness, and you must walk in it."

"I'm sorry, Dad. I understand."

Daniel looked at her with a proud smile.

"So who's Ben?"

"He's the commander of Criminal Investigations up here and my brother." Daniel caught a herd of wild horses out of the corner of his eye and did a double take. When he looked again, they were gone, a cloud of dust the only evidence that they may have been there.

"Wait, your brother?" she asked, giving him a look of confusion.

"He's actually my best friend, the one I told you about in our group. In the Navajo tradition, a best friend is considered a brother. My sicheii is my mom's father and the tribal elder."

"Okay," she acknowledged. "Do I call Ben uncle?"

"Yep. He's married to Christiana. Call her auntie."

Daniel turned into the dirt driveway of a modern hogan and turned off the engine. A Navajo man and woman came out of the house to greet their guests. Ben, in his early fifties, sported a Khaki short-sleeved shirt with a badge over the left breast, blue jeans, and cowboy boots. The woman, Christiana, his wife, wore a traditional skirt and blouse with tall moccasins.

"*Sheila!*" Ben called. Jessica looked at her dad.

"Brother," Daniel translated for her.

She gave a slight nod and a smile as she looked at Ben. Daniel got out, and the two men gripped each other's forearms and patted each other's shoulders.

"Ben, good to see you. It's been a long time! Christiana!" Daniel grinned, offering Christiana a gentle hug. She smiled, returning the embrace.

"Yes, it has!" Ben agreed, and then he looked at Jessica. "Is this Jessica?"

"Yes, it is. Jessica, this is your uncle, Ben," Daniel told her, putting a gentle hand on her back and ushering her forward.

"Welcome back to the rez, Jessica." Ben smiled, offering his hand.

Jessica was too caught up in the spirit of the family reunion to settle for just a handshake and excitedly hugged him. Ben was surprised for just a moment, keeping his arms from encircling her until Daniel nodded his consent. Then he hugged her gently.

"Nice to finally meet you," she told him.

Jessica greeted Christiana in the same fashion.

"We ran into Hawkeye at the trading post," Daniel said. He gingerly pulled a duffel bag from behind the driver's seat.

Jessica pulled one of hers from the back seat as well. The four then headed into the hogan.

"I bet that was interesting, eh?" Ben chortled.

"To say the least," Daniel agreed.

When they stepped inside, Lukas White Wolf, Daniel's great-grandfather, greeted him. He only spoke in Navajo and to Daniel's surprise, Daniel found himself understanding.

"Red Tears," he said, "the blood of our people cries through you."

Daniel stopped in his tracks, feeling something stir in his heart. Lukas continued to speak to his grandson. "Let the Great Creator cry through you for them."

Daniel, while taken aback at the odd greeting, shook himself and went to the old man who was sitting on a chair. Daniel knelt before him, taking the position he had when with the eagle earlier that day. He understood the power of his elder's blessing, having learned it from his sicheii and the Old Testament.

Lukas lit some white sage and placed it on the floor in an abalone shell in front of Daniel, who drew the smoke toward him with his hands. His sicheii had taught him that the smoke represented the Great Creator's presence as it had in the Old Testament. "Great Creator, Father of all, bring forth the spirit man of my grandson and give him the courage to carry your burden."

Ben translated for Jessica's sake as Lukas continued. "You shall live and not die and declare the works of the Lord," Lukas finished. He then placed a gentle hand on Daniel's shoulder, indicating he could get up.

Daniel stood and then ushered Jessica up to Lukas. When Lukas looked at her, tears fell from his eyes. "Yanaba," he said quietly.

Jessica looked at her dad uncertainly. He smiled and gave her a nod to kneel the same way he had. She knelt in front of her great sicheii, and he spoke a blessing over her in Navajo. "*Yanaba Chenoa.*"

Daniel translated for her. "Brave Dove."

"You are his prophetess. You will see things in the Spirit."

Lukas made a motion with his hands, indicating that she could get up. Daniel and Jessica embraced, both realizing that God, the Great Creator, had his own plans for bringing them back to their true home.

CHAPTER 7

The sun was setting over the western mesas of Arizona, painting their walls with hues of red and purple. Red Tears, half Navajo and half white, sat on top of a flat rock with his wife, Meda, sharing the colors of the fading day. As young children played soccer nearby, the couple's reverie was interrupted by one of the children urgently motioning to the south. There in the near distance, wavy images like a mirage sped toward them—a cloud of ominous dust billowed behind. Red Tears and Meda quickly climbed off the rock, grabbed the youngest of the children, and ran to the nearby village.

"Get the children and women to safety!" Red Tears shouted in Navajo to the villagers. The men sent the women and children out of the village to the safety of a nearby canyon dotted with ancient caves. Red Tears and the men of the village then took a stance, shoulder to shoulder, forming a line to face their enemy. Red Tears stood beside his brother-in-law, Bannin Hawkeye, and waited.

The trucks pulled to a stop in front of the brave men. Skinheads stood up from the back of the trucks and aimed rifles at the Navajo warriors. Red Tears and Hawkeye looked at each other, knowing the end was near.

"Hokahay!" Red Tears said to his brother.

Hawkeye nodded once.

Suddenly, the armed men opened fire. Warriors fell in a heap, but Red Tears and Hawkeye remained standing, untouched by the bullets. The brothers looked up to the sky and began to sing in Navajo as the armed men climbed from their trucks, surprised and annoyed that these two had not even been scathed. Ten white men descended on the two Navajos, beating them and then loading their unconscious forms into the back of one of the trucks. The men drove to the edge of a mesa, backed up to it, and opened the tailgate. The brutes stood up the barely conscious men and then pushed them off the cliff.

Daniel sat upright with a jolt, his breathing heavy and sweat drenching his body. He drew his right hand over his face and blinked in the dark room. After his eyes adjusted, he realized he was alive and safe in his new home, next door to Ben's home. *How* safe, he wasn't certain. He threw the sheet aside, walked to his still unpacked duffel bag, and pulled a t-shirt out. He pulled it on as he quietly walked to Jessica's room. He opened the door, careful not to let it squeak as he looked in on her. She was asleep, oblivious to her dad's newest torment.

Daniel went to the kitchen and sat down at the table, bathed in moonlight. He went over the nightmare he'd just had. First, he was with a woman he'd never seen before, and second, he died as a warrior with Hawkeye by his side. The most disturbing part wasn't that he had been killed but the fact that it was skinheads who killed him. He would have to inform Ben about the McKinleys. The dream had to be a warning. He drank down a glass of water, showered, and spent the remainder of the early morning hours praying about the dream.

At daybreak, Daniel, with Ben's help, moved his and Jessica's things into the manufactured home next door to Ben's place. It had been built by some missionary volunteers for a couple, but after a year, the occupants had moved off the reservation. While Daniel did his best to try to hide the pain he was in, the stitches on his cheek and lips hinted that he was more injured than he was letting on.

"You getting old, Shelia?" Ben asked Daniel as he watched him step outside with Jessica.

"What do you mean?" Daniel feigned innocence but dropped his hands from his ribs self-consciously.

"I mean you're moving like an old man. You didn't do that much."

"I just got caught in a minor brawl a couple of days ago," Daniel said. "I took a couple of hits."

Jessica wouldn't look at Ben. Ben noticed her response but said nothing further. Suddenly, the end of their conversation was interrupted by Hawkeye's erratic drive toward them. He pulled into Ben's driveway with a crooked skid. He got out and strode over to the three of them. Daniel was just putting his duffel bag into his SUV.

"Where you going, half-breed?"

"Hawk!" Ben barked sharply.

Daniel put his hand up, ignoring Hawk. "It's okay, Ben."

"You're drunk this early?" Ben had to ask.

Jessica started toward the house after giving her dad a kiss good-bye.

"Breakfast of champions!" Hawk replied, wiggling a beer bottle by its neck. He then refocused on Daniel when he saw Jessica walking to her house. "You dumpin' your daughter now?" Hawk asked in disgust. "Can't handle the pressure of raising your girl, so you leave her here with us, eh?" He slapped Daniel sharply on the back, causing Daniel to wince.

"Whatever you want to believe, bro." Daniel stepped away and got into his SUV.

"Ain't your bro, apple," Hawk spat back. Daniel wouldn't have expected less from Hawk. Using such a nasty jab and inferring that Daniel was white on the inside and red on the outside raised Daniel's ire, but he had more pressing things to worry about at the moment.

"See ya, Ben." Daniel gave a wave and then pulled out.

"You're too easily insulted, Hawk. Why do you always have to pick a fight?" Ben said.

Hawk ignored Ben. "You're still running, huh?" Hawk hollered after Daniel.

"Shut up, Hawk, and put some food in that trap of yours," Ben suggested.

Jessica returned from inside her house and started to head out for a jog while Hawk staggered past her into Ben's house.

"Jessica!" Ben called.

She stopped and turned. "Yes, Uncle?" She smiled and trotted over.

"Jessica, I'd rather you didn't go anywhere alone, especially when your dad's not here. When he gets back, we'll be looking into a situation we have here on the rez."

"The missing clansmen?" she asked.

Ben cocked his head. "Just one. Your dad told you?"

"Of course. We don't keep secrets." She stretched out her legs as she talked.

"That's wise. Did you eat yet?"

"Yeah, Dad and I had breakfast earlier."

"You two know family. That's very good."

Jessica offered an appreciative smile

"Ever been to work with your dad?"

Jessica shook her head.

"Good. You can come with me. I'll tell you some stories about your dad." He chuckled.

"That could be entertaining." She grinned as they walked to Ben's SUV.

As Daniel drove back to Stake Town, he had time to go over again the recent dream he'd had and what his sicheii meant about the Great Creator's burden. Flashes of his dream haunted him. All he could sense from it was hatred. The one good thing he saw in the dream was that he and Bannin Hawkeye were on the same side. He pulled his vehicle to the side of the road and prayed that the images of the dream would stop.

Tommy quickly packed a military duffel bag and loaded it into his car. He had parked it around the block on a route he knew his dad and Jeff never took. He wasn't expecting his good-bye to go very well, and he even considered just leaving without a word. Tommy was just finishing a small breakfast when his dad and Jeff came in for the morning.

"Why didn't you wait for us?" Tom Sr. asked him.

"I have to go, Dad."

"Go where?"

"I found a place with some friends."

"What does that mean? You're moving out?" his dad asked, looking genuinely concerned. It was the softest expression Tommy had seen his dad carry in a long time, and it caught him off guard.

"Dad, I'm nineteen. I think it's time for me to be out on my own."

"Jeff's still here."

"I'm not Jeff, Dad."

"So you just want to leave?"

"Dad, I…" He paused, realizing words, no matter how grateful they sounded, were not going to work. "Yes," he said, standing up.

Jeff shoved Tommy back down into his chair, signaling that the discussion was still open. "That's no way to treat Dad!"

"It's part of growing up, Jeff. Kids move out!" Tommy shot back.

"You're trying to make me look bad, aren't you?" Jeff retorted.

Tommy rolled his eyes with a sigh. "Whatever, Jeff." He then looked at his dad. "I'm not asking for anything but that you let me go, Dad. I don't want to be a burden to you anymore."

"What if I don't want you to leave? You're my son, and family stays together," Tom Sr. said with a hint of threat in his voice.

A chill ran down Tommy's spine.

"You aren't planning on going after that half-breed's daughter, are you?"

"Dad, I'm an adult. Who I love really isn't your business." Tommy's impatience was growing, but he remained calm.

"I taught you better than that!"

"No, Dad! What you tried to teach me is wrong. I have my own heart. I can't be brainwashed like Jeff!" Tommy hadn't meant for the good-bye to become an argument, so he stood again and started for the back door.

"You watch your tone, boy!" his dad snarled, grabbing Tommy and turning him back toward him.

Jeff grabbed his other arm after his dad had released him and slammed him in the face. "Say you're sorry!"

Tommy wiped the blood from his mouth and just stared at Jeff. His dad remained silent, observing. Tommy knew he had to get out. "I won't apologize for what's true!" he said. He looked at his father. "I know what you did to Jessica's dad. You set him up." Tommy tried to go for the door, but Jeff grabbed him.

"We'll just have to make sure you understand our idea of truth," Jeff said, shoving his little brother against the wall, pinning him there.

His dad walked up and stood by with his arms folded over his chest. "Now, son, I think you're confused."

"I'm not the one who's confused!" Tommy struggled in Jeff's hold. "You said we're family, and look at the two of you. You're going to beat the truth into me?" He tried to get them to see reason.

"That's how I was raised, my father before me, and on down the line. It's part of growing up in the McKinley family. Y'see, son, we're part of a proud heritage of Native American slave owners."

"Four hundred years, right, Dad?"

"That's my boy, Jeff." Tom Sr. smiled at his eldest. Then he turned to Tommy. "Now why can't you remember family history like that?"

Tommy's eyes were pleading but went unnoticed.

"What's the right color, son?"

Tommy's face registered confusion. "What?"

Jeff pressed him harder against the wall.

"What's the right color? Come on. We've been over this." His dad was a sea of calm as if this line of interrogation was a part of his lifestyle.

"Red," Tommy said defiantly. Tommy surprised himself. He'd meant to say white. But at that moment, the answer he gave he knew was the right one.

Tom Sr. shook his head in regret, stepped back, and allowed Jeff to beat his younger brother into submission. Tommy tried to fight back and got a couple of good strikes in. However, Jeff was a head taller and known for his brawn. Eventually, Tommy stopped fighting back. Jeff threw his exhausted and bloodied brother out the front door into the dirt. His dad then surveyed Tommy as he stood over him. "When you come back to your senses and figure out the right answer, you can come inside and have a meal with us."

Tommy lay there hugging his ribs, breathing hard, his eyes closed tightly in pain. He could just make out his dad turning and leaving as the horrific mind-set of his family sunk in. He couldn't believe that a father and a brother could be so consumed with hate that they could treat him like they had. A wave of nausea washed over him, and he lost his breakfast. He moved away and tried to stand, but he was too hurt to move any farther and passed out near the side of the house.

A couple of hours later, Tommy regained consciousness and rolled to his back, tears mingling with the blood on his face. He saw his dad's SUV and knew he and Jeff were still home. He staggered to his feet and made his way down and around the block to his car.

Daniel stopped by the real estate office to see if there was any interest on the house yet. There were some hits on the Internet but no offers to date; after all, it had only been a day. Daniel headed to the diner to grab some lunch and then started for the house. As Daniel arrived at his house, he stopped the SUV in front of it before pulling into the driveway. He bowed his head in frustration. On the front of the adobe, scrawled in red paint was the epitaph: "Go home, half-breed!" He took a deep breath and pulled into the driveway. He got out and went to the front door.

The hair on the back of Daniel's neck bristled when he entered. He sensed someone was there. He pulled his .45 and cautiously checked each room. When he looked inside the kitchen, he noticed the glass on the back door had been broken. There was some blood on the floor, only a few drops, but he observed the direction of the splatter and followed it. He made his way upstairs and saw a body on the landing. With his gun raised, he slowly took the last few stairs. When he made the landing, he could see it was Tommy. Daniel holstered his gun and knelt beside the young man.

"Tommy!" Daniel said, lifting the young man's head slightly.

Tommy opened his eyes, one of them bruised and swollen, and he smiled through a fat lip. "Dad wished me well," he tried to joke, and then he broke down into sobs.

"What happened?" Daniel asked as he held the broken boy.

"They beat me, Mr. Patterson."

"Who?" Daniel wanted clarification.

Tommy grasped Daniel in a desperate hug, "Dad and Jeff. They said that I should have learned their ways," he cried. "They might hurt Jessica."

"Don't worry, Tommy. I won't let that happen," Daniel promised.

Daniel realized that the broken-spirited young man in his arms needed all the fathering he could offer. He helped Tommy into the bathroom, giving him a washcloth and towel so he could clean up. Daniel retrieved one of the shirts he'd left behind and brought it to Tommy. As Tommy cleaned up, Daniel then packed the remainder of his clothes, blankets, towels, and food. The rest would sell with the house. When Tommy was ready, they left and headed back to the reservation.

"Does your dad know where you are?"

Tommy was reclining in the passenger seat holding his stomach. "I don't think so. They left me in the front yard of our house. When I came to, they were still inside. I got out of there as fast as I could."

"Hopefully they won't think you're headed for the rez." Daniel gave a reassuring smile to Tommy. "And even if they did, they'd have a real hard time getting to you."

"Why's that?" Tommy asked.

"Because family is very important to the Navajo."

Tommy looked at him, curiosity in his expression, but he said nothing. He closed his eyes and tried to sleep off the pain. Daniel prayed the rest of the way to the rez and called Ben to give him a heads-up on their arrival.

❖ ❖ ❖ ❖ ❖

Two hours later, Daniel pulled into the driveway of his new home. He hadn't had much time to recover from his own injuries, and the labor of loading his SUV again and then supporting Tommy had strained him to his limits. Ben met them at the house with Jessica.

"Oh my God!" she exclaimed, seeing Tommy's condition.

Ben gently pulled her back. "Go tell Christiana, and help Sicheii with the preparations for his injuries."

She nodded, forcing back tears. She hurried back into Ben's house. Daniel let Ben take most of Tommy's weight as he helped get the boy into the house. Once they got him inside and laid his unconscious frame on the couch, Daniel slipped off into a corner and leaned against the wall with a quiet groan. Jessica noticed her dad's attempt to hide his pain. She went up to him and touched his arm, concerned by his trembling. "Dad? You don't look so good."

"I'm okay," he breathed out.

"You don't lie so good, either."

"Well," he corrected, and he forced himself to stand up straight just to prove to her that he was okay. "Let's see to Tommy."

Lukas White Wolf, Daniel's grandfather, had just come out of the kitchen with some herbal tea and a jar of brown goo called rez mud.

"You okay, bro?" Ben asked Daniel as he returned to the scene with Jessica.

Daniel nodded, waving him off.

"Don't lie to me."

"Relax, will ya? I'm fine."

Daniel and Jessica sat down and watched Sicheii light a bundle of white sage, called a smudge, and pray over Tommy. Ben translated the prayers and words of the song. Lukas sang over Tommy for Jessica's sake. Lukas also waved the smudge, asking Jesus to heal the boy. Tommy finally opened his eyes and looked around at the two Navajo men he didn't know and then smiled in relief when he saw Jessica's familiar face. Lukas was given a chair, and the elder sat down next to Tommy.

"Open your shirt," he said, and Ben translated.

Tommy looked at Daniel for assurance.

"It's okay. It'll help," he told him.

Jessica winked at him. Tommy unbuttoned his shirt, and then Lukas proceeded to slather the warm mud onto his torso.

"It's herbal mud. It will speed the healing," Ben said.

"This is my brother, Ben, and Sicheii, or grandfather, Tommy. You can trust them," Daniel told him.

Though Tommy cringed at the smell, the immediate relief he felt was visibly remarkable. "Wow, this is great stuff," Tommy commented.

Daniel hadn't used the mud in years, but he was about ready to submit to asking for help.

"I'll take some of that," Daniel said.

Ben grinned, and Lukas handed him the jar. Daniel dipped his fingers into the sticky mess and dabbed it onto his stitches on his cheek and lips, wincing at the sting. Ben chuckled.

Lukas looked at his grandson with a serious face, which always worried Daniel. He spoke to him in Navajo. "You will soon have to soak in it. You must let pride die in you."

Daniel needed no translation. He knew what had been said. The language was flooding back to him at an alarming rate. He thought he'd completely forgotten his tribal language. It had only been asleep inside of him, and now the Great Creator was reawakening it. Daniel's humble reply was in Navajo. "Thank you, Sicheii."

Jessica looked at him in surprise.

Daniel suddenly rushed outside, needing air, having a sense of urgency as his heart pounded in his chest. He knew the Great Creator was speaking to him, but he didn't understand it yet.

Ben had followed Daniel outside. He leaned against the bumper next to Daniel. He remained silent, waiting for Daniel to speak up. Daniel closed his eyes breathing deep. He was a man who wasn't afraid to cry, but he had never cried so much in recent days.

Resolution was the word he kept hearing.

"Ben, my heart is aching. I'm crying a lot lately, and I don't know why." He threw up his hands in exasperation.

Ben nodded. "There is someone you need to meet," he said simply.

Daniel wiped his face, careful to avoid the stitches, expecting something more profound than that from his close friend and responded, "That's it?"

"That's it." Ben shrugged with an amused grin.

Daniel looked at his brother and gave a sigh, shaking his head. "Okay," he submitted.

"But first, we'll go for the best ribs around," Ben invited, clapping Daniel on the shoulder.

Daniel tried to hide the pain it caused.

"And you're going to tell me how badly you're hurt."

"I'm telling you, I'm fine," Daniel said. The fact was, he didn't know just how badly he was hurt, but for some reason, the pride he was told he'd have to swallow was growing. The doctor had told him his ribs were bruised, but without X-rays, a guess was the best he could do, and Daniel had refused to go to the hospital. "Ribs sound good," he admitted, hugging his midsection. "But not mine," he joked.

The two men walked back to the house. "Hey, Jessica, we're going for ribs," Daniel told her. "Tommy, are you up for it?"

Tommy sat up, obviously feeling relieved of any pain he'd been in. "Yes, sir. I am now!" He smiled. "This mud stuff is incredible! The pain is almost gone!"

CHAPTER 8

Rez Ribs wasn't technically on the rez. It was just over the reservation's border by two miles, near Window Rock. It was owned and operated by an enterprising Navajo businessman. It was dimly lit and hopping with mostly the younger crowd of residents from various parts of the rez and a small mix of "outsiders." A small band supplied the music with a mixture of contemporary and Native sounds. Daniel was surprised that it wasn't as smoky as he had expected, but the owner didn't smoke, so those who did had to take their cancer sticks outside. Outside meant just that, so the smoke easily wafted in each time the door opened.

Daniel, Ben, Jessica, Tommy, and Lukas found two tables and pulled them together with chairs before seating themselves. They had a temporary audience due to Daniel. There had been murmurings that Red Tears had returned.

A jovial Navajo woman arrived at their table shortly thereafter, placing cloth napkins, utensils, and glasses down for the group.

"Water all around," Ben ordered.

"You guys are gonna put us out of business," she teased with a smile. "You're all goody-two-shoes!"

"On the rocks," Ben added with a smirk, just to appease her.

"Sure, cuz, live dangerously." This made Ben grin at her. She then looked Daniel over with a smile but addressed Ben, "Hey, cuz, who's the cutie?"

"Taken," Ben told her, causing the waitress to put on an exaggerated pout. She trudged away, and the group then turned its attention to the band on stage. They sang a song about returning to the rez.

Daniel could smell the meal even before it reached the table. He turned with a nudge to Tommy. The waitress and another server carried two trays out with plates of steaming, saucy ribs, green beans bathed in butter, and corn bread with chili on the side. Bibs along with the cloth napkins were supplied simply by the understanding that the rib joint would go under if it relied on supplying paper towels to guests. The ribs were well known for their sauce, and it got everywhere. Tommy rubbed his hands together in anticipation of his first meal since breakfast. Daniel cracked a smile at his enthusiasm. They blessed their meal and dove in.

"So what's been going on since I've been gone?" Daniel asked after swallowing a mouthful.

"You know, progress." Ben ripped at the ribs. "They put more electricity toward the north of Chinle as well as more double-wides. More water wells and wood stoves."

"If they would just set up some solar grids, it would be cheaper in the long run," Daniel pointed out.

"True, but in the long run is not the now run. Donations are what they are." Ben wiped his mouth while Daniel smiled, watching Jessica interact with Tommy and his sicheii. "Oh yeah, and some crazy guy bought up a huge parcel of land near Aztec about four months ago."

"Isn't that where that supposed gold mine is?" Daniel said, sipping his water.

"The one and only. I guess they're out to prove it's not a myth."

"Anyone we know?"

Ben shrugged. "Probably not. We have silver, and everyone I know is pretty content. I doubt anyone of ours would have the money to make such a purchase anyway."

Something didn't sit right with Daniel about the mine purchase. He couldn't put his finger on it and so pushed it to the back of his mind for a matter of prayer later. "You forgot the reason I'm here."

Ben gulped down his mouthful and wiped his chin. "The only reason?"

Daniel ignored the comment.

"Okay, his name is Simon. He's got a wife and kids, and he's been missing for two days."

Daniel stared at his hands for a moment. "Bill McKinley said there were clansmen, plural."

"Slip of the tongue? He's not known for his concern for non-whites, after all. He may be *hoping* it's more than one."

Daniel scoffed. "Yeah, you're probably right."

"We'll check it out tomorrow, eh?"

Daniel nodded.

Hawk sauntered in after a half an hour of bliss at the table. He shouted to the group and said hello to others he knew as he made his way to their tables. "It figures you'd bring your daughter here!" He swayed in front of Daniel and the group, smelling too much like a keg. "Thisss ain't nooo place for a young lady," he slurred, getting in Daniel's face. "All the alcohol, tobacco, you know."

Daniel was forced to sit back, repelled by his brother-in-law's breath and behavior. "And you're just an exemplary specimen yourself."

"I'm fine, Uncle!" Jessica jumped in.

"Nooo, noo." Hawk wagged a finger at her. "He needs to take better care of you." Hawk stopped short, spying Daniel's plate of food, and grabbed a couple of ribs for himself.

Daniel pushed the plate away, visibly annoyed. He wiped his hands and face clean and yanked the bib from around his neck.

"What's the matter, too good to share with a poor drunk?"

Daniel stood up. "I need some air," he said to his friends.

"Dad?" Jessica checked with concern.

"I'll be fine," he said, kissing her forehead. As Daniel stepped aside, Hawk took his seat almost before he was out of the way and then helped himself to Daniel's plate.

"Like a vulture," Ben observed.

"Hawk! It's Hawk," Hawk said with a full mouth of ribs, sauce dripping down his chin.

Jessica cringed but tried to be polite despite the situation. Hawk finished quickly, wiped his face, and then abruptly stood up with his bottle of beer, knocking his chair over. He then strode purposely out the door. Ben looked at Lukas and could only shake his head with a sigh.

Hawk found Daniel sitting on the bumper of his SUV. "Look at the hot-shot sheriff," the drunk saluted. "Too polluted in there for you?"

Daniel chose not to answer.

Hawk smacked Daniel's leg, slopping beer on his pants. "Too good to talk to your drunk brother-in-law?"

"We can talk when you're sober," Daniel said.

"How about I talk and you listen." Hawk shoved Daniel, causing him to slide off the vehicle and stand up. He grimaced at the quick move, not letting Hawk see. "If that girl was mine, I'd never take her to a dump like this!"

Daniel recovered and turned to face him. "Good for you, Hawk. You're a better father than I am."

"Don't patronize me!" Hawk yelled.

Daniel turned away from him, but Hawk clamped a strong hand onto his shoulder and turned Daniel back to face him. "I said, I'll talk to you when you're sober and thinking straight," Daniel breathed out in pain.

Hawk took a swig of his beer and then shoved it in Daniel's face. "Have some! That way we can both be drunk and understand each other better!" He snickered. "It'll heal up dem scratches, too!"

Daniel tried to avoid the bottle, turning his face away, but his vehicle was directly behind him. He was trapped.

"You're going to make that girl a whore just like you did her mother!" Hawk seethed with hatred.

"What did you say?" Daniel growled.

"You heard me, half-breed!"

Daniel was near the end of his rope and really wanted to hit him, but he knew a fight wouldn't solve anything and would only encourage Hawk more. "You'd…you'd call your own sister a whore?" Daniel asked, incredulous. He pushed Hawk out of his face.

"She wouldn't listen to me! She had to marry a white boy!" Hawk ranted. He grabbed the front of Daniel's shirt, his knuckles banging against Daniel's bruised chest.

"She married for love. Something you know nothing about!" Daniel answered, grabbing Hawk's wrists to try to protect his wounds.

"You deceived her into thinking you loved her!" Hawk sneered into Daniel's face.

"You're crazy! Get out of my face, Hawk!"

"Or what? The white boy's gonna kick my butt?"

"I'm more Dineh than you," Daniel said, looking him in the eye. "You're the real apple around here. Face who you are, Hawk!"

Hawk blinked, stunned.

"That would require you to be a man and admit it though." Daniel paused for a moment and then finished. "Half-breed."

Hawk pulled his right fist back and slammed Daniel in the face, breaking open the gash on his cheek. Daniel hit the ground face-first with a grunt as Hawk staggered back from his effort.

"Them's fighting words, half-breed!" Hawk's anger was fueled by what Daniel had said because it was true.

Hawk was really Sarah's half brother. Her father had died when she was three, and her mother had remarried a Japanese-American man. Hawk was born soon after, and so he was technically Japanese and Navajo. "So you got out of school while we had to stay! You betrayed us, left us. You used your status to get away from us!"

"You don't know anything about it!" Daniel shot back.

"I was there!"

"Were you, Hawk? Were you really there?" Daniel got himself to his feet, only to be shoved back against the hood of a truck. Daniel couldn't hide the pain every assault on his body caused.

Jessica's leg was bouncing a mile a minute, nervous about her uncle being outside with her dad. She looked at her watch and then at Ben, Tommy, and her sicheii. Her concern was verified when two patrons entered with a casual announcement.

"Hey, Hawk's out there wailin' on the new guy," one of them said. They sidled up to the bar, apparently used to such displays of his behavior. Ben stood, but Lukas grabbed his arm. "He must fight this battle on his own, or he will not be able to stand in the war."

Ben cocked his head and then gave a nod of understanding. Jessica, tired of waiting, ran outside, with Tommy close on her heels. When Ben got outside, he found Jessica crying into Tommy's chest. Sicheii emerged calmly from the building.

"Daddy!" Jessica cried.

Daniel had just dragged himself upright after a third visit to the dirt. He was staggering away from Hawk when Hawk broke his beer bottle on a nearby fender.

"Hawk!" Ben boomed at him.

Hawk turned, startled, and looked at Ben.

"Fight fair," he warned.

Jessica looked at Ben, shocked that he hadn't made a move to help her dad. Since Ben didn't indicate that he would help, Jessica broke from Tommy's embrace and stormed up to Hawk.

"Leave my dad alone, you drunken creep!" she yelled at him, slapping at him. Ben pulled her back from Hawk as the inebriated man studied her for a minute and then refocused on Daniel. Daniel was unable to do much else aside from hug his ribs and try to breathe.

"Let him fight," Ben told her.

"He can't fight!" she cried desperately.

Hawk charged Daniel and body slammed him against the side of the bed of a pickup truck. Daniel cried out in pain. He collapsed to the ground.

"What do you mean, Jessica?" Ben asked, urgency in his voice.

Hawk proceeded to kick Daniel as he lay on the ground. He was in such a rage, he didn't care how much damage he was doing to the brother-in-law he hated so much. Jessica stared at the brutality, in shock at her uncle's madness.

"Jessica!" Ben shook her.

Jessica looked at him in a daze.

"Tommy! Take Jessica inside and get my guys. They're the big ones sitting at the center table."

"He was beaten up by his unit a couple of days ago!" Jessica yelled over Hawk's angry ranting.

Tommy gave a nod and took Jessica inside. He had to put his arm around her to get her to leave the scene. Ben rushed up to Hawk as Hawk landed one last stomp on Daniel's ribs before Ben grabbed him and pulled him away. Ben handcuffed Hawk.

Shortly, two husky and very tall Navajos hurried out to the parking lot. Ben shoved him at his men. "Book him for assault with intent to kill."

Hawk protested and struggled. "I was defending myself!"

"You were defending your pride!" Ben said.

Hawk struggled more.

"Chill, cuz," one of the men told Hawk. Joe, one of Ben's investigators, pinned Hawk against a truck until he relaxed.

Lukas White Wolf stepped up to Hawk with sadness in his eyes. He shook his head. Hawk's demeanor changed quickly. His shoulders slumped as he was led away. Ben rushed to Daniel, who was attempting to get off the ground. Ben helped him to his feet, Daniel's face betraying the agony he was in. Tommy and Jessica returned to the scene after hearing the fight was over.

"Jessica, how bad was Daniel hurt?"

"I don't know. The doctor said his ribs were bruised, but he couldn't tell for sure unless he got an X-ray."

"He didn't, I take it?"

"No, sir," she confirmed through tears, looking at her dad. "Daddy, are you okay?" she asked him, wiping some dirt from his bloodied face.

Daniel hugged his ribs and gave a weak nod, but he couldn't breathe. He doubled over in a fit of coughing, bringing up blood. He passed out, falling back to the ground.

"Don't argue this time, Jess. He's got to get to a hospital!" Tommy told her. Ben knelt beside his friend, pulled his phone, and dialed 911.

The next morning, Daniel lay in a Banner Page Hospital ICU room with Jessica by his side. Daniel had been airlifted to Page, Arizona, three hours from Window Rock. He was still unconscious from the surgery to repair his broken ribs and re-inflate his collapsed lung. He was on oxygen to help speed the healing of his lung. Various lines and tubes connected to a bank of machinery monitored his heart and blood pressure. His face bore signs of further repair. Jessica looked at her dad, her eyes puffy from crying most of the night. Tommy had remained behind at Lukas's hogan with him to pray for Daniel and Jessica.

She closed her eyes for a brief prayer. "Thank you, Great Creator, that you saved my dad. He's a mess, but he's alive, and for that I praise you." When she opened her eyes, Hawkeye was sitting on the other side of Daniel's bed from her. She was stunned at his audacity.

Angry, she asked, "What are you doing here? Come to gloat?"

Hawk was fully sober now, having spent the night in Ben's jail. His face held concern and regret, and after a moment, he held his handcuffed wrists up, showing her he was still in custody.

"No, Jessica. I came to apologize."

"A forced apology," she answered sardonically.

"Hey, give me a chance."

"Like you gave Dad?" she snapped. "You've hated my dad for eighteen years for something that was none of your business," Jessica growled.

"I was trying to protect my sister."

"From what?" she interrupted. "From the 'half-breed'?" Jessica wiggled her fingers in quotation marks.

"I lost my sister because of him," he whispered.

"I lost my mom, and it wasn't Dad's fault!" she snapped at him through clenched teeth. "It was because of people like you who hate him. Don't try to justify yourself."

Hawk dropped his head at her piercing words. She noticed his shoulders starting to shake as he broke down in remorse. Jessica started to cry as well.

Finally, Hawk looked up at his niece. "I'm sorry," he said. He got up from his chair and left the room.

Ben was waiting for him outside and handed him off to his men. He then peeked inside the door to check on Jessica. "You okay?" he asked her.

She nodded, wiping tears from her face.

"Can I get you anything?"

"Can you bring Dad back?"

Ben gave her an understanding smile.

"Only the Great Creator can. I think you know that."

"Yes," was her reply.

Ben checked the corridor and then stepped inside the room. "You know, he is not alone right now," Ben told her. "He is with the Creator to discover his heart."

"Why did he have to get hurt to discover his own heart?" she questioned.

Ben was quiet for a moment as if listening to a silent voice. He looked intently at Daniel, and then after another moment, he looked at Jessica. "The Creator knows just how to reach each one of us.

Sometimes he must get us still in order to connect with us. Your dad is being taught deep lessons."

"You mean the Great Creator did this?" She pointed upward.

"No, Yanaba." Ben smiled patiently. "He is a loving Father, but he will use certain things for his purposes. He wants his son healed more than you do," he assured.

"I know. Mom and Dad taught me this," she said quietly. "I trust him. It's just that…" She paused, trying to put her feelings into words without revealing too much. "I feel alone. I know I'm not, but…"

"I understand. We've all been there," Ben said. "He, too, understands."

Jessica let a smile of relief cross her face.

"Now, you need to eat, young lady. Your dad will have my scalp if he finds out I didn't take care of you." He grinned.

She looked at her dad fondly. "Okay, I'll take a sandwich."

"Good!" Ben said, standing up and moving to the door. "I'll be back soon."

Jessica had finished her sandwich, but she refused to leave her dad's side, so Ben went back to his motel room. Worn out from her vigil, she made herself as comfortable as possible on the pull-out couch, grateful for the pillow and blanket a nurse had brought to her earlier. She got up and went to her dad's side. She leaned in and kissed his forehead.

"I love you, Dad. I need you." She went back to the couch to settle in for the night and was quickly asleep.

Jessica sat up in a dream, seeing her sicheii standing beside Daniel's bed. He was waving a prayer fan and shaking a rattle. She watched and listened intently as he sang a Navajo prayer song. He then prayed in Navajo for his grandson, and somehow she understood.

"Great Creator and father of us all, I call on you for my grandson, Red Tears. The dark evil is trying to kill him. Invade with your true light, O Great One. He has much to do here for you and our people. Guide him

back to us with your light, for he carries your heart. Thank you, Great Creator. We eagerly await his return."

Jessica blinked in disbelief. Her parents hadn't taught her the Navajo language except for her name and her grandparents' names. Her dad hadn't even remembered the language until recently, and yet she understood perfectly the words that had just been spoken. She wondered what other surprises she might discover in this deeply spiritual climate.

Lukas looked at Jessica with a knowing smile. "He is returning," he told her in Navajo. She gave a quick nod and looked to her dad expectantly, but he didn't stir.

Daniel was standing on a plateau wearing only his jeans. No shirt, bare feet. An eagle feather hung from his hair, and a bone choker with a silver medallion depicting the four directions hung from his neck. The cross at the center of it was painted red. Lukas appeared in front of him, sitting on a dapple gray mustang. Daniel looked at his sicheii and waited. Lukas dismounted and walked up to Daniel as a wind kicked up, causing Daniel to put his arm up to shield his face. He couldn't see Lukas for a moment, but then the wind died down, Lukas was holding a long spear with a bronze head.

Lukas stepped back from Daniel and then suddenly thrust the spear into his grandson's heart. Daniel's eyes opened wide with surprise and questioning as he grasped the shaft of the spear. He fell to his knees. Daniel sputtered in disbelief as Lukas pulled the spear back, taking Daniel's heart out with it. Lukas's face was expressionless as, again, Daniel wondered at his actions. Daniel fell to his back, struggling to remain coherent. He watched as his sicheii took his heart in his hands and offered it skyward as he spoke in Navajo.

"Great Creator. My grandson offers you his heart today as you have pierced it. Let your blood flow though his."

Daniel's eyes closed as his last breath left him, but Lukas knelt beside him and touched his chest. The wound disappeared, and Daniel's eyes fluttered open to see the old man smiling down at him. He gave a nod of assurance to Daniel, offered his hand, and helped him to his feet. Lukas then turned and got back onto his horse. The horse turned and walked off, vanishing into thin air.

CHAPTER 9

Tommy felt strange being in an unfamiliar house with unfamiliar people; as a matter of fact, the whole culture was a shock. Everyone, apart from Hawkeye, was so laid-back. It was a very different world from his "white" world, yet he was attracted to it. He wasn't so sure he liked the stares he received when he went out, but he supposed that because Daniel's family accepted him, the rest of the clan eventually would as well.

Tommy especially liked Lukas White Wolf. He was learning quite a bit from Lukas. He loved having a great-grandfather with such a rich, clean history. He wanted to quickly forget his own. Christiana naturally took on a mother role; she and Ben never had children of their own. All he was learning would almost cover a semester of college. While there was a language barrier, somehow Tommy was picking up Navajo in bits and pieces. Daniel told had him that Lukas knew English but chose only to speak his native language. Tommy purposed to learn Navajo, eager to feel a part of the family, though Jessica had assured him that Navajo wasn't a prerequisite to becoming part of the family.

Jessica woke up with a stiff neck from sleeping on the small couch. She was expecting to see Lukas and her dad awake. Daniel still slept soundly in his bed, and Lukas was nowhere to be found. She folded her blankets and went into the bathroom to shower and change.

When she emerged a half hour later, two nurses and her dad's surgeon were standing around Daniel's bed.

"Is he okay?" she asked, alarmed at the gathering.

The surgeon stepped aside.

She then looked at her dad and saw his eyes fluttering open. "Dad!" she exclaimed, hurrying to his side.

He was just coming around, and the surgeon was injecting something into the pic line in his IV.

"What are you giving him?"

"It's just a pain killer. He's going to need it now that he's conscious."

"When can we go home?"

"In a couple of days."

"Okay." Jessica calmed as she stroked her dad's hand.

Daniel turned his head toward her and gave her a smile.

"Hey," she said, "welcome back."

"Yanaba," he said, squeezing her hand.

Ben entered and smiled. "Welcome back to the land of the living, Sheila."

After the nurses and surgeon finished with Daniel's care, they left. Ben joined Jessica at Daniel's bedside.

"Dad can go home in a couple of days," she told Ben with relief and joy.

"That's good to hear." Ben beamed. He then addressed Daniel. "You have an interesting way of getting out of a meeting."

Daniel narrowed his eyes. "What meeting?" he asked.

"You'll see."

Daniel closed his eyes and shook his head. "I give up."

Angel Green drove through the rez for the millionth time as a minister to the Native Americans. She had first come with a small group of like-minded and like-hearted people who had also felt the calling of the Great Creator to bring peace, healing, and reconciliation to the First Nations People on the Navajo reservation. Years later, she remained behind when the others left. This gained her the confidence and trust of the Navajo people. Because of her dedication, she had earned the title of Meda, meaning prophetess of the Great Creator.

Angel stepped into the local grocery store with her supply list.

"Hello, Stewart. How are you today?" She smiled at the clerk. She'd gotten to know him over the years, and he and his family considered her a true friend and spiritual mentor.

"Can't complain, Angel darlin'," he answered. "Hey, did you hear what Hawk did to his brother-in-law?" he asked her with a voice of conspiracy.

"His brother-in-law is here?"

"Not now," he explained. "Poor guy's in the hospital recovering," Stewart told her as he boxed her order from behind the counter. "Yeah, Hawk was drunk as usual and beat the sh— crap out of him."

Angel frowned at what he said. She thought she had made some progress with Hawk. She sighed.

"Turns out the guy had already been beaten up by some skinheads working with his sheriff's office from Stake Town. He didn't even fight back. He just let Hawk wail on him."

"Really?" Angel was intrigued by this bit of information. She picked up a box of wood matches from the counter and placed them with her list.

"From what I hear, Daniel Red Tears could have beaten the drunk out of Hawk but chose not to." Stewart carried the box for Angel while she took a canvas bag of the remainder of her items as together they loaded her car.

Angel then drove out to Lukas's hogan to see how he was and to talk to him about Daniel Red Tears Patterson. As she expected, he didn't tell her much.

"Years ago, you were meant to know him," Lukas said in Navajo.

Angel stood by the window, listening intently. She always found solace, looking out onto the Plains, and Lukas's window afforded the perfect view. "Know who?"

"You will find out when he tells you."

"Who?" Angel realized that what she was supposed to know would be found out from the Great Creator in prayer. Sometimes she wished that every visit with Lukas wasn't a spiritual mystery, but she usually ended up grateful for the lessons she learned from them.

She headed home after making her usual visits to some elderly natives. While on the road, she pulled over with a strange feeling and quickly got out of her pickup. She looked up into the sky and saw a golden eagle soaring high above as he gave a cry. It was rare to catch a glimpse of one of these majestic birds, and she had a feeling he was there for a reason—Daniel Red Tears Patterson.

Ben picked Daniel and Jessica up at the hospital. It was obvious they were eager to get home. He found them both sitting in the room, luggage and prescriptions in hand.

Daniel had taken a pain pill before leaving the hospital. He was asleep in the back seat as Ben and Jessica talked. Jessica had many questions. She was quiet at first, delving into her own thoughts about recent events and about what was stirring both hers and her dad's hearts.

"When we were driving here, I felt very attached to the land and the rez," she finally said.

Ben nodded but didn't say anything.

"My heart was pounding like all of my emotions were going to explode, and when I asked the Great Creator what was going on, he said..." She paused, closing her eyes and heard the voice again.

Ben glanced at her and noticed the serene smile plastered on her face. "Heritage," he said for her.

Jessica looked at Ben. "How did you know?"

Ben shrugged. "Because he talks to me, too."

"He talks to you about other people?"

"Sure."

Jessica was new to that concept and was ready to learn about it. "Would he tell me about other people?"

"If he knows he can trust your heart."

Jessica looked out the passenger-side window and considered the meaning of what she had just heard. "Why would he do that?" she asked him.

"He will tell us about someone so we will pray for that one or, if he chooses, speak his words to them."

"Why doesn't he just talk to them himself?"

"He talks to his children all the time, but they don't always listen," Ben explained. "They're not ready to hear the Great Creator directly. It scares them."

Jessica felt a great wave of compassion sweep over her, and a desire to be his mouthpiece welled up inside of her. "I hope someday he can trust me," she said softly.

"He already does, Yanaba," he assured her.

She smiled. "Thanks for letting me know."

"You are ready to hear him."

Again, Jessica looked out the window as the desert flew by. She thought about the responsibility and the magnitude of carrying something like that for the Great Creator and what it all meant. She knew she could never live the same way again. She resolved to get to know the Great Creator and be serious about her pursuit of him. After all, he was the one who created her and knew her before she'd been born. He was the one who gave her breath, and she vowed to set special time aside to build her relationship with him.

"He will meet you whenever you call," Ben told her.

Jessica gave a nod of understanding feeling honored. "My dad stopped and sang to an eagle," she told him. "In Navajo. He says he doesn't speak Navajo."

"He used to," Ben revealed. "What you saw was an answered prayer," he explained. "The eagle carried our prayers to the Great Creator, and he communicated that to Daniel."

Jessica nodded thoughtfully, remembering the scene. "God is far from boring, isn't he?"

Ben chuckled. "Never a dull moment," he agreed.

"Tell me about my uncle Hawkeye," she changed the subject.

Ben sighed and settled in for the last hour of the drive. "He never used to drink, you know," Ben began.

Jessica knew deep down in her heart that Bannin Hawkeye was a good and caring man.

"Yeah. Dad told me."

"Your mom was his half sister. Her dad died when she was three years old, and her mom remarried a Japanese-American man, your uncle's dad. His name Bannin means watchman in Japanese, and, of course, Hawkeye is his Indian name. When Hawk grew old enough to understand his heritage, he became ashamed that he wasn't full-blooded Navajo," Ben explained.

"But why? Who would put shame on him?"

"I don't know, Jessica, but maybe that's why you're here. Maybe you're here to pray for him, and perhaps the Great Creator will tell you what he needs to hear."

Jessica remembered the night Hawk beat her dad. Did Hawk deserve more mercy than Tommy's family? She struggled, knowing that if she forgave Hawk, she'd have to forgive the McKinleys as well. She realized that they were all connected as family. She remembered her dad's words, that family shouldn't hate each other. A tear streaked her cheek, and then a slow smile spread across her lips. She decided to do all she could to help her uncle.

"He used to like Daniel. The four of us—your dad, mom, me, and Hawk—went through a lot on the rez together. Then they took us away to the Indian boarding school, and when they found out that your dad was half white, they sent him back to the rez."

Ben looked out his side window and grew silent. When he didn't continue, Jessica looked at Ben, noticing his expression had grown hard. "Uncle Ben? Are you okay?"

Ben gave her a forced smile. "I was remembering the day they separated us."

"Will you tell me? I mean, if it's not too painful." Jessica brushed her hair back and turned in her seat.

"We were outside playing ball when the headmaster came and got Daniel. We thought he was in trouble. I followed and hid behind the building. I was able to look in the window without being noticed. I saw the headmaster waving a letter around. Daniel tried to run for the door, but they stopped him." Ben looked out the window again as his knuckles grew white, gripping the steering wheel.

Jessica looked at her dad, reached over the front seat, and took his hand.

"I saw your dad literally fight to stay with us. They beat him and warned him to leave quietly, and his leaving is all Hawk knew. Daniel even wrote to us, but the school never allowed us to see the letters. I found out later from his mom."

"So Uncle Hawk thinks Dad wanted to leave the boarding school?" Jessica surmised.

"Uh-huh. We all went to high school off the rez, near Stake Town, and that's when your dad and mom really fell in love. Hawk already felt betrayed, so when Yanaba wanted to marry Daniel, Hawk couldn't stand it."

"That's why he refused to go to their wedding?"

Ben nodded.

Jessica could easily discern the root of bitterness in Hawk. "So God will sometimes speak through people to give us insight?"

"Yes," Ben confirmed.

Jessica prayed for Hawk and her dad the remainder of the ride home to the rez.

CHAPTER 10

Ben and Tommy helped Daniel into his new house, next door to Ben's. All three were thankful it was a single-story dwelling. They walked him into the bathroom. Daniel stopped short when he saw the tub filled with the reddish mud they'd used on Tommy.

"What's the matter, Sheila?" Ben asked him.

Tommy had an amused grin on his face. Daniel looked at the young man. "What are you grinning at?"

"You're going to love it," Tommy assured him.

Ben began to unbutton Daniel's shirt. Daniel batted at his hands. "Wh...what are you doing?"

"You're getting in, bro," Ben informed him.

"Okay, okay! If I need help, I'll ask!" he said, stepping backward.

Ben raised an eyebrow at him. "We'll be right outside," he told Daniel with a smirk.

Daniel gave a nod and, with great effort, was finally able to get his shirt off, but he couldn't sit without help, and he certainly couldn't bend over to reach his boots. He realized he was going to have to ask for help to undress. His first piece of humble pie came to him as a mouthful. His sicheii's words accompanied it.

"You will need to soak in it soon. You must let pride die in you."

Daniel sighed and called for help. Ben teased him as he and Tommy helped him sit on the edge of the tub so they could get his boots and socks off. They stood him up again to remove his pants.

"You make an ugly wife," Daniel said as Ben eased his jeans down. Daniel stepped out of them, relieved the ordeal was over.

"You sure could use one right now." Ben chortled. "You can keep your skivvies on. But we need to get this wrap off," Ben said as he began unwinding the Elasticon from Daniel's torso. Daniel let out a yelp of pain as pressure was released from his rib cage. "They shaved you nice and clean. At least now you look more like an Indian." Ben and Tommy snickered.

"Hey now, that's funny, ha, ha," Daniel offered.

The surgeon had screwed two plates on his rib cage, one on each of his broken ribs, and then closed the wound with glue rather than staples. By the time the Elasticon and gauze wrap were removed, Daniel was trembling and no longer laughing at Ben's jokes.

"Sorry, bro. The mud will make it all better." A look of compassion crossed Ben's face.

"Yeah." He grimaced as Tommy and Ben carefully lowered him into the tub. "Okay! This is hot! And muddy!" he whined.

"I wouldn't complain. Soaking in this mud will make you better in a week as opposed to eight," Ben advised.

Daniel looked at him with uncertainty, but he trusted his best friend and gave a silent nod. Tommy chuckled at Daniel, submerged up to his neck in mud. He and Ben had left Daniel to soak when Daniel realized they had taken all of the towels from the room.

Jeff sauntered into his dad's cubical at the sheriff's office in Stake Town. "Just heard that Patterson took a beating from his own brother-in-law. Put him in the hospital." Jeff was obviously happy about it.

"Ya see how dangerous law enforcement is? He may not last through the summer." Tom Sr. snickered.

Jessica knocked on the bathroom door. "Dad?"

"Yeah, Jessica, it's all clear."

Jessica cautiously entered. When she saw her dad, she muffled a snicker.

"Really funny," he mumbled in self-pity.

Jessica sat on the edge of the tub with an amused smile and dipped her finger into the mud. She held her finger up to study the red goo.

"Did Ben put you up to this?"

"Up to what?" she said. Her face was a mask of innocence. "Dad, I'm here to cheer you up. I wouldn't tease you in this condition." She paused for effect. "At least not until you're a little better." She giggled. She gently wiped the mud from her finger over the stitches on his cheek and lips. He closed his eyes with a wince, feeling the sting. "I'm on your side, okay?"

"Okay." He lifted a muddy hand menacingly toward Jessica, causing her to jump back with a yelp.

"Dad! Come on!" she begged, putting her hands up in surrender. "Seriously, I need to talk to you."

He searched her eyes and relented, lowering his paw back into the mud. She hesitated a minute, but he motioned with his head for her to sit back down. She finally returned to the edge of the tub.

"So what do you need to talk about?"

"Uncle Hawk came to the hospital while you were still unconscious…to apologize."

Daniel stared at the tub of mud he was immersed in. He never answered.

"Dad?"

"I heard you," he said. He was actually shocked that Hawk had come by to offer an apology, but he felt something in his heart that said shock was the wrong response to have. He realized that he'd given up on Hawk. Even though he'd forgiven the man, he still had lost hope that he would ever change. He'd reached the point of believing that Hawk was a hopeless case. "Forgive me," he mumbled, lost in his thoughts.

"For what?" Jessica asked him.

Daniel looked up at Jessica absently, having forgotten she was there. "Oh. I was asking the Great Creator to forgive me."

"Dad. What could you have done that you need his forgiveness?" she questioned with slight amusement.

He collected his thoughts and then spoke. "Jessica, always remember. God can do anything. We should never pray without faith, and we must never label anyone as hopeless," he reminded. "That's judging, and it's wrong."

Jessica looked at him for a long moment.

"I gave up on Hawk, and it became a silent curse." He quickly wiped a rogue tear. He then continued after a moment. "Our Great Chief, Jesus, said to love our enemies, to bless and not curse." He sniffed. He realized the magnitude of what he'd done. "Jess, he isn't my enemy. He's family."

"I understand what you're saying." She cried. "Oh, Dad," she squeaked out, "you're such a gift to me." She smiled and put her hand out to him.

Daniel took her hand in his. She wiped her eyes with her free hand. "Sicheii wants to pray over you. I'll go get him. I'll also send Ben and Tommy to help you out."

Daniel gave her a smile of appreciation as she left.

Ben and Tommy came in shortly and assisted Daniel, getting him out of the tub and into the shower. By the time he'd cleaned up and dressed, the mud had relieved enough of the pain that he was able to dress himself, a simple act he rejoiced in. He put his pouch on but left his shirt off. Lukas came into his room, finally, with a cup of herbal tea and a smudge. Daniel took a long sip of the tea and then knelt carefully in front of his sicheii.

Lukas lit the smudge and placed it in an abalone shell and held it in front of Daniel as Tommy and Ben stood in the doorway with Jessica. Daniel waved the smoke toward his face and chest, deeply inhaling the aroma of the white sage and giving silent thanks to the Great Creator. To the Navajo and other tribes, the smudge held spirits to ward off evil, but they also believed that the smoke carried their prayers up to the Great Creator. For Lukas and Christian natives, the smoke from the smudge represented the presence of God and his Holy Spirit. Ben explained this to Tommy when he asked what they were doing.

"In the Bible, the Old Testament says God often rested on the Ark of the Covenant in a thick cloud of smoke called his glory. The high priest was the only one allowed inside the holiest place, and he had to fill the room with the smoke of sweet incense to protect himself from the glory of God."

Ben began to play gently on a hand drum as Lukas sang a prayer song. Daniel kept his eyes closed but recognized the song. It was the same song he'd sung to the eagle right before arriving. Now he understood the words as his native tongue came rushing back. He couldn't help but sing along.

After the song, Lukas prayed, "We thank you, Great Creator, for bringing Red Tears back to us. Now we ask you to heal his body and his heart so he can help his people." Lukas stopped for a moment and peeked at Daniel, letting a grin split his face, and then he continued. "And help him see the new good woman you have for him."

Daniel tried to be reverent, but the last part of the prayer got his attention. He opened his eyes, staring at his sicheii. He got up slowly. Jessica helped him with his shirt, noticing the pouch around his neck and smiled. Daniel kept staring at Lukas as Jessica took hold of his hands and directed them to his buttons.

Ben stepped up to him and put a hand on his shoulder. "Was it the part about your heart or the 'new woman' that got to you?" he asked with amusement at the expression still plastered across Daniel's face. Daniel finally pulled his gaze away and glanced down at his buttons as he closed his shirt.

"I'm not sure," he answered. He didn't bother tucking in his shirt; he was still too preoccupied by what had just been said.

Jessica picked up the cup of tea and handed it to her dad. "It sure got me wondering."

Daniel took the tea, drank it down, and then stepped up to Lukas. Daniel spoke to him in Navajo. "Thank you, Sicheii."

"Thank your Creator." Lukas smiled as he gathered up the abalone shell.

"Come on," Ben said. "We've got some work to do."

"Mind if I come along? Maybe observe? I'd like to help," Tommy said.

Daniel looked at Ben and nodded. He'd almost forgotten they had a missing clansman to find. "That's up to Sicheii."

Tommy looked to Lukas with hope in his eyes. Lukas gave a nod.

Later that afternoon, Ben and Daniel sat on a dilapidated couch in the doublewide belonging to Simon and Roberta. Tommy remained outside. His stark-white presence would have been uncomfortable for the woman. But since he asked to go along, he'd have to learn what it felt like to be an outcast—a lesson Lukas felt everyone should visit at least once.

Roberta sat across from the two detectives as her three young children played a board game behind them. The children were well behaved and were doing their best to stay quiet. Daniel smiled, remembering how Jessica, when she was a child, would pretend to play in the background while he and Sarah were on the couch talking.

"Roberta, thanks for talking with me again for Daniel's sake. Did Simon say anything unusual or act differently than normal the day he disappeared?" Ben said.

Daniel pulled his attention back to the investigation.

"No. He's been goin' to a pool hall a lot lately though. Off rez, near Lupton. Been winnin' pretty good, too. He was gonna buy us a new couch. He normally plays poker with the guys."

"Why did he start going to the pool hall?" Daniel asked.

"There was a notice about a pool tournament. Mostly white folk there, but because Simon was winnin', well, who could resist?" She paused for a moment, wringing her hands. "Simon said there were drugs there, too."

Daniel and Ben exchanged a look. "He would come home at the same time every night?" Daniel asked.

"Sure. He loves his family. He'd call if he was gonna be late."

"So when he didn't call, you knew something was up?"

"Yep."

Ben closed his notebook. She'd said almost exactly the same as before. He and Daniel stood up. "Roberta, we'll find Simon, but give us some time. Now that I've got my brother here…"

"Red Tears. Heard a lot about you. Lukas White Wolf says you will bring us hope."

Daniel was momentarily stunned. "No pressure, eh?" He let off a nervous chuckle. "Nice to meet you," he said and left the house.

"He's been away for a long time. He's getting his bearings again," Ben said.

Roberta nodded. "Thanks, Captain. I know you can find 'im, eh."

Daniel and Ben left the house and met up with Tommy at the truck. "Maybe we can catch a dealer at the pool hall and get some info that way. Otherwise, I'm out of ideas."

"Well, let's get crackin' while there's daylight." Daniel motioned for Tommy to get in the truck.

"I'd rather go with full light. Besides, it's not my jurisdiction."

"What about the state troopers?" Daniel said as he climbed in.

"I know they aren't interested in my theories from past experience." Ben closed his door, started the engine, and looked past Tommy to Daniel. "Time to meet someone."

They returned home to pick up Jessica and to drop off Tommy, who would be kept busy with Lukas and Christiana learning "the ways", and then drove over to Angel Green's hogan.

When they got there, dinner was waiting.

"Welcome to my home," Angel greeted them warmly.

Ben cleared his throat. "Daniel, Jessica, this is Angel Green. The clans call her Meda."

"Prophetess," Daniel translated for his daughter.

Angel looked at him in surprise, her smiling eyes penetrating his soul. "Just call me Angel."

Daniel ushered Jessica in and then entered himself, inspecting the main room.

"Call me Dan or Daniel," he began but then fumbled, "but don't call me Danny."

Jessica nudged him. "Dad," she whispered.

"Sorry," he mumbled.

Angel motioned for them to sit at the table. Ben sat next to Angel, and Daniel seated himself next to his daughter. He watched Angel as she put food on the table, noting her mannerisms. He looked down at his plate, obviously trying to cover a smile that threatened to betray his feelings. Angel snuck a look at Daniel and then smiled at Ben as she put some fry bread on the table. Jessica watched the whole scene with delight.

Ben grinned at Angel. He had tried to set her up before, though not too often. She knew that when the Great Creator released her to be married, she wouldn't have a doubt. This was the night, and she felt almost giddy inside. She had a small concern about leaving the safety of the Great Creator's special vow, but she also knew that he'd been preparing her for this moment in time, the moment she would meet the man who was to be her husband. She wondered if Daniel understood yet. It wasn't her place to tell him, and until then, she would remain focused on God. She was confident he'd do all the work for her.

"Wow, fry bread!" Daniel exclaimed. "We haven't had that since—" He stopped as Jessica looked down at her plate. Daniel's exuberance disappeared. He looked at his daughter with a sad smile, taking her hand and squeezing it. "Sorry."

"It's okay." She forced a smile.

"Let's pray," Ben suggested. They all joined hands as Ben began. "Great Creator, Father of us all, thank you for bringing new friends and old friends together to share your gifts and to share your love. In the name of your Son, the Great Chief, Yeshuah, amen." After the collective amen, the food was passed around—steaming mashed potatoes, creamed corn, beef, and the fry bread.

There was an awkward silence that followed, so Ben broke the ice. "Angel came here with a group of missionaries. Your sicheii took her under his wing," Ben told Daniel and Jessica.

"You know my great-grandfather?" Jessica asked with wide eyes.

"I do!" Angel answered with just as much wonder. "I've learned so much from him. He's a wise man and mentor."

"Where are the others?" Daniel asked her.

"They felt called to go out to other tribes and reservations," she said.

"But not you?"

"No. Not me. I was called to stay here. This is my home," she said.

Daniel gave a nod and took some fry bread.

"What about your family?" Jessica asked.

"I'm an only child. My parents died when I was young."

"I'm sorry," Daniel said.

Angel gave a bright smile. "Well, I know I'll see them again. When it's my turn."

"Do you miss them?" Jessica asked.

Angel was the one to be careful this time. "I do, Jessica, but I don't let it stop me from living. I know they're with the Great Creator, and that's better than here any day."

Daniel looked down at the food on his plate, moving it around with his bread.

Angel glanced at Jessica, but she focused on Daniel. "It's okay to miss her and still love her."

He remained fixed on his plate.

"But the Great Creator wants you to be able to love him more so he can love through you."

Jessica nodded in understanding. Daniel finally looked up and met Angel's eyes as Ben busily shoveled food into his mouth while balancing a grin.

"Careful there, bro. You're going to choke yourself," Daniel said, trying not to chuckle.

Angel was relieved, knowing Daniel had received the message. She sat back with a chuckle and clap of her hands, quite pleased with the way the evening was unfolding.

Jessica snorted at her uncle as Ben wiped his mouth.

After dinner and a decadent chocolate mousse, one of Angel's specialties as well as her favorite, the small group adjourned to the living room of the hogan. Since the room was round, they formed a circle as they sat down in simple but comfortable chairs.

"So how long have you been on the reservation?" Jessica asked.

"I've been here for fifteen years. How about you, Daniel? How does it feel to be back here?"

"Eighteen years is a long time. Things haven't changed much. That can be good and bad in my book. I'm always open to change." He redirected the subject. "So you came to save the Navajo?"

"Why do you say that?"

"Because no whites choose to live on a reservation unless—"

"They have a God complex," Angel finished. She smiled to herself. Daniel was trying to figure her out, and she found herself liking that. "Sounds like you're not very fond of missionaries."

"They do tend to try to make us white," Daniel mumbled.

Jessica elbowed him with a warning look.

"We don't do that anymore. There are some missionaries who actually hear and obey the Great Creator. I am sorry that ever happened, and I'm here to show that the one true God is not the one that the missionaries of old have said he was. I know the damage we did. I'm sorry."

"We?" Daniel asked.

"When a person or a group has sinned against another, it's the church's responsibility to repent on behalf of them and become them." Angel sensed that Daniel had such a burden in his heart from God.

Daniel nodded. He was quiet for a moment as he sat forward, resting his arms on his knees. He began to rock back and forth. "Accepted," he said.

Ben helped the conversation to move forward. "So what about the rest of the missionaries? You said they left?"

"Yes. They felt it was what God wanted them to do, to try to help other tribes as well. I knew as soon as I stepped foot on this land that I was to stay. Your sicheii was honored by that."

"Dad began telling me about Sicheii when we drove up here." Jessica looked to her dad. Daniel was staring at the floor.

Angel smiled. "I'm sure your dad will tell you a whole lot more. Lukas is a man rich in history and culture. But what I'll tell you is that he was like a father to me. He taught me Navajo traditions and spirituality and then showed me what traditions the Great Creator had taught him to integrate into his faith and what was not to be integrated. It's really quite amazing, the insight he has."

"I hope he teaches me that, too."

"I'm sure he will," Angel assured. "I met Hawkeye through Lukas."

"How?" Jessica asked.

"Lukas was trying to teach Hawkeye the Navajo traditions like he did me, but he always seemed more interested in drinking than anything else. I mean, Hawk went to him for guidance out of respect, but he was really bitter against religion. Lukas asked me to see if I could reach Hawk."

Daniel snorted.

Ben spoke up, "If you'll excuse me, I need a siesta. Besides, you don't need me to keep you going anymore." He gave an exaggerated sigh and a stretch. "Yeah. My job here is done." The group watched Ben leave, their faces all holding a look of dismay.

"So tell me about Bannin Hawkeye," Angel said as the door slapped its frame in the background.

"Is this a counseling session?" Daniel questioned with slight irritation. He wasn't sure where she would take the subject, and it scared him.

"No. I just want your take on him. You know him better than I do."

"I don't think so. You two are friends. I haven't seen him for eighteen years. I came back, and the first thing he did was beat the crud out of me," Daniel answered, getting up from his chair. The sudden move caused him to wince.

"That's true." Jessica nodded in support of her dad.

"Maybe he has too much hate in his heart for you to help him," Daniel said.

"That's not my problem. It's God's," Angel answered.

Daniel paced as he looked over the pictures and books she had adorning the shelves on her walls. Daniel then stopped and looked at one particular picture of Angel and Hawk. He was actually smiling. He then moved to a picture of his sicheii saying a blessing over Angel from years earlier.

"You're right about that," Daniel agreed.

"You gave up on him, didn't you?" Angel asked.

Daniel turned to Angel, not appreciating her question. "Who told you that?"

Jessica watched her dad's irritation level rise, so she began to pray.

Daniel then stared out one of her windows at Ben who was taking a snooze on the hood of his truck. Deep inside he now knew what Lukas had meant by the "new woman." His theories on why he'd been returned to the reservation were multiplying, but he definitely knew by whom he had been sent. "I did. I know I shouldn't have," he said in a quiet tone. "I already had this discussion with my Father," he confessed.

"So has he renewed your hope?"

"Yeah," he said, softening, "In fact, Jessica told me that Hawk came to the hospital to apologize for the beating he gave me."

"How'd you take the news?"

"That's when I realized I'd given up on him. I was surprised that he'd apologized. He was pretty pissed...sorry, angry with me."

Angel hid a chuckle. "You're fine," she assured him. "I'm not perfect either, and I strive to please him, just like you."

Daniel smiled with a nod. He really was beginning to like this woman who was getting under his skin. He realized he was spilling his guts to her, and he hadn't planned on cooperating.

"Why didn't you fight back?"

Daniel shrugged.

Jessica answered for him. "He didn't want to hurt him," she said. "Dad could have wiped the floor with him," she beamed.

"Jess!" Daniel shushed her.

Angel smiled at their interaction.

"What? It's true!"

Angel had a way of asking questions that put Daniel on the spot. Or was it the Creator putting him on the spot? He searched his heart for the threat of pride and then shrugged. "I don't know. Why do you care?"

"There was a reason you let him beat you up," she pressed. She was silent for a moment when he didn't answer. He watched as she stood from her seat and then turned to face one of her walls with her eyes closed. She then slowly turned back to him. "You believe you deserved it. It was like your penance."

Daniel glared at her. "Come on, Jess. It's time to go," he said in a low voice of annoyance. He motioned for Jessica. "Thanks for your hospitality." Daniel left, but Jessica lingered.

She walked over to Angel. "Thanks for dinner. It was really good, especially the fry bread," she gushed and then softened. "Sorry about my dad. Being back on the rez is doing something to him."

"I know. I've been praying for him. The Great Creator has something he wants him to do, and right now he's getting your dad ready. It's a painful process."

Jessica nodded thoughtfully.

"Come by any time you want more fry bread. Maybe you could teach me your mom's recipe," Angel suggested.

Jessica's eyes lit up. "Really?"

"Really," she confirmed with a smile.

Jessica hugged Angel and felt a sudden and strong love for her and emanating from her.

Daniel was in the truck, drumming his fingers impatiently on the open window frame. Jessica had been standing beside the passenger door for several seconds without him noticing her, so she cleared her throat, startling him. He got out and let Jessica slide in.

Father and daughter sat there while Ben remained snoozing peacefully on the hood. After a moment, they looked at each other with mischievous smirks. Daniel nodded to Jessica, who leaned on the horn. The effect was quite humorous as they watched Ben nearly jump off the hood and disappear over the side of the truck. He popped up suddenly, dusting himself off, trying to protect his dignity. Daniel and Jessica laughed hysterically. Ben got in and started the truck, unhappy about his rude awakening.

"Beware, bro. When you least expect it…" he mumbled to Daniel. "It's good to see you laughing though," he added.

"Yeah, Dad," Jessica chimed in, hugging his arm.

That evening, Daniel sat at the kitchen table of their new home going over the notes he and Ben had collected from Roberta and Simon's friends. He thought about looking over the village to see if anyone seemed scared or concerned. He wanted to blend in, though. Jogging had been part of his regular routine since high school, and the beatings had set him back. With only a day's worth of rez mud soakings, he hoped he was up for a jog. That would allow him to observe the villagers but not be obvious. He couldn't wait any longer.

Jessica sat across from him, studying him without a word. Eventually he felt her gaze and looked up. "What?"

"I just want to know why you got upset," she said.

He ignored the question and went back to his papers. After a few more moments of her pointed gaze, he finally answered. "I don't like people reading my mail," he mumbled.

"But that's how God works. He'll use people to talk to us. You know, 'word of knowledge,'" she reminded him.

"I know. I know."

"So really," she prodded, "you're miffed at God."

Daniel looked at her in amazement. "What were you two talking about after I left?"

"Fry bread." She smiled. She got up from the table and kissed her dad on the cheek.

"Fry bread," he repeated, not believing it. He shook his head, pretending to refocus on his papers. "Are you going jogging in the morning?"

"I've been wanting to. Uncle Ben wouldn't let me go alone. Why? You want to come along?" she asked him.

"I'd like to give it a try. See how well this rez mud really works. Is seven too early?" he suggested.

"I don't want you to get hurt, Dad."

"Jessica, I need to try. Besides, it'll give me a chance to scope the area and see if there are anymore skinheads sneakin' around."

"Like I said, I don't want you to get hurt!"

"Jessica, I won't. We'll be perfectly safe. They're not going to try anything on the rez. They're too afraid of us. That's why I need to jog around and see what I can find."

"Can't you drive?"

"Too obvious. I'm looking for stealth."

"Oh yeah, I can see you all stealth-like. Groaning with every step. Yep, that's my dad, the picture of stealth."

Daniel sat back, unsure if he should be offended or amused. "So, seven?"

Jessica sighed. "Do I have a choice?"

"Not really," he told her, concealing a smirk.

She walked down the hallway to her bedroom.

"Good night," he called with amusement in his voice.

She gave a wave and disappeared into her room.

CHAPTER 11

Daniel was surprised that he could handle a jog so soon. He thanked God for the rez mud. He couldn't go the five miles he was used to, but once his ribs were completely healed, he'd get back on track. After a mile and a half, Daniel had to stop. Rez mud or not, wisdom had to dictate his decision in this case.

"Are you okay?" Jessica asked.

"Yeah. But I won't be if I keep going, so let's head back and end on a good note."

Jessica gave him a nod before they turned around and walked back toward their new home.

Hawk came barreling up the road in his pickup truck and pulled up alongside them. "Need a ride?"

"Yeah, thanks!" Daniel answered.

"I was talkin' to Jessica!" he said with a sternness that surprised Daniel. He then laughed at their bewildered expressions. "Ha! Gotcha! Get in."

Jessica snorted, and Daniel tried not to smile. They climbed into the bed of the truck and settled in, after kicking aside the various offerings of discarded beer cans and trash.

"Hey, have I got BO or something?"

"Yes!" Daniel and Jessica shouted in unison and then laughed.

"Try to be nice!" Hawk said in mock offense.

Daniel looked at Jessica. "So how's Tommy?"

"How should I know? You're the one who's got him holed up with Sicheii and Ben. Not to mention keeping him busy with you doing police work. How *is* he, Dad?"

"An idle mind is the devil's playground."

"That's a new one. Is this how to protect your daughter from her boyfriend 101?"

Daniel smiled as he looked out at the distant mesas. "I'm going to take you out there once I know it's safe. Soon, I hope."

Jessica looked at her dad and smiled. "That'll be nice, Dad." She looked at the mesas for a moment and then spoke again. "So what do you think of Angel? I mean aside from her prophetic gift." She smiled with a lift of her eyebrow.

"I don't know. We only spent a few hours with her."

"I saw you looking at her, Dad. With *that* look."

"What look?" he asked as if his hand had been caught in the cookie jar.

"The *look*. The look every guy has when they think the woman or girl they see is hot."

"Jessica!" he said. He was horrified to think his daughter knew so much about men and that she could read him so easily. He wasn't lusting after her as the phrase implied, but he was definitely attracted to her. He looked down at the truck bed trying to hide a grin. He had been found out.

"You like her!" Jessica gushed.

He looked away from her, his grin growing. He cleared his throat and looked at Jessica. From the way she was acting, it was obvious she approved, but he wanted to make sure before he actually confessed. "What do you think about her?"

"I like her. A lot."

"What about Mom?"

Jessica was quiet for a moment, and Daniel felt he may have hurt her.

"I'm sorry, Jess."

"No, Dad. It's okay. You know what makes me love Angel?"

"What?"

"She was considerate of Mom and our feelings for her. So fess up."

"Yeah. I like her."

"Cool!"

Jessica kissed her dad on the cheek. "She asked for Mom's fry bread recipe. Maybe you should come along when I bring it."

Daniel looked at her with a raised eyebrow.

"You know, in case I can't remember it."

"Are you setting me up on a date?"

"Would that be so bad?"

He thought about it for a moment. "No."

"How's tomorrow night?" She grinned.

He looked at her. She had it set up already.

"Great." He smiled with a chuckle at her exuberance. "Tell me this. When did you suddenly get so keen on me dating?"

"Dad, you seem so sad. It's been two years. I just thought maybe you might need to move on. I feel like the Great Creator has helped me heal and move on." She flailed her arms as if fighting a swarm of bees. "You shouldn't be alone."

"I have you."

"You know what I mean." She gave him a look.

Daniel hadn't thought about dating. He had expected to be with Sarah for the rest of his life, and when she died, he shut down those ideas or any ideas of marriage. "Don't you miss your mom?"

Jessica looked away for a moment, and again, Daniel was sorry he'd said it. This time he felt he really had hurt her. "Sweetheart, I'm sorry. I only want to understand your enthusiasm."

She looked at him curiously.

"You caught me off guard. I had no idea."

"Dad, aren't you lonely?"

Daniel grew quiet. "Yes," he said. "For your mom."

Jessica wrangled her long hair as it whipped in the wind. "Dad, God doesn't want you to be alone. *I* don't want you to be alone."

Daniel listened. He knew what she said was true. He was surprised by her words, though. "I don't like being alone."

"Then it's settled!"

"What is?"

"You're going on a date with me and Angel." She flashed a triumphant grin.

"So you want me to find you a new mom?"

"No. I want you to find a new wife."

Once home, Daniel and Jessica got ready for their day. Lukas was going to take Tommy and Jessica out on the rez for a tour de force of learning. And since it was an unusual curriculum, not set in a school building, Tommy and Jessica were more than willing to go on the field trip. Ben warned Lukas to stay away from the northeast area of the rez and to not go off rez without him or Daniel.

Jeff McKinley and Johnny Smith sat in a small café in Aztec. In the farthest rear booth, they looked over a map of the reservation and New Mexico. "Here's where we'll keep your clan. They'll be safe and well fed. The guy we already have is fat and happy."

"How do I know you're not lying?"

"Johnny, come on. We need your help, and if we were to lie to you, you wouldn't trust us. It's all about trust, my friend." Jeff pulled an envelope from his back pocket and handed it to Johnny under the table.

Johnny opened it and counted five hundred dollars. He looked at Jeff and gave a nod. "I want to see Patterson pay for my sister's death."

"There's more where that came from, especially when Patterson steps into our trap. Now here's what we'll do." Jeff explained the McKinleys' plan as Johnny gripped the envelope with white knuckles.

Bill and Tom McKinley sat in the sheriff's office looking at maps. "That's a damn big reservation, Bill. How are we supposed to find my boy?"

"Don't forget why we have Johnny Smith," Bill said. He took a pinch of tobacco.

Tom's smile turned to a grin. "We just up the ante for him. He's probably ready to bring Patterson in for us. Why would this kid be so willing to help us, Bill?"

"Revenge is a cancer, Tom. He believes we're not going to hurt his people, and we did promise we'd release 'em after, didn't we?" He winked at his brother.

"We sure did, didn't we?" Tom snickered.

"I guess he figures this is the best way to finally get back at the man who let his sister die. So maybe the first one wet his appetite." Tom shrugged his thought off.

Bill placed his finger on the map at Aztec. "How's the mine doin'?"

"I heard from Ralph the other day. Once we get Patterson and the rest of those we need, we'll be makin' sweet time. Gold should be ready to ship in the next couple of weeks."

"Your boy is wanting some revenge of his own. We'll let him have some fun with Daniel before he has his accident," Bill said, spitting a wad of tobacco juice on the floor.

Daniel and Ben drove to the pool hall in Lupton.

"So what's the plan?" Daniel asked as they parked across the street from their target. Daniel and Ben wore jeans, tank-tops, and casual button downs on this run so they wouldn't scatter any lawbreakers inside the bar when they walked in. Each hid his badge on his belt for necessary identification and carried their handguns on the backs of their belts. Daniel was glad to finally be a respected equal with someone and grateful it was Ben.

"You play pool?" Ben asked.

"Maybe a little," Daniel said with a grin.

"Did you soak in the mud this morning?" Ben asked as they got out of his truck.

"Now there's a question!" Daniel exasperated. "How am I supposed to get that crud out of my bathtub?" He leaned against the front of the vehicle and waited for Ben's answer.

"Have you ever heard of a bucket?" Ben shrugged as he surveyed the hall. "You mean to tell me you haven't changed the mud?"

Daniel looked at him mystified. "You actually expect me to carry buckets of mud out of my house with broken ribs?"

"Don't worry, bro. By the time we get back, there'll be a whole fresh tub of it."

"Great," Daniel said without a hint of enthusiasm. "So the mud works better as it ages."

"That future son-in-law works hard for you, bro, and you don't even know it." Ben chuckled.

"What? He's been changing the mud?"

"You oughta thank him when we get back."

"Great. I've been soaking in cold mud when I could have had hot mud."

"Shall I call for a masseuse, too?"

Daniel gave in, shaking his head.

The two men started across the street. They stepped into the dark pool hall, a far contrast to the brilliant light outside. They had to remove their sunglasses in order to see in the gloom. They looked the place over, taking note of how many were there. Jeff was nowhere to be found. Aside from two pool tables, a bar, and a jukebox, there were only about seven white boys occupying the hall. Based on the tip, he half expected the place to be full of natives, but Daniel could easily understand why no Indian in his right mind would visit there, even with the lure of money. There was no sign of a flyer, either. There was quite a bit of wagering at the tables, and the bar was being held up by obvious regulars. Except one.

Daniel noticed a man in his mid-twenties leaning over the bar counter and casually snorting cocaine as if it were perfectly legal. Daniel nudged Ben on the arm and gestured toward the scene at the far end of the bar. The two investigators casually strolled over to the man and took a seat on either side of him. When he came up for air, he noticed his two visitors. Daniel and Ben looked at each other with a raise of an eyebrow.

"Blow's illegal in these parts, innit, bro?" Daniel asked, leaning across and forward to speak to Ben. He snorted and added, "Heck, any parts."

Ben leaned forward to answer. "I do hear it is."

The man in the middle chuckled as he licked a finger and cleaned up the remainder of the powder, careful not to waste any.

"That's a fine grade," Daniel noted. "Is there more, or shall we shop somewhere else?"

"Naw, man. I can set you up with anything you want," the dealer said. "Shall we step into my office?" He slipped off the bar stool and gestured to the back door.

"After you," Ben said.

Ben and Daniel exchanged looks of curiosity and caution. They put on their sunglasses and stepped outside. There were a number of cars in the back dirt parking lot, all roasting in the hot morning sun. The dealer led them to his car. He immediately lit a cigarette, hinting at his nervousness as he pulled his keys from his pocket and walked to his trunk. He opened it up and pulled out a leather briefcase, closed the trunk, and set it atop the back of his car. He popped the case open to reveal quite a presentation.

The case was lined with black velvet and sported on the inside lid, specific loops to hold vials of different sizes. On the floor of the case were several piles of plastic baggies of varying sizes, containing from one-half to three grams of cocaine, a couple of baggies of rock cocaine, all cordoned off by separate compartments.

Daniel and Ben snuck a look at each other. It seemed too fancy for a man of his apparent standing. There was a floating divider with bands on both sides sporting syringes, needles, bongs, and rubber tourniquets. Both Daniel and Ben had one hand on their guns, ready for anything.

"One-stop shopping for all your hallucinogenic needs," Daniel said. He pushed his un-tucked shirt aside to reveal his badge. "Too bad you're going out of business."

The dealer's eyes widened in shock before he quickly shut and locked the case. The man took off running, leaving the case behind.

"Aww, dude! Don't make me chase you!" Daniel whined after him, blinded by the glaring sun. Suddenly, Ben was there, standing with the shackled fugitive. "How'd you do that so fast?" Even with his sunglasses on, he'd been looking right into the sun in the direction the dealer had run, so he never saw Ben move.

"I'm an Indian, remember?"

"Yeah, well, no one taught me that!" Daniel grumbled.

"Maybe they only taught you *half* of it." Ben chortled.

Daniel nodded with a look as if he were annoyed at the comment. Daniel grabbed the briefcase, and the two men walked the dealer to Ben's vehicle across the street. No one had seen the transaction or arrest.

"If you'd stayed even *half* as long as you should have, you might have learned something," Ben continued the joking.

"And you're not *half* as funny as you used to be," Daniel retorted.

The man was placed between them as they drove back to the police station in Ben's unmarked pick-up truck. They booked the man for possession and dealing.

"Nice digs, don't you think so?" Daniel said to the dealer as they stepped into Ben's Criminal Investigations office.

The dealer sneered but didn't answer. Daniel handed him off to Joe, one of the deputies who had arrested Hawk. Pete turned on the fingerprinting machine and stood by as Joe un-cuffed the man's hands from behind him and then re-cuffed them in front of him.

"I'm impressed, Ben. We were still using ink in Stake Town. I should have moved back here a long time ago."

"No accounting for taste, I guess," Ben said, sarcasm dripping from his words.

"I'm offering you a compliment, and you slam me. Some friend." Daniel put on a pout, knowing Ben was razzing him. Yet, there was some truth in what Ben had said. Daniel walked into the holding block and inspected the very clean cells—four in all and looking as if they'd just been built. "Give, bro. You got an in with a construction company?"

"I've got a friend at the Bureau."

Daniel gave a silent nod and narrowed his eyes, considering Ben's reply. He'd been away so long he couldn't read his friend on that one.

"All prepped for interrogation, Ben," Joe announced. "Shall I get the knives?"

"Nah, let's see how much he gives up with just the noose first," Ben joked. The dealer's eyes were widening with every comment. Daniel had to hide his grin.

"You have a choice. You can tell us who and where your supplier is, or we can put you in a cell with a really mean Indian," Ben offered. "Risk your scalp and all that."

"I ain't talkin' to you, pig!"

"Old school," Daniel pointed out and then shrugged. "At least he didn't call you chief."

Ben frowned. "He's too young for old school. What are you, twenty?" Ben didn't wait for his answer. "Maybe he learned it from his boss."

Daniel pulled a long knife from the sheath on the side of his belt and walked up behind the dealer. The man's towhead had a receding hairline for his age, and Daniel had to search for a good grip. He laid the cold steel against the man's scalp, covering a row of ten small swastikas.

"I don't know, bro." Daniel clucked with pity. "There's not much to work with."

"That's why they shave their heads," Ben teased. "So we can't scalp 'em when we kick their white Aryan butts."

The man growled at Ben and attempted to move, but Daniel reminded him of the blade.

"I was so looking forward to this," Daniel gave a dejected sigh, putting his knife away and hoisting the dealer to his feet.

He walked him into the separate room where the holding cells were. He shoved him into one and slammed the door closed. "Good thing it's Sunday tomorrow," he told the criminal. "The judge goes to church." Daniel smiled.

The dealer spat at Daniel as he turned to leave, hitting his pant leg with a very large wad of saliva. Daniel stopped, cringed in disgust, and then turned back to the man in the cell. "Now that wasn't very nice." He smiled. "I didn't scalp you and yet you spit on me. I'm disappointed."

The dealer sat with a confused expression, apparently expecting a different reaction. Daniel grabbed two paper towels from a nearby dispenser and wiped the spittle off his jeans and then exited the room.

"Hey!" the dealer called. "I get a phone call! And what about some food?"

"Do you know how to use smoke signals? That's how we Indians communicate," Ben answered as he and Daniel chuckled to each other. "Restaurant's already closed, too. You should really try to get arrested during business hours next time."

Joe and Pete had their feet up on their desks, enjoying pancakes. "Wow, these griddles are good, ain't they, Pete?" Joe said.

"Mmm!" Pete murmured through a mouthful.

"Hey!" came the cry from the holding cell.

"We'll be in my office," Ben said as he and Daniel headed for the large-windowed room.

Joe gave a casual wave of acknowledgment, concentrating on his breakfast.

"I love the laid-back feel in there." Daniel grinned.

"They do, too," Ben said.

Daniel and Ben sat in Ben's office, debriefing their experience from the pool hall and what their course of action should be. "What do you think about Stanley White Powder?" Daniel asked.

"I have a feeling it was a lure of some sort," Ben said while munching on some fry bread.

"Good point. The briefcase setup was very high end and too neat for a guy like him," Daniel added.

"Right," Ben said. "Let's check out what the nightlife is like, and then we'll go from there."

CHAPTER 12

Lukas, Jessica, and Tommy arrived home after a long day on the mesas, a classroom to be envied by anyone choosing to study. They used a Navajo translation dictionary that Ben had given them, but Lukas was gracious enough to speak in English for them. Lukas had taught them how the Great Creator had made the mesas for the sun to paint as it rose and fell each day and how all of his creation was made for his people and animals to enjoy. He made them study the sand and the dirt and all of the details God had put into his masterpiece called earth.

Both Tommy and Jessica had never really thought about that aspect of God, nor of the intimate detail and design of all he had made. "Sicheii, I never really saw the Great Creator in this way before, how much he cares for me by why and how he made the earth."

"You know, I've never really thought about all this before, either. I mean, I'm surrounded by it every day," Tommy began. "I've always thought of God as distant and aloof. He sure didn't fit into my family even though my dad uses God as an excuse to justify his beliefs. I never thought God would be interested in me. I'm just a speck in the universe."

"But an important and beloved speck," Jessica said with a smile.

Tommy smiled back. "I want to know more. I want to know the Great Creator."

Lukas was pleased at the young man's pliable heart.

As they finished bringing in their various specimens of dirt, sand, rocks, bones, and plants and placing them on the kitchen table of Ben's hogan, they were excited to learn more as Lukas finished telling them of some of his experiences at the Sherman Indian School. There was much to digest, and the two young people had a million questions, but Lukas ended the day with a lesson on rest.

"Even the Great Creator had a time of rest, and he called it sacred. It was a time to enjoy what he had made, and he wants his people to enjoy it and him as they rest. It refreshes the spirit and soul to rest,"

Lukas explained. "When we rest in the Creator's presence, we learn who he is without any effort, and that is the best part of learning."

Jessica and Tommy looked at Lukas in awe. "Thank you, Sicheii," Jessica said reverently.

Daniel pulled into the driveway of Ben's home. Jessica rushed out of the house to greet her dad.

"Dad!" she whined. "It's four o'clock!"

"Okay, when are we supposed to be there?"

"Five!" she emphasized.

"Well, you can blame Ben for making us late."

"Hey!" Ben said.

"I'm trying to save you from making a bad impression! Go!" She pushed her dad across the yard to their house.

"I'm going! I'm going!" He chuckled.

"No soaking tonight. There's no time!" Jessica ordered, both disappearing inside.

Ben and Tommy watched from his front door. "See what you're in for?" Ben slapped Tommy on the back. Tommy nodded with a grin.

Jessica had set out her dad's attire for him, allowing him jeans and a nice southwestern shirt, but when he arrived in the kitchen with a tie, she protested. "Where'd you get that?"

"What?"

"That tie!" Jessica quickly stepped up to Daniel and removed it. "There."

"I thought it looked okay."

"Dad, how would you know? You've never dated anyone but Mom, and you haven't dated since. Ties are so two centuries ago."

"How was I supposed to know?"

"Did I put a tie out for you?"

"I thought you forgot."

Jessica, hands on hips, gave him a look of disbelief. "We need to go."

"Dad, how can you give me advice on Tommy when you're so nervous that you're sweating?" she asked as they drove to Angel's.

"It's hot out!" he reasoned.

"The air conditioning's on," she pointed out, making sure all the vents were hitting him.

"Look, just relax. It's not like you're getting married tomorrow." She chortled.

"If Sicheii had his way, we would be." He chuckled half heartedly and then looked at Jessica suspiciously. "We're not, are we?"

Jessica let out a loud laugh, clapping her hands together.

Daniel pulled their SUV to a stop in front of Angel Green's hogan and turned off the engine. Jessica climbed out and bounded to the front door while Daniel remained behind the wheel, holding it with a death grip. Jessica knocked on the door and then noticed that her dad had failed to follow her.

She looked at him, hands on her hips, head cocked. "You've got to be kidding!"

She walked back over to the vehicle to the driver's side. She opened the door and began to pry Daniel's fingers from around the steering wheel. At that moment, Angel opened her door but found an empty stoop. She stepped out and looked at the SUV.

"We'll be there in a minute!" Jessica assured.

Angel gave an amused smile, waved, and then stepped back into her home. Jessica finally got his hands free and led him to the front door. Once there, she had to nudge him inside quickly to ensure she wouldn't have to pry his fingers from her doorframe or, worse yet, tackle him if he made a run for it, although she was pretty sure he wouldn't take it that far.

"Everything okay?" Angel asked with a sparkle in her eyes.

Jessica greeted Angel with a hug. "Oh yeah. Dad was just giving me some last-minute instructions for how to behave at the table."

Daniel stood there, looking around the room with an awkward smile.

"You can come in," Angel offered.

Jessica stepped up to her dad, telling him with her eyes and not so many words to get with the program. "Dad," she whispered through clenched teeth, "she doesn't bite."

"That's not my take on it," he whispered back and moved toward the kitchen. He looked at Angel. "I would have worn a tie, but Jessica assured me that that would be a sappy move." He smiled. "So I insisted on flowers." He handed her a small bouquet that Christiana had put together for him.

"Well, I can certainly understand you not wanting to appear sappy. The flowers saved you. They're beautiful, Daniel. Thank you," Angel said.

Daniel studied her for a moment and then looked to his daughter for clarification. Jessica only shook her head quickly.

As Daniel and Jessica sat down at her kitchen table, Angel set cold glasses of water before them. "So. Did you bring that fry bread recipe with you?"

"It's all up here," Daniel said confidently, tapping his temple.

"Well, everything else is ready. I just need that recipe." She smiled at him. "Jessica, would you mind setting the table in the dining room?" she asked with a wink.

"Sure!" She winked back.

Angel handed her a stack of plates and the needed silverware for dinner and pointed her to the small dining room. Jessica performed the task as slowly as possible, wanting to give them some time alone.

Ben drove to Rez Ribs and found Hawk there, just as he expected. The barkeeper held up three fingers, indicating how many beers Hawk had consumed. He sidled up to the bar next to Hawk as he was finishing his third beer and calling for his fourth.

"I'm out. Send another one down, would ya?"

Ben caught the bartender's eye and with a look told him not to send it. "Hey, bro, we need to talk."

Hawk looked at Ben with a sour expression. "About what?"

"Come on," Ben said, putting a hand on Hawk's shoulder and guiding him off his stool.

"What about my beer?"

"Later," Ben told him, hoping later wouldn't come. Hawk acted reluctant but followed Ben out to his truck.

Ben drove them out to an old hideaway he, Hawk, Daniel, and Sarah used as kids. It was an old cave overlooking a canyon. They got out, and Ben sat down on a flat rock near the entrance.

"What are we doing, counting stars?"

Ben ignored Hawk's sarcasm. "Has Daniel acknowledged your offer?" he asked.

"You mean when you took me to the hospital to see him?"

Ben nodded.

"I've only seen him once since he got back. Yesterday I offered him and Jessica a ride back from their jog. He didn't seem mad. Why?"

"Were you really sorry about what you did?"

Hawk thought about it and then shrugged. "I guess."

"You guess?"

"Yeah. What's all this about? When did you become a counselor?" Hawk asked, annoyance edging his words.

"I need to tell you something," Ben said slowly.

Hawk threw his hands up with a shrug. "If it'll get me back to my beer and get you to shut up."

Ben forged ahead. "Do you remember when we all went to school together?"

"You're kidding, right?"

"Answer."

"Yeah, yeah, that's why I hate him." Hawk stopped, realizing what he'd just said.

Ben looked at him.

"Yeah. I remember," Hawk amended.

Ben went on. "The day they made Daniel—"

"Whoa, wait! *Made?*" Hawk's question was incredulous.

"Made," Ben repeated. "I was there, Hawk. He didn't want to go. He begged them to let him stay."

"Yeah." Hawk snorted.

"I was there, bro. Shut up and listen!"

Hawk was surprised by his tone. He adjusted his position on the rock and prepared for a long story.

"I watched him crying to stay at the school so he could be with us. They beat him and made him leave."

Hawk looked at Ben in stunned silence and then looked away. "It's the first I heard of it." He stared up into the night sky. "Truth?"

"Truth," Ben affirmed.

"I'm sorry."

"Really?" Ben now asked.

Hawk nodded, looking at the ground.

"I believe Lukas has something for you two tonight."

Hawk looked at Ben. "Okay," he submitted.

They headed back to Ben's house to wait for Daniel.

Daniel washed his hands and then, with Angel by his side, began his lesson on Sarah Yanaba's fry bread recipe. "First, I need garlic salt, sage, oregano, and some shredded cheese." Daniel stopped for a moment as a wave of emotion threatened to wash over him.

Angel went to the refrigerator and pulled out jack and cheddar cheese. When she put them on the counter, she looked at Daniel.

"Daniel, are you okay? Is this too difficult for you?" She waited, but he remained, staring at the counter. He saw images of Sarah, laughing in the kitchen while making the bread.

"Daniel." She touched his arm. He looked at her hand on his arm. She pulled away. "I'm sorry if this is too difficult. We can just eat what I—"

"No. No. I'm sorry. I just didn't expect these emotions." He straightened and leaned against the counter to face her. "I mean, I would expect it from Jess, but she's handling this better than I am. It's been two years, but this is all sudden."

"I'm really fine with serving what I have. It is just dinner, after all."

"Is it? Really?" Daniel's smile softened.

"What do you think?" Angel said, focusing on shredding the cheese.

"I believe this is from the Lord. I...I want to share this joy with you. It's a good memory of a great woman, and you're the one I'm to share it with." Daniel took hold of her delicate fingers and wiggled her hand playfully. "So…" He turned, looking at the cheese. "Okay, we need the garlic salt."

Angel pointed to the cupboard. Daniel opened it and found a plethora of spices. He removed the needed ones and began to instruct her on the finer aspects of Sarah's fry bread. "So we just mix this with the flour to taste. I like garlic, personally." He looked at the smirk on Angel's face and added, "But I also like to brush my teeth."

Jessica listened intently from the other room as her dad cracked quiet jokes, a sure sign he was feeling more comfortable. She could hear Angel laugh. She would occasionally peek into the kitchen when it got too quiet. She finally finished setting the table and cautiously approached the kitchen. She smiled at what she saw.

Daniel and Angel were each leaning on opposite counters facing each other.

"She would throw flour on her face to make us understand how hard she worked in the kitchen."

"How'd you know she did that? Maybe she did work really hard." Angel's defense of Sarah was touching to Daniel.

"I saw her do it. I loved to watch her cook, but she didn't like it when I watched, so I would peek in every so often. So when I saw her do it one time, I cleared my throat. Sarah turned around all flustered." He chuckled at the memory.

"What did you do?" Angel's face held fascination.

"It's not what *I* did. *She* threw flour at me, and as you can guess, we made a mess of the kitchen."

Angel broke out into laughter. Jessica couldn't help but laugh as well but covered her mouth and ducked back into the dining room.

They had just finished the belly laugh with the slow calm of realization between them that they were enjoying each other's company. Then they remained fixed on each other's eyes, soft smiles playing on their lips.

They didn't even notice Jessica standing in the doorway. She observed them with a smile for a moment before clearing her throat.

"So how's the fry bread coming along?" she said, pretending to be just entering the kitchen.

Daniel and Angel straightened as if being caught in the act of something forbidden. Angel turned to the counter and began to wipe it down while Daniel turned to the hot oil and batter.

"Dad?"

Daniel turned, as if hearing her for the first time. "Hmm? Oh hey, Jessica."

Jessica handed him his water. He took a long drink. "Thanks, I needed that."

"I know." She winked at him with a wry smile. She then stepped up to Angel. "So how's the fry bread going?" she asked again.

Angel gave her a sideways glance. "Not bad," she whispered, sneaking a glance at Daniel for Jessica's benefit. Jessica grinned.

The three finally sat down to dinner, and Daniel had the women in stitches, telling them stories of his childhood with Ben, Hawk, and Sarah.

"So there we were, stuck in the tree. The dogs had given up on having us for dinner hours before."

"What did you do?" Angel laughed with excitement.

"We would have spent the night there if it hadn't been for Sarah's dad." The women laughed more.

"Leave it to the heroic dad!" Jessica said.

"Yeah, and don't forget it," Daniel said, pointing a teasing finger at her.

"If it's okay, may I ask what happened to Sarah's parents?"

"They passed a couple of years after we married."

"I'm sorry. You seem to have had a lot of sorrow in your life."

"Sicheii taught me to remember the good in the bad and to let that heal me. I think it's working, don't you?" he asked Jessica and Angel. Angel and Jessica exchanged a smile.

After dinner and dessert, they played a rousing game of Pictionary and vowed to get Ben and the rest of the family in on the next visit.

"We should do this more often," Jessica said.

Daniel and Angel got the message and shared another long gaze at each other. It was 10:00 p.m. by the time Angel conceded her championship. Daniel and Jessica almost didn't want to leave. It had been a long two years since they'd really laughed with someone.

"I really have to go. I've got an early start tomorrow," he said with obvious reluctance in his voice as he stood up.

Angel and Jessica stood with Daniel between them, but Jessica stepped around to her, hugging her good night.

"I was hoping you two could come back soon," she said to Jessica.

"I'll work on him," Jessica assured, "but don't be surprised if he asks you out on his own."

Daniel was putting the game away, all the while sneaking glances at the two women who were obviously plotting something, judging by the long embrace. When he cleared his throat, Jessica hurried to the door.

"I'll meet you in the truck, Dad," she said in a lilting voice. Before he knew it, she had rushed out, not giving him a chance to protest being left alone with the woman he was falling in love with. He was surprised that over the course of making the bread and having dinner, he had realized such feelings for Angel. The front door opened and closed in a flash, and there they stood. He knew the Great Creator was behind it, but it was moving so fast. The one thing that most endeared him to her wasn't her looks, though she was beautiful, but that Angel respected the memory of Sarah. It was as if Sarah had been *her* friend. Again, he surmised it was all the Lord's work. He wasn't one to fight the Lord's will.

"She's a sly one." Angel smiled and bit the bottom of her lip.

Daniel let out a soft chuckle of agreement.

"You didn't have to clean up. I am the hostess, after all."

"I don't mind." He shrugged. "I'm pretty domestic." He looked at her. "Thanks for the great evening," he said.

"Thanks to you," she said.

Again there was an awkward silence and nervous smiles. They both moved for the door at the same time and ended up closer to one another than expected.

"Ever have a feeling," Daniel began but then stopped, inciting a curious look from Angel. "Uh…" he stammered, "like the Great Creator's up to something?" he finished with a gulp.

"I'm a little nervous. I've never really been alone with a man before."

Daniel raised an eyebrow.

"I mean…that seemed to care about me," she finished.

Daniel reached for her right hand and kissed it gently. He looked at her again, seeing her smile. Somehow she didn't seem so confident anymore, so Daniel treaded carefully. He leaned in and gave her a soft kiss on the cheek. He pulled away slowly to check her reaction. Her eyes were just opening while she held a content smile.

"Would you like to go out sometime, for dinner?" he asked her. He was still holding her hand. It seemed so natural.

Angel looked at him. "I'd like that," she replied.

"It will be Wednesday before I'm free. Will that work?"

"I'll be right here," she assured him.

"Okay then, Wednesday it is." He cleared his throat. "I'll pick you up at five o'clock." He opened the door and stepped out.

His gaze remained fixed on Angel's sweet smile.

Jessica watched from their SUV and giggled as her dad backed out of the hogan and nearly fell on his backside when he missed the step. He gave an awkward wave and then hurried to the vehicle. He didn't even notice he was taking the passenger side.

Once inside, Jessica grilled him. "Okay, give!" She grinned as she started the SUV.

As she backed away, Daniel kept staring at Angel's front door. She was still standing there, and she gave him another wave. He returned it.

"Hello! Earth to Dad!" Jessica said a little more loudly. Daniel turned to his daughter slowly, revealing the smile of a smitten teen. He still hadn't heard his daughter.

"Dad!" she said sharply, quite amused.

He finally snapped out of it. "What?"

"Give."

"Give what?"

"Did you kiss her?"

"Jessica!" he replied with surprise. "That's none of your business."

"If she's going to be part of the family, I think it is."

"Now that's where you're wrong," Daniel corrected her with a raised eyebrow.

"Wrong about her being a part of the family or wrong about it being my business?" she dared to ask.

Daniel flexed his hands several times, studying them, as if the action would give him clarity. "Wrong about it being your business," he mumbled.

Jessica had to strain to hear him over the road noise, but she did hear him and grinned. "Yes!" She punched the air with a fist.

Daniel put his right hand to his forehead in amusement and shook his head.

Jessica pulled into their driveway. She and Daniel walked over to Ben's house where Lukas, Ben, Tommy, and Hawk were awaiting their arrival inside. Tommy stood and greeted Jessica with a hug.

"Careful," Daniel warned.

Tommy released her and stepped back. "Sorry, sir."

"Dad," Jessica scolded him.

"So Red Tears has returned from his excursion," Lukas said in Navajo. Tommy, Jessica, and Daniel sat down.

"Yes, sir," Daniel answered.

"Does Red Tears know who the Meda is?" Lukas questioned him.

Daniel was silent for a long time as he looked from his sicheii to Ben and then to Jessica. He gave a tense glance to Hawk.

Hawk snuck a look but glanced away, a look of shame on his face. "Yeah, who is she to you?"

"Hawkeye is jealous?" Lukas asked. Hawk clammed up.

Daniel glanced out the window, stood, and walked up to it. He stared out at the black desert. He finally turned to his family.

"She belongs here," he said in Navajo, tapping his chest. "A gift from the Great Creator."

"You're so full of—" Hawk started.

"Hawk!" Ben said. "Speak up plainly. Do you love Angel?"

Daniel turned to Hawk, waiting for his reply.

"No, but she's my friend. She was my friend before he ever got here."

"You sound like a spoiled child," Ben said. "Let Lukas finish."

Jessica and Tommy took hold of each other's hands. Jessica's expression was pensive. Hawk rolled his eyes. "Fine." He made a motion of zipping his lip.

"Red Tears, you are ready to give your heart," Lukas told him. He looked at Hawk. "Bannin Hawkeye!"

"Sir!" Hawk sat up, startled.

"You are not ready. But you will be," Lukas told him.

"Come," Lukas invited Daniel and Hawk.

Daniel looked at Ben with concern and then to Jessica and Tommy.

"Don't worry, bro. I'm staying. They're safe," Ben assured him.

Daniel sighed in relief, and Jessica stepped up to her dad, giving him a kiss on his cheek. "Don't worry, Dad. I'll be fine. Just learn well," she said.

He kissed her forehead tenderly. "I will."

Lukas was out the door and waiting in Hawk's truck for Daniel and Hawk. Hawk walked around to the driver's side, but Lukas spoke up. "Red Tears drives," he instructed in Navajo. Though Hawk didn't speak Navajo, he understood the gesture that Lukas gave and looked with annoyance at Daniel. With a sigh, he conceded and tossed him the keys. As they drove, Lukas gave directions, and after a half an hour of driving, they ended up back at Ben's house.

"I thought you understood Navajo," Hawk complained.

Daniel leaned forward and looked past his sicheii. "I do."

"Then what are we doing back here?"

Daniel didn't answer but looked at his sicheii's expression. "Maybe it's a test." Daniel shrugged. He sat back and gave his sicheii a wink.

Hawk drummed on his window frame, clearly annoyed as Daniel pulled out again and followed Lukas's directions to a hogan on the east side of Chinle. After an hour's drive, they ended up in the middle of nowhere. Daniel pulled to a stop twenty-five yards from a low in-ground building. Lukas gestured for Hawk to get out. Daniel was already out and walked to the other side of the truck.

Without a word, Lukas started walking toward the hogan. He removed his shirt as he walked toward the low small sweat lodge while Daniel and Hawk watched.

"So. Stealing Angel away from me too, eh?" Hawk said once Lukas was out of earshot.

Daniel watched his sicheii disappear into the sweat lodge. He remained silent.

"Truth hurts, don't it?"

"What truth, Hawk? What you perceive as truth and what really is the truth are two different things. Besides, if you're such good friends, me being in the picture shouldn't disturb that."

"You've always got an answer." Hawk turned to him, his eyes burning with anger. In Hawk's opinion, Daniel was always the one getting the girl, the rewards, and the best of everything, and he was tired of it.

"No, Hawk. You just have so much anger in your heart you can't see straight." Daniel took his shirt off and tossed it into the cab of the truck and followed Lukas.

In the dimming headlights, Hawk stared at the bruises on Daniel's torso, knowing he'd been a part of inflicting the injuries. And while Daniel's ribs were no longer wrapped, the scar over the left side of his rib cage urged a flood of remorse through Hawk. He shook his head, bewildered, and then followed suit. By the time Hawk entered, Lukas had a fire going, heating four large, smooth rocks. Daniel was seated on his sicheii's right side so Hawk sat down on Lukas's left.

Lukas spoke in Navajo while Daniel translated for Hawk. "It is time to give your hearts to the Great Creator as brothers. No man can rule or own his own heart. God has given you each a heart so that you may have only him rule it."

Lukas poured water on the hot rocks, causing steam to fill the lodge, and lit white sage, mingling its smoke with the steam. He continued in Navajo, "Red Tears will pay a price for giving his heart. Will you, Bannin?"

Hawk flinched at the Japanese word that meant watchman. Lukas didn't look at him, but Hawk knew he was waiting for an answer. Hawk looked at Lukas and Daniel and then gave a nod of affirmation.

"Now we will sit in his presence and seek his counsel."

Lukas picked up a hand drum and mallet and began to sing, "Welcome our Creator."

Daniel closed his eyes, obviously trying to focus. Hawk knew the concept of the sweat lodge and that Daniel was allowing his body to sweat and be purified physically and spiritually. Hawk wasn't much of a believer in God and spiritual things, but he did his best to participate. He closed his eyes and relaxed.

Daniel sang the song with his sicheii. It was the song he'd sung when he first returned to the rez a couple of weeks earlier, but he hadn't known what it was then or that he even knew it. After the song, Daniel received a vision. It was almost the same as the one he'd had of himself and his sicheii; in fact, it started out the same way.

Daniel stood shirtless and barefoot on top of a plateau. His sicheii rode up to him, spear in hand, atop a dapple gray Mustang. Lukas got off the horse and walked up to Daniel. As he moved to thrust his spear into him, Hawk appeared in front of Daniel, his back to him and dressed in the same manner, as if stepping in to take his place. The spear pierced Hawk's chest, shoving him back into Daniel, who caught him as they both went down. Daniel held the same look of surprise as before as Lukas removed Hawk's heart and offered it up to the Great Creator. Daniel and Hawk watched as Lukas spoke to the Great Creator.

"Here is the heart you gave your son, O Great One. He has given it freely and purely." Daniel watched the heart become like ashes, and

a wind took the dust from Lukas's hand, swirling them up into heaven. Daniel looked at Hawk, feeling his body relax into death.

Daniel's eyes shot open, and he took a gasp of air as if he'd been underwater trying to reach the surface. He looked at Hawk. His eyes were still closed, as were Lukas's, but Lukas smiled.

"You will learn the meaning of this vision soon," he told his grandson.

Hawk then opened his eyes and took a slow deep breath. Both Daniel and Lukas looked at him expectantly.

"I got nothing," he told them.

Daniel gave him a disbelieving nod. Somehow he knew that Hawk had seen something but was choosing not to admit to realizing his spiritual side. Lukas told Daniel to sit beside Hawk. He complied and took a seat to Hawk's right. Lukas gestured for them to put out their neighboring arms, Hawk's right and Daniel's left. Lukas then stood and pulled out a long narrow strip of leather from his jeans pocket and began to tell them a story in Navajo, which Daniel translated for Hawk. He was stunned at the gift of interpretation the Great Creator had given him.

"One evening, an old Indian told his grandson about a battle that goes on inside people. He said, 'My son, the battle is between two wolves inside us all.'" Lukas began to wrap the leather around Daniel's and Hawk's wrists. "One is evil. It is anger, envy, jealousy, sorrow, regret."

Lukas spoke the words, looking intently into the two men's eyes. While Hawk would not hold his gaze, Daniel did.

He continued. "Greed, arrogance, self-pity, guilt, resentment…" He spoke slowly, purposely. "Inferiority, lies, false pride."

With each word, Daniel prayed to the Great Creator to cleanse his heart as Lukas tied him and his brother together.

"Superiority and ego. The other wolf is good. It is joy, peace, love, serenity, humility, kindness, benevolence, empathy."

Daniel noticed that Hawk appeared more uncomfortable by the moment and watched him stare at the leather that was binding him to Daniel. "Generosity, truth, compassion, and faith."

Lukas put his hands on the men's shoulders, still looking intently at them. "The grandson thought about it for a minute and then asked his sicheii, 'Which one wins?' The old Sicheii simply replied, 'The one you feed.'" Lukas finished, giving their shoulders a squeeze for emphasis. "For the next three days, you will starve your bodies but feed your souls. What part of your souls is your choice. You will cleanse your bodies and souls with water, natural and spiritual," he further instructed.

"Great," Hawk mumbled.

Daniel nudged his disrespect.

Lukas spoke up. "You agreed to this, Hawkeye. A man does not give his word only to grumble about it and then desire to back out, unless he is a coward," Daniel translated.

Hawk gave a grunt. "Translated like a pro."

Lukas motioned for them to stand and then led them outside to a nearby pond. The moon reflected off the perfectly still water. Lukas indicated the water and spoke.

"We are to baptize ourselves for the journey," Daniel said.

Hawk looked at his wrist bound to Daniel's and then yanked Daniel into the pond with him. After breaking the surface, they struggled to climb out. Both men being tied together would present some interesting challenges.

Being evening in the Arizona high country, their bodies reacted to the cold, causing them to shiver as the water cascaded off them. The next challenge came as they tried to change into the dry pants that Lukas had brought along. Lukas chuckled, watching Daniel and Hawk stumble around, fighting to keep balance and tugging at each other's wrists, vying for control of the situation.

Once they accomplished the wardrobe change, Lukas put a blanket around each man and then pulled out two necklaces of leather with hammered silver medallions. They were about an inch and a half in diameter, and each was stamped with a wolf on the front. On the back was the simple question in Navajo, "Evil or Good?" He placed a necklace around each man's neck and gave them bedrolls and canteens. He also handed Daniel a smudge of white sage.

"You must follow the signs and find your way," Lukas said, and then he pointed to the moonlit desert plains beyond the pond.

CHAPTER 13

Daniel and Hawk pulled their blankets tightly around them and started walking. They heard the sound of Lukas's truck come to life and then drive away.

Daniel wondered about Hawk's commitment to this quest. He thought he himself wasn't afraid, but he knew it wouldn't be easy to have to face what was inside him. As they walked, he considered what might be inside of his own heart and realized he *was* afraid.

"Hey, give me your knife," Hawk said to Daniel.

"Why?"

"So we can cut this crap off," he answered as if it were obvious.

"I don't think so."

"You want to stay like this for three days?" Hawk tugged on his wrist. The sharp bite of the leather made him realize he didn't want to do that too often.

"There's a point to all of this, Hawk. You just want the easy way out." Daniel tugged back.

"Go ahead and say it," Hawk interrupted.

"Say what?"

"As usual. That's what you wanted to add, wasn't it?"

"Hawk!" Daniel snapped. "Let's just focus on the task at hand. Together, okay?"

"Fine," Hawk answered uncertainly. He gave another tug just to irritate Daniel.

With a strong yank back, Daniel cast a warning look Hawk's way.

"Touchy," Hawk mumbled.

Daniel and Hawk walked for about an hour. In the moonlight, they found a rock outcropping.

"Guess it's Boy Scouts time." Hawk yanked on Daniel and grabbed a batch of scrub.

Daniel tugged back, dragging Hawk over to a small dead myrtle wood. He forced his left hand and broke off several small branches. "You mean Indian time."

"I joined the Boy Scouts," Hawk informed him. He found a piece of tumbleweed and proceeded to stomp it into kindling.

"Then *you* can get the fire going," Daniel said. He picked up some of the kindling and pulled Hawk toward the large outcropping.

Hawk dropped his treasure in a heap and sat down. Daniel dropped his and tugged on Hawk's wrist again. "We need rocks, Boy Scout."

Hawk cursed under his breath but got up. "I knew that." He helped Daniel carry some of the rocks back over to their makeshift camp so they could start a fire.

Daniel, after arranging the rocks in a neat circle, remained on his haunches and looked up at Hawk.

Hawk yawned.

"How's that fire comin'?" Daniel asked.

Hawk scowled and squatted next to Daniel. "I didn't bring any matches."

"That's the Boy Scout way?"

"It's one way!" Hawk sat down and crossed his legs. "You're the one with all the police training. Didn't they teach you how to survive in this desert?"

Daniel released a heavy sigh. He put his head down. Hawk heard him mumble something.

"Don't tell me God's gonna light the fire."

Daniel ignored Hawk. Hawk watched as Daniel took some fine grass, a narrow strip of bark, and a straight stick from among their finds. He split the bark enough to hold the grass and then knelt in front of his project. He set the stick into motion by rubbing it back and forth on the bark as fast as having one hand would allow. "Mind giving me a hand?"

Hawk shrugged and put his tied hand next to Daniel's left hand so Daniel could hold the bark. After several attempts, the grass began to smolder. Hawk held his breath as Daniel leaned down and blew softly on it until a flame burst forth.

"Yee haw! We got fire!" Hawk proclaimed, throwing his hands in the air with triumph. This caused Daniel to drop the small flame, snuffing it out. Hawk dropped his hands quickly. "Oops." He swallowed.

Daniel scowled at Hawk and then started the whole process again. Again he was successful. He got a strong roaring fire going and then sat back. "You see?" Daniel said.

"What?" Hawk acted dumb, annoying Daniel.

"Nothing," Daniel huffed, tossing a small twig onto the fire. They put their bedrolls out and settled in, though uncomfortably, for the night.

"Hey, half-breed," Hawk said.

Daniel really wanted to reply in kind but figured that wouldn't feed the good wolf, and besides that, Hawk needed to first admit that he himself wasn't full Indian. "What?" Daniel answered.

"How are we supposed to follow the signs? You know I'm not all that spiritual."

"Are you serious about this journey?"

Hawk was silent for a moment. "I haven't cut us free, have I?"

"I didn't give you the knife," Daniel reminded him.

Hawk rolled his eyes. "Okay. If I had my own knife, I wouldn't have cut us free," he amended.

"Great. Then don't worry about it," Daniel said. He closed his eyes.

"Hey, half-breed?" Hawk said again.

"What?"

"You don't toss and turn, do you?" He tugged on Daniel's arm as if wanting to roll to his side.

"Go to sleep, Hawk," he ordered.

Later, before Hawk fell asleep, he noticed Daniel trembling and speaking urgently in Navajo. He seemed to be having a distressing dream. Even though Daniel already had his blanket over him, it obviously wasn't enough, so Hawk took his own blanket and covered his brother with it.

Daniel was the first to awaken in the early morning. He looked at the extra blanket covering him and then at Hawk and gave a smile. He nudged his brother-in-law awake.

"Hey, Hawk," he said.

Hawk grumbled and tried to roll over, forgetting that he was tied to someone.

"What, man? I'm trying to sleep."

"Well, it's time to get up."

"Why?"

"Because nature calls."

"How can you be spiritual so early in the morning?"

"I'm not being spiritual," Daniel emphasized and sat up, yanking on Hawk. Hawk looked at him for a minute, and it finally dawned on him as he felt the call as well.

"Oh, right."

He and Daniel got up and walked a distance from their camp, both thanking the Great Creator that they were only consuming water for the next three days. Once nature was appeased, they broke camp, rolled up their blankets and bedrolls, and headed out again, searching for their first sign.

The day was long, hot, and dirty. Daniel didn't like the added discomfort of the tight leather strap tethering him to a man who hated him. He would be surprised if Hawk chose to stick it out. He remained silent as they walked, lost in his own thoughts. The sun beating down on him kept him from focusing on one thought for more than a few minutes. He winced with almost every step, feeling his ribs healing and his back burning.

Hawk made it difficult on Daniel for the first few hours the first day. He made Daniel drag him along, and then he would get ahead of Daniel and tug on him. He didn't want to think about what lessons he might have to learn on the journey, realizing the very real possibility of being humbled before the man he hated. He felt his body craving beer, which agitated him more. He took it out on Daniel, continuing his game of tug-of-war.

That night, the temperature dropped quickly, and Hawk welcomed a fire. He cooperated with Daniel for his own purposes as his alcohol withdrawal intensified. Hawk could only hope to get through the night without tearing his hair out or hinting to Daniel the pain he was really in. He discarded his blanket as cold sweats gave his condition away. Hawk finally drifted off to sleep, feeling his blanket resting upon him and a faint echoing voice of prayer filter into his subconscious.

The first torturous day and second night had ended in a silence that Hawk felt had wasted his time and energy. He believed he hadn't learned anything, and Daniel's complete silence had annoyed him to the point of wanting to hit him. He sat up with a jolt as the sun peeked over the mesa, resting its heat on his eyelids. He yanked on Daniel's wrist. "Get up, choir boy."

Daniel stirred, and then the sun caught his eyes as well. He winced, wiping the sleep away. "Choir boy?"

"Okay, how about holy man?"

"Whatever. What's your problem?"

"I'm sleeping tied to you, I can't have my beer, and the ground is hard!"

Daniel just shook his head. "So call the front desk." He yanked on Hawk's wrist as he began to gather his bedroll.

"So what's today looking like, o great one?"

"Shut up, Hawk. We'll walk till we find the first sign."

"Yeah, great."

Daniel and Hawk walked three hours, feeling hunger and thirst setting in with a vengeance. Daniel prayed, scanning the path they were on for anything that would bring him hope.

It wasn't long before they happened upon the first sign. Literally. There in their path was a wooden stake with a piece of paper tied around it.

"You're kidding!" Hawk said.

"What? It's our first sign." Daniel smirked. His sicheii certainly had a sense of humor.

"You're in cahoots with Lukas, aren't you?" Hawk accused.

"Do you honestly think I'd want to be tied to you for three days?" Daniel shot back and then added, "Do you really think I'd want to deal with nature tied to another guy?"

"No. I guess not," Hawk said. "Since you put it that way. So what does it say?" he asked as Daniel opened the paper.

"I don't know. I can't read Navajo."

"What? What are you talking about? You speak it, but you can't read it?"

"Something like that," Daniel said, looking out onto the horizon and squinting, wishing he had his sunglasses as the first rays of the dawn began their intense dance across the mesas.

"Well, shi…oot," Hawk corrected quickly.

Daniel didn't look at Hawk but smirked at his attempt to change. "I need to pray," Daniel said and then looked at Hawk. "We both do."

"Can we at least find some shade?" Hawk complained. "You know, because if your brain fries, I'll never find out what the note says."

"Would you care?" Daniel asked.

"Maybe!" Hawk snapped.

Daniel considered him for a minute, remembering not to give up on him. "Come on," Daniel said, yanking on Hawk's wrist and heading for a large distant rock outcropping that afforded plenty of shade.

Daniel and Hawk sat down, and Daniel pulled the smudge from inside his bedroll to light it. Hawk was more cooperative, which made creating a flame somewhat easier. Daniel waved the smudge around and in front of him and then set it on a small flat stone in front of both of them. He attempted to wave the smoke toward him, but Hawk had reclaimed his hand.

"Do you mind?" Daniel asked in exasperation.

Hawk responded by rolling his eyes and letting his bound wrist relax.

"So why do you use these wicked ways if you're a Christian?" Hawk asked with sarcasm.

"It isn't wicked if you understand how to honor God with it," Daniel answered. "The smoke and sweet aroma represents the presence of the Great Creator. I'm surrounding myself in his presence. In the Old Testament, God's presence was represented in a cloud of smoke and a pillar of fire. Back then, it was dangerous to be in his presence. A man could die if he wasn't clean and pure before him. Back then, only the high priest could enter his presence," Daniel explained. "Now, we can all be in his presence if we want to," Daniel finished.

"At the school they said Jesus died on a cross," Hawk said.

"Yes. He's our Great Chief. He paid for our way because of his love for us. That's how we are able to come into his presence and fellowship with him whenever we want, without fear."

"They left that part out," Hawk mumbled.

Daniel looked at him with a smile of understanding.

"Is that why you don't believe in him?"

"You could say that. The Savior they preached was not the Savior they showed to us."

"But Lukas was able to get past the hypocrisy and find the truth. He's the example we need to follow. We can't let ignorant men destroy our belief in God. We have to look to the Great Creator and trust him only. Men are dust and full of deceit," Daniel reminded Hawk.

Hawk followed Daniel's movements, inhaling the sweet smell of the sage. Daniel closed his eyes and prayed to the Great Creator as Hawk observed and then closed his eyes and offered his own prayer. After a few moments, Daniel opened his eyes and took a deep breath.

"Now, I can read the note," he said.

"How do you know?"

Daniel shrugged, unfolding the letter again. Hawk looked at him as Daniel began to read. "We call liberty allowing the other man to please himself to the same extent that we please ourselves."

Hawk groaned. "It sounds awfully deep. Too deep for you to have made it up on the spot."

Daniel raised an eyebrow at him.

"I'm listening, okay?" he insisted. "Just read."

"True liberty is the ability, earned by practice, to do the right thing."

Another groan from the Hawk camp.

"There's no such thing as a gift of freedom. Freedom must be earned. The counterfeit of freedom is independence. When the Spirit of God deals with sin, it is independence that he touches. That is why the gospel awakens resentment as well as craving. Independence must be blasted right out of the one who follows the Great Chief, Jesus. There must be only liberty, which is a very different thing. Spiritually, liberty means the ability to fulfill the Law of God, and it establishes the rights of other people."

There was more written that Daniel read to himself. *"Grandson, a great father of our faith, Oswald Chambers said that, not me. But don't tell Hawkeye."* Daniel chuckled to himself.

"What's so funny?" Hawk asked, trying to absorb what he'd just heard.

"Nothing," Daniel said, getting up.

Hawk snatched the note from him, and he stared at the Navajo letters, but he couldn't read any of it. Daniel looked at him, noticing he had the shakes from being deprived of his alcohol. This wasn't going to be easy for either of them. Daniel sat back down since Hawk wasn't budging from his position.

"So what now?" Hawk asked. Daniel handed him a canteen.

"Drink some water."

"I need a beer."

"You need water," Daniel corrected. "Let it cleanse you."

"Yeah, okay." Hawk took a long drink, letting the water drizzle out the sides of his mouth and down the front of him. "Now what?"

"Sicheii told us to apply what we got from the signs over the next three days," Daniel looked at the ground. "I think forgiveness is the whole point of this journey."

"I guess I'm supposed to do some soul searching?" Hawk asked.

Daniel shrugged.

"Tell me why you left us," Hawk said.

Daniel didn't look at Hawk but rather stared at the leather binding their wrists together. "Because they told me to," he answered quietly.

"There's more, isn't there?" Hawk pressed.

"Not really."

"You're lying."

Daniel slowly looked at Hawk and then looked away.

"Hey. You're the one who's all spiritual. What are you afraid of?"

"Nothing. Let's get moving." Daniel stood up, pulling Hawk with him. "We can talk as we go."

"That's funny 'cause it doesn't sound like you're doing any talking. I think forgiveness is your issue."

Daniel picked up his bedroll and slung it over his shoulder, remaining silent.

Hawk jerked his arm, forcing Daniel to look at him. "Who's the serious one here? I want the truth!" he shouted.

Daniel said nothing.

"You said we'd talk when I was sober! Well, I am! So start talking!" Hawk grabbed Daniel's medallion and pulled him closer.

Daniel glared at Hawk.

"Talk!"

Without a word, Daniel slammed Hawk across the face. Hawk staggered back, dragging Daniel with him. An awkward brawl ensued. Daniel, being right handed, had the advantage. He pushed off Hawk and slammed him again in the face. Hawk brought his right leg up between Daniel's legs and threw him over his head. Daniel landed hard, stunned. Hawk crawled over to him and punched Daniel in the stomach. Daniel yanked on Hawk's arm and tripped him as the momentum of the forward motion threw Hawk off balance. Again Hawk was in the dirt. The two rolled several feet attempting to gain a hold of each other. Hawk managed to bloody Daniel's nose and Daniel returned the favor.

Daniel's rage came because the Great Creator revealed the anger and bitterness inside of him. Daniel threw a final punch at his dazed brother as he pinned Hawk to the ground. Daniel then pushed himself off Hawk and collapsed next to him. Despite the fact that he still wasn't healed from Hawk's previous beating, he'd won this round.

But as he sucked in air trying to compose himself, he didn't feel like a winner.

Angel drove to Daniel's home to spend the day with Jessica. She was eager to get to know the young woman and perhaps learn more about Daniel. Jessica ushered her into her home and showed her around. "It's not quite the same as our adobe in Stake Town, but it is nice for a manufactured home," Jessica said. "I've got fruit salad. I thought it would be something cool to eat."

"Sounds refreshing." Angel smiled, following Jessica into the kitchen. "Can I help?"

"It's all made. But you can grab a couple of bowls in that cabinet." Jessica pointed. She pulled a larger bowl from the refrigerator.

"And the utensils?"

"Second drawer, left of the sink." Jessica grabbed two glasses and then took them to the large open room that made up their living and dining areas.

As the two sat down, Angel noticed Jessica's laptop opened on a desk across the room. "Do you like the internet?"

"Oh, I love it. I love being able to go all over the world and learn and research," Jessica said as she dished a bowl for Angel.

"What are you researching?" Angel filled their glasses with water and then took her bowl.

"It's for dad this time. He asked me to find information on a Senate Joint Resolution that's currently in the House. It's called SJR 14."

"Wow, I would have never figured your dad as the political type."

"He's not really." Jessica offered her hand, and they blessed their food. After the blessing, she looked up. "He found a leather pouch he used to wear as a kid. He was going through some old photos when we were packing, and it was in the box. He said the Great Creator had given him a burden regarding a little scroll inside the pouch."

"So what have you found out about...SJR 14, was it?" Angel was intrigued.

Jessica nodded. "It's called the Apology to the Native Americans."

"Oh, yes, I've heard about that. Didn't Senator Sam Brownback draft that?"

"It's amazing, Angel!" Jessica picked up her bowl and glass and strode to the computer. Angel followed, sensing an excitement in the air.

Jessica sat at her computer as Angel pulled up a chair next to her. Angel put her bowl down and pulled out her glasses. She leaned in, looking at the screen.

"Listen to what I found. Senator Sam Brownback from Kansas introduced then Resolution 15 to the senate in 2005 and has been trying to get it voted on ever since. It seems the government is afraid to put it into play," she summarized from what she'd just read. "Now it's SJR 14. Listen to this," and she continued to read from the website, Native American Resource Network.

"This is a report from Jean Steffenson who runs the site. There's a scripture here. 'If they confess their iniquity and the iniquity of their Fathers with their unfaithfulness in which they were unfaithful to me and that they have also walked contrary to me…then I will remember my covenant…I will remember the land,'" she read. "From Leviticus 40:40, 42. Jean Steffenson then says: 'For over eleven generations, the Native Americans have suffered much injustice by the actions of the US Government: Congress, office of the president, and the courts. This is the generation to break that cycle.'"

At that point, Angel thought of Daniel and the burden Jessica had mentioned.

Jessica continued. "'In the past, few Christian have sought reconciliation, healing, and justice for the Native people. We need to take a stand now with the senators and representatives who are willing to acknowledge these injustices. Your continued prayer is needed. Action is needed.'"

"This is your dad's burden." She said it more as a statement than a question.

Jessica looked at her for a moment and then responded, "Yes."

Angel and Jessica breezed over some of the information before leaving for their planned outing into New Mexico. "How do you think your dad will respond to all of this?"

Jessica closed her computer. "I'm not sure. He's really been quiet about the subject. That usually means it's bothering him. I guess we'll find out when he reads about it."

As Daniel lay in the dirt, he put his right arm over his eyes in an attempt to stop the onslaught of emotions that was bringing him to tears. "God! Forgive me. Forgive me," he cried repeatedly.

Hawk opened his eyes but didn't move, listening to Daniel's sobs and cries for mercy. Daniel finally calmed, and both men stared up at the painted clouds for a long time. Eventually, Daniel sat up and put his right arm around his knees. Carefully, he searched his memories. He jerked and winced as he saw the headmaster, a priest, slap him across the face when he was seven. He jerked again as he recalled the razor belt that he was lashed with. Finally, he remembered sitting in the back seat of his dad's Buick, being driven away from the boarding school as he cried quietly.

He never told his mom or dad what the school had done. He told them he'd gotten into a fight to cover for his bloody nose and welted back. Daniel knew Ben had seen it all, though, and had stepped from around the building of the headmaster and given him a sad wave. Sarah and Hawk had not been witness to any of it.

His memories flowed to Sarah—her smile, her laugh, the day they married. That day and the day Jessica was born were two of the happiest days of his life. He smiled but it soon faded as he then saw himself rushing, sliding down a steep embankment to try to free his wife and a little girl from a burning car. Once again, he'd failed Sarah and Hawk; only this time he'd failed his daughter as well. He finally noticed that Hawk was sitting up next to him.

"I'm sorry," Daniel whispered.

Hawk wiped blood from his nose. "I'm tough. I can take it." He shrugged.

"No. I mean about Sarah."

"What?"

"Sarah. I couldn't get to her," Daniel clarified and then continued. "They murdered her."

"What do you mean?" Hawk gave him a hard look.

Daniel stared out at the brightening plains and finally spoke. "I was supposed to meet Sarah and Jessica for lunch, but the sheriff called me away to a meeting. They went back to the youth center to wait, but then Sarah had to drive one of the kids home. She was run off the road by Tom McKinley."

Hawk looked at Daniel. "How do you know?"

"I found two sets of skid marks on the highway, and Tom immediately had his cruiser repainted. Bill McKinley said it was an accident of Sarah's own making. I snooped in his office after hours one night and found the report he'd written, along with the coroner's report. They said she'd been driving drunk. The meeting was just to keep me away." He dropped his head, feeling defeated.

"Why would they want to kill her?"

Daniel raised an eyebrow at the question. "Everybody knew Bill and Tom McKinley were Aryans, and killing me after just arriving would have been a little too obvious. I'd found out that they had dealings with a white supremacist group and were preparing to put a small army together," he explained.

"I remember those brothers. They constantly harassed the Navajo kids at the high school until we put a stop to it. So why not just kill you? They didn't have to kill her."

"They discovered that I'd found out about their activities, and her death was a warning to me to keep quiet. They may have intended for Jessica to be next." Daniel finally noticed his own nose was bleeding and wiped it with the back of his hand.

"Tell me about that day at AZ Prep," Hawk said, more gently this time.

Daniel kept his head down. He knew that it was the Great Creator prying his heart open and that it was time to tell someone. He sighed deeply before he began. "They'd called my dad when they found out that he was a white man. So they called me in and told me I was going back home. I begged them to let me stay. Told 'em I was full Navajo. When they said no, I tried to run and hide. They stopped me, and I fought back."

"What happened?"

"They beat the crud out of me." He shrugged.

"Ben told me. I couldn't believe it. I never knew, and it's still hard to believe they'd do that to a kid. I mean, they gave us beatings for speakin' the language, but because you wanted to stay?"

Daniel realized how painful the searching light of the Great Creator was and now understood Hawk's tendency to run. If he himself was surprised at what had been revealed inside of his own heart, he could only imagine what Hawk was afraid to find.

CHAPTER 14

As the day grew hotter, they continued to follow the path laid out that was to bring them around a large lake and back to the lodge.

"Why were you asking for forgiveness?" Hawk asked Daniel as they walked.

"A lot of reasons."

"Give me a few."

"Because of the anger I found inside of me that I didn't know was there. I've been bitter and holding a grudge against the boarding school for not letting me stay. For telling me I wasn't Indian enough," he continued, raking his hand through his hair, "for them keeping me from my friends, for not suffering what you guys did, and for not protecting Sarah," he finished.

They kept walking. Daniel's ribs were hurting, which wasn't helping his mood, and he really wanted to get home and soak in the mud. The fact that he had to stay out on the desert for three days, deprived of any pain relief, only added fuel to his anger.

Daniel and Hawk had found few places to rest that day. They both knew that once they stopped, they wouldn't want to go on. So they trudged on at a steady but cautious pace in order to make it to a safe place for the evening. The shade of a rock outcropping was a welcomed relief from the relentless sun that had tanned their skin all day.

Later, they continued east as directed by Lukas; they eventually came upon another stake and note next to a promised body of water. The heat of the day lingered, causing the leather binding on their wrists to chaff and hurt. The fact that they were covered in dirt added to the chaffing, but they knew they couldn't get the leather wet again or it would shrink and cause them serious damage. The sun was preparing to set, so they filled their canteens and washed the blood from their faces and then made camp nearby.

"I suppose this note's in Navajo, too?" Hawk said.

Daniel nodded with a smirk.

"You gonna pray again so you can read it?"

"Naw. It all came back to me with the first one. But—" he smiled in amusement—"I know we're going to need to pray after it."

"Let's have it," Hawk surrendered.

Daniel opened the note and read it silently for a moment, anticipating another footnote from Lukas. He began to read. "It is an incredible moment in a man's life when he knows he is explored by God."

"We'll see," Hawk mumbled.

Daniel ignored the comment and continued. "The thing in us that makes us look inside ourselves and know the springs of our thoughts and motives takes the form of the prayer, 'search me, O God.' The psalmist speaks of God as the Creator who knows the vast universe outside and of his omnipresence, but he does not end there."

"Here it comes," Hawk whined quietly.

"Will you shut up and listen? Just for once!" Daniel said in exasperation.

Hawk looked at him, wide eyed. "Okay." His answer was quiet and submissive.

Daniel stared at him to make sure he'd stay quiet, and when he was satisfied he would, he went on with the note. "He asks the Great Creator to explore him. There is something much more mysterious to him than the great universe outside, and that is the mystery of his own heart. There are mountain peaks in my soul, he implies, that I cannot climb. There are ocean depths that I cannot fathom. There are possibilities in my heart that terrify me. Therefore, O Great One, search me out."

Daniel stopped. That was exactly what he'd made a habit of asking God, and it was exactly what God had given him. "Be careful, Hawk."

Sarcasm dripping from his lips, he answered, "Well, that sounds encouraging. Okay, why?"

"Because God is in the habit of answering prayers, and it's never the way we expect them to be answered."

"Thanks for the warning."

They shared a chuckle and then fell quiet, each man reflecting in his own heart.

"That's why you were crying for mercy," Hawk said quietly in revelation. "Because he showed you your heart."

Daniel nodded in affirmation.

"That must really hurt."

"More than you know," he answered, and then he looked him in the eye. "You still in?"

"Yeah, I'm in. Pain makes the warrior, eh, bro?"

"*Hokahay*," Daniel said half-heartedly.

They watched the sun set behind the mesas in a short silence, and it was Hawk's turn to bear his soul.

Daniel broke the silence. "So why do you hate me and yourself?"

"Did," Hawk corrected.

Daniel looked at him with a raised eyebrow.

"Ben told me about the school…yesterday," Hawk confessed.

Daniel chewed his bottom lip.

"I hated that school, and I thought you were glad to get out of it and just left us."

"I tried to write," Daniel mumbled.

"He told me that, too. He was there, you know. He saw them beat you and send you away."

Daniel nodded. "Why didn't you want me to marry Sarah?"

"By then, I hated you because of school, and I hated those whites and anyone else white." He looked at Daniel. "And since you were part white, it only fueled the hatred. I didn't trust you with her anymore. I figured that if you left her before, you'd do it again. I only helped you and Ben out in high school to protect Sarah." Hawk tossed a twig on the fire that was now illuminating the two men. "I was wrong."

"It happens to the best of us," Daniel said. "You still didn't answer why you hate yourself."

Hawk was silent as he stared at the fire, the occasional spark spitting upward to the sky, reaching for its place in the stars. He felt like that burning wood—being consumed by a fire he didn't and couldn't control.

"I hate drunks, man. When Sarah died, I became what I hate. I thought it would numb the pain."

"It didn't," Daniel said.

"No, it didn't. It caused more," he admitted. "But it seems the truth was made to cause more pain as well."

"It's a momentary pain that hopefully changes us for the better, if we let it," Daniel assured. "And then, it's like real freedom." He smiled.

Hawk was quiet for a moment. He realized that he too was, in fact, a half-breed and that part of his pain was from hiding it. It was again like a fire burning up his insides. "I guess I need to get this out."

Daniel looked at him, waiting.

"I've hated the fact that I'm not full Navajo."

"But you're not white either."

"True. But I'm not full Navajo, and that's been eating at me. I guess I haven't felt complete or that I fit in."

Daniel nodded but said nothing.

"You must feel like that."

Daniel shrugged, his silence very telling to Hawk. He rubbed his tethered wrist.

"I haven't helped matters, calling you half-breed, when I'm one, too. It's the pot calling the kettle black. Here I call Christians hypocrites, and I'm one myself."

Again, Daniel remained silent. Hawk could sense his brother's discomfort and wanted to fix it. "I'm sorry." When Daniel only nodded, he said it again. "I'm sorry." Hawk asked another question of Daniel to get off the subject. "Do you think the hate is gone from inside of you?"

"God, I hope so. But there's something else inside."

"What?"

"I don't know," Daniel said quietly. He grabbed his bedroll and laid it out. "Let's call it a day. Maybe you'll have a dream."

Hawk said nothing but set his bedroll out and lay down. He had become used to the chafing of the leather on his wrist, considering it his just reward for all the pain he'd caused Daniel.

The two men stared up at the stars.

"We go home tomorrow, eh?" Hawk asked, already knowing the answer, but for some reason he felt he needed the assurance.

"Yeah," was Daniel's answer.

"Hey, Red Tears."

"What?" he answered, almost asleep.

"I was pretty harsh, you know, about Sarah and Jessica," Hawk said.

"Mmhmm," he agreed.

"I'm sorry. Do you forgive me?"

"Only if you'll shut up and go to sleep."

Hawk grinned and closed his eyes.

Early the next morning, the two men were up before the sun. Daniel was especially quiet. He'd had the dream about Hawk again and had a sense of dread concerning it. They headed out for the last "sign" of their journey, and then they planned to return to the sweat lodge. As the sun crested the horizon, they found another stake, and Daniel pulled it from the ground and removed the attached note.

Daniel read it. "Which wolf have you been feeding?"

The two brothers looked at each other for a moment, knowing they had learned their lessons.

Daniel continued to read. "Which one will you now feed? Cut your bonds and ride on true freedom." Daniel knew there was a message there but frowned because he wasn't sure if Lukas was being symbolical or literal.

Daniel reached behind him and drew his knife. "Ready?"

Hawk grinned.

Daniel carefully slipped the glinting blade between their wrists and cut the leather. They silently watched the leather fall to the ground, both relieved to be free.

Hawk offered his hand to Daniel. "Peace, brother."

Daniel looked at Hawk for a moment. A slow smile appeared on his lips. Moisture glinted from his eyes. Daniel gripped Hawk's forearm in an Indian handshake. "Peace." The gesture became a willing hug with pats on the back. They were now truly brothers.

Ben sat in his office, having spent the entire day going over facts and evidence or the lack thereof regarding the missing clansman,

Simon. He couldn't figure out why no one had seen anything. He'd combed the entire reservation before Daniel had arrived, took Daniel to interview his wife, and still he came up empty. Normally, he could solve a missing person's case, but this one had him stumped. The man had vanished into thin air.

"Hey, Boss, we asked everyone again about Simon, but they all either didn't know or they told us what they said before." Joe put the SUV keys on his desk as he sat down and removed his cowboy hat.

Ben sat back from his desk with a heavy sigh. "Okay, Joe, thanks. Maybe a fresh pair of eyes will help. I'm almost sorry I introduced Daniel to Angel now. He's coming home soon, and then he's got a hot date with her."

"Maybe it's for the good, innit? I mean, maybe he needs a good woman to help him focus."

"She'll help the investigation, eh?" Pete added.

Ben chuckled at his men.

Daniel and Hawk filled their canteens and then walked for about an hour until they came upon two mustangs grazing a short distance from them.

The men froze as the two horses' heads shot up and snorted an alert. The mustangs stared at them but then slowly moved toward them.

"Don't move," Daniel whispered.

"Why?"

"You'll scare 'em. Do you want to walk home?"

"What? We're riding these home? How is that supposed to happen?"

"Have you been so far from your roots that you even lost sight of the miracles that happen every day?"

"What are you talking about?" Hawk shifted, and one of the horses snorted. He froze again. "How do you know about horses?"

"I'm an Indian. It's in my blood." He paused and then added, "And I may have learned a thing or two from my friend Pat Parelli" The Great Creator is giving us a gift. These horses should be running in the opposite direction, but they're not."

"That's the miracle?"

"I'd say it is."

"How come I never saw stuff like this before?" Hawk started to squirm.

"Quit moving," Daniel reminded him. "You never wanted it before. Maybe this journey has opened your eyes to the Creator's ways."

Hawk gave a nearly imperceptible nod.

One of the mustangs, a dapple gray, tentatively stepped up to Daniel and reached his nose out toward him. Daniel slowly turned sideways, reaching the back of his hand out to let the animal greet him. It took several minutes, but the mustang finally touched his hand. Hawk had broken out into a sweat having to stand there frozen.

"Can I move now?" Hawk whispered.

"No," Daniel whispered back.

"I gotta go," he insisted.

"Hold it."

"I'll pee my pants."

Daniel relented. "Okay. Turn away slowly."

Hawk gave a slight nod and did as he was told. While Hawk was retreating, Daniel slowly began stroking the mustang's nose. The other mustang, a sorrel, became curious and joined her buddy in front of Daniel.

Hawk disappeared behind a large boulder as Daniel made steady progress stroking the horse's neck. He knew this was the Great Creator at work because no wild horse in its right mind would have ever approached a predator.

After several minutes, Hawk peeked out from behind his sanctuary and saw an amazing sight. Daniel was sitting atop the dapple gray mustang. He took a step out from behind the boulder and stood wide eyed. He was afraid to speak but finally got the nerve to and slowly approached his brother

"May I have a ride too, O great master?"

"Not funny." Daniel scowled.

"How'd you do that?"

"I didn't do anything. Remember the gift?" Daniel told him.

Hawk shrugged. "I guess I need to thank him?" He moved a little too quickly toward the sorrel mustang, causing her to snort in alarm and run away. "Hey!" Hawk protested as Daniel smothered a chuckle. He quickly cleared his throat when Hawk shot him a look and put on a serious face as if trying to help him figure out the situation.

"Maybe you should move slower."

The mustang stopped fifty yards away, looking alert at the approaching, smelly predator. Hawk reached out his hand to her as he'd seen Daniel do, but she didn't reach for him. Rather, she backed away. Daniel and his mount both watched the scene unfold before them with growing interest.

"Hey, maybe you need a bath," Daniel suggested deadpan.

"And you don't?"

"Who's on the horse?"

Hawk sighed deeply. "All right. What do I do?"

"Move slowly. Approach sideways and look friendly," Daniel instructed. "Then offer the back of your hand and let her touch you. Don't reach for her until she sighs. Then you can gently rub her nose, face, and neck." Daniel sighed when his horse sighed, mirroring his moves, indicating his partnership with the animal.

"Then what?"

"Let's get through that first."

"This is going to take forever," Hawk bemoaned.

"Walking will take longer." Daniel smiled.

Tom McKinley strode over to a stall inside an old barn and wracked the bars with a broom handle. "Hey, red skin, here's your supper. Your brothers'll be here soon to keep you company and then go gold diggin' for us. Sound like a plan?"

Simon took his bread and water and shrugged.

"Yeah, I figured." Tom snorted. "You were the only one who took our bait, so we'll have to change our strategy. How about a Help Wanted sign?" Tom chuckled, not needing an answer.

Jeff walked in to put some pad locks on the other stall door in preparation for their captives.

As Hawk conceded to Daniel's directions and started the process, Daniel had unconsciously taken hold of his leather pouch, gripping it firmly with his right hand as it dangled from his neck. Once he realized his action, he felt the contents through the leather, remembering and picturing each piece inside. As he focused on the symbols and what they meant, Hawk was calling to him, but he didn't notice at first. That was until Hawk used his Indian name.

"Red Tears!" he said as loudly as he dared.

Daniel finally snapped out of his trance and looked at Hawk who was now gently but proudly rubbing his horse's back.

"Now what?"

"Are you going to walk her home or ride her home?"

Hawk blinked at Daniel. "What if she throws me?"

"I thought you could handle it." Daniel enjoyed teasing Hawk. They were the old friends they started out being so many years ago.

"I can handle it!"

"Then shut up and get on!" Daniel said in exasperation. Daniel and his horse started moving off as Hawk looked at the mare. "You sound like a cry baby," Daniel mumbled.

"I heard that!"

"Good!" Daniel replied. He chuckled under his breath.

Hawk leaned slightly toward the mare's face, addressing her. "Make me look good, okay?" She turned her head toward the strange man about to get on her back. Once Hawk got atop her, she remained where she stood, unmoving. She sighed once as if she were bored.

"Sighing," Hawk said quietly to himself, remembering seeing Daniel and his horse do it earlier. "Sighing is good, right?" he asked the horse.

The mare cocked her right rear leg and got comfortable. Hawk didn't want her to get frightened again, so he relaxed with her. After a few moments, Daniel circled back around with his horse and saw Hawk sitting on his horse but getting nowhere.

"Who are you posing for, bro?"

Hawk only scowled at him.

"You coming?"

"How do I make her move?"

"You don't *make* her do anything," Daniel replied. "She's allowing you to ride her, so just ask."

"Okay. How?"

"Just bring life into your body, but whatever you do don't—"

It was too late. Hawk brought too much life up, and when she moved, he got nervous and squeezed her rib cage.

"Squeeze," Daniel finished.

Hawk's horse bolted, leaving him on the ground in the dust. Daniel couldn't hide his laughter as Hawk got up and wiped himself off. The sorrel returned to Hawk with a nervous snuffle.

"No squeezing," Hawk verified.

"Right."

"I suppose the Great Creator is teaching me a lesson in all of this?"

"At least *she* is." Daniel gave a nod toward the mare.

Hawk looked at his horse, carefully got back on, and asked her to move without squeezing her. She complied, and the two men were on their way again.

A few hours later, Daniel and Hawk found the last sign. Daniel read it.

"This ride home will be silent. That means no talking, Hawk." Daniel tried to hide his grin.

"That's not in there," Hawk protested.

"It is!" Daniel held the note up for him, pointing to the line he'd just read as if Hawk could read what was there. Then he put his index finger to his lips and looked coolly at Hawk. "Shh!" He then continued reading. "As you return in silence, you will learn to hear the Great Creator. He will speak to your hearts. Do not forget what he says, and do not run from it." Daniel folded the note and put it into his jeans pocket. Daniel and Hawk looked at each other and began their silent journey home.

As they rode, Daniel focused on the tiny scroll inside his leather pouch. Again, he unconsciously gripped it, but this time he opened the bag and pulled out the tiny parchment. He unrolled it and stared at the red words printed there: *RES.*

"Resolution", a voice said. Daniel looked up, thinking Hawk had said something, but he was several paces away and too focused on not falling off his ride to say anything.

"You will be a bridge for the white brothers and your brothers to come together in peace."

The horses delivered the two men back at the sweat lodge in the late afternoon where Lukas White Wolf was waiting for them with a grin. Hawk had gone over the previous three days during his silent time and was surprised and yet excited to discover that he now had an anticipation and hunger inside of him to relearn his native language and some of the Navajo traditions.

He carefully dismounted and strode up to Lukas but stopped short, uncertain if the vocal fast had ended yet. Daniel got off his horse, giving the animal a smile and a rub on the neck and then watched the two mustangs take off into the desert. Hawk looked at Daniel for an answer, but he only smiled in amusement. Lukas squeezed Hawk's shoulders and spoke in Navajo. Hawk turned to Daniel again.

"He said welcome back, Watchman, and you can talk now," Daniel told him.

Hawk turned back to Lukas. "I want to learn our traditions. How old is this journey tradition?"

Lukas answered, humor in his voice with a pat on his bare back and then walked toward the lodge.

"Long enough for you to need a shower," Daniel translated.

"You mean for *us*," Hawk corrected and then stopped a minute. "Wait, long enough?"

"Three days, bro." Daniel chuckled. "The Navajo don't have a journey tradition or vision quest. He made this up, just for us."

Lukas turned from the lodge and waved for them to follow.

They spent an hour in the lodge before Lukas spoke again with Daniel translating.

Daniel's thoughts were on Jessica and Angel.

A voice in his heart spoke to him. *You will marry Angel.*

"You will marry the Meda," Lukas said aloud. Daniel looked at him but said nothing.

"Whew-hew! We're gonna have a wedding!" Hawk slapped his hands together, eager for a celebration.

"I haven't even asked her yet. Relax," Daniel said.

Lukas chuckled and then changed the subject. "You are brothers now. You have fed the good wolf, and with it, you will fight the bad wolf. But beware. He bleeds red just as you do."

CHAPTER 15

Hawk would normally have gone to the store and bought a couple of six packs of beer, but he no longer needed it. He would now depend on Ben and Lukas to occupy his time by teaching him the language and traditions of his people. He was eager to put to use what he had learned and to live in his newfound freedom, the freedom he gained from forgiving his brother, Red Tears.

Daniel was anxious to go on his date with Angel, knowing this too was a continuation of the journey. Daniel pulled the truck into Ben's driveway and watched Hawk honor Lukas by walking with him to his door.

Jessica ran outside to greet her dad. "Dad!" she said excitedly. About to hug him, she stopped short when she got a whiff of him. "Welcome home. You can have a hug when you smell a little better."

"Yes, dear, it's good to be home." Daniel smiled at her repugnance. He headed into their home, eager for a shower. Once the water began to massage his sore body, he realized the true blessing of the element and its partner, soap. Daniel took a long shower, and when he finally emerged, he found a bottle of men's cologne on the dresser with a note:

> *Dad, I already know she's hooked on you, but this will help keep her. Besides, I'm sure you'll need this after three days in the desert.*
>
> *Love, Jessica.*

He chuckled out loud and shook his head. He opened the bottle and sniffed. It smelled pretty good. He slapped some on and then finished dressing, remembering not to include a tie. He checked himself in the mirror. He felt like a nervous schoolboy. Jessica wouldn't be there this time, and it was all up to him. He went next door to

Ben's to officially greet his family. He'd missed Jessica and hugged her tightly.

"I missed you, kiddo," he said.

Jessica smiled. "You smell good, Dad. I missed you, too. I bet I know someone else who missed you." She winked at him.

"That must be my cue. I'm off to see an angel," he announced, heading for the door.

"Hey, don't forget you're supposed to be helping me investigate Simon's disappearance," Ben said.

"Ben, my friend. I am here to help, but it seems to me you were the one who pushed me through this door in the first place. Now I know it's in the Great Creator's hands. You gonna fight him, because I'm not?"

"Okay, okay. Marry the woman already and get your butt to my office." Ben grinned as he slapped Daniel's shoulder.

"Tomorrow, I promise."

Ben waved him off with a nod.

As Daniel drove to Angel's, he realized he was more nervous than he had been when he'd asked Sarah to marry him. After all, he'd grown up with Sarah, and he'd only just met Angel. This was a whole new ball game. God was moving things along at a rapid pace, and Daniel had been caught in the whirlwind. The dream he'd had of Angel and himself sitting on the rock with the children playing nearby came to his mind. He smiled for a moment, but concern edged his thoughts as he remembered how the rest of the dream had played out. He shook it off and concentrated on the task at hand: making conversation with a stranger he knew was to be his wife.

Jessica turned to her uncle Hawk with a huge grin on her face.

He looked at her, his suspicion obvious. "What?"

"I have to tell you something," she said. She was excited about the message she knew was from the Great Creator. She had told Lukas, and he'd agreed with her that Hawk could receive it when he returned from his journey.

"Okay, I'm listening."

"You might want to come outside with me for a minute," Jessica said, hinting at the private nature of the message. Hawk shrugged and followed her outside to the front yard. They sat down at a picnic table there.

Jessica hesitated for a moment, feeling her heart pounding in her chest. "Uncle Hawk, the Great Creator wants you to know that he is proud of you."

Hawk sat staring at her, dumbfounded.

"He sees you as his son and has a very special purpose for you. He asks that you open your heart all the way to him—" Jessica looked up from the table at him, and he was still staring wide eyed—"and he will speak to you. You're not a drunk. You were specially made by him," she said.

Jessica saw a warm breeze blow over her uncle, pushing his hair back. She got up to go into the house, not expecting a response; his look of amazement was enough for her.

"Hey, Niece," he called, his voice quiet.

Jessica stopped and turned. "Yes, Uncle?"

"Thanks."

Jessica walked back over to him and kissed him on the cheek. "You're welcome."

Angel Green looked in the mirror for the fifth time, adjusting a stray hair here or looking critically at her mineral makeup, trying to decide if she looked natural or made up. She realized that for the first time in her life, she was uncertain and nervous. She had reason to be. This was her first official date since she'd given her life over to the Great Creator to be only his. Daniel was a stranger and quickly becoming a friend, but he was the man she knew she was to marry.

There was a knock on her door, and she jumped and then giggled to herself. She felt like a teenager going to her first prom, although her white blouse and denim skirt were a far cry from the elegant gown she might have worn. And while she'd never experienced that milestone in a young woman's life, she had a feeling that this was what it felt like. There were butterflies in her stomach, and her skin tingled with anticipation. She hurried to the door, stopping only long enough to regain her composure. She opened the door, and a huge smile lit up her face at the handsome man on her doorstep.

"Hi," they said at the same time and then chuckled nervously.

"Come in," Angel invited, stepping aside.

Daniel walked inside, unable to take his eyes off her. "You look... incredible," he said.

"Thank you."

"Are you ready to go?"

"I am. I didn't know where we were going, so I hope I dressed appropriately." Daniel was wearing black jeans, boots, and a southwestern-print cowboy shirt, so she felt reasonably assured that what she was wearing was an acceptable outfit for the evening.

"You're perfect," he said, obviously enamored.

"You don't look bad yourself." She smiled as Daniel ushered her to his SUV.

When he opened the passenger side door for her, she had to ask, "Are you going to tell me where we're going?"

"We're going for some Italian about an hour off the rez, and then we're going to the rock."

"The rock?" Angel asked. "Is that a dance club or something?"

"You'll just have to wait and see." He smiled at her. He put his sunglasses on and started the engine.

"A man of mystery." She grinned. "Interesting."

Angel looked out the window, enjoying the scenery, always glad for the opportunity to be a passenger so she could take in the sights of the painted desert she so loved. It was only five, but already the sun played with the colors on the rocks.

At dinner, Daniel and Angel talked and laughed about the joyful parts of their lives, and on the way to the rock, which looked very much like returning to the rez, both were quiet and thoughtful.

Angel grew more curious as Daniel drove onto the rez and toward the setting sun. This was not the way to any social establishment she was familiar with. Finally, Daniel pulled up to a gently sloping and very tall rock. Angel looked at Daniel nervously, uncertain as to what he was planning. She'd only been alone with him one other time, but she could see he was more nervous than she was. She knew he was a man who feared God, so she forced herself to relax, sensing she could trust him.

He looked at her with a smile and then got out of the SUV. "The rock," he said, gesturing toward the large sandstone slope.

She looked at the rock and realized it was the same rock from a dream she'd had. Daniel was at her door before she knew it and had it open.

He had a blanket tucked under his arm. "Is something wrong?" he asked, noticing her hesitation. He removed his sunglasses for a moment.

"I...this rock was in a dream I had," she told him, stepping out but still staring at the formation.

Daniel waited for a moment until she gave him a smile of reassurance. He offered his hand, and he helped her up the slope. Once they reached the top, he released her hand, laid the blanket out, and then helped her sit down. He sat down next to her, but not too close, and smiled at her. He adjusted his collar several times and cleared his throat. He put his sunglasses back on.

"I thought we'd watch the sun set." He shrugged. He looked out over the valley the rock rose above. A small herd of horses grazed lazily below. Though the ground was rarely green, the light created shadows of varying shades to play tricks on the eyes of those taking it all in. "Tell me about the dream you had."

Angel studied him for a moment and then looked at the fading orange and pink light of the descending sun. "I was sitting here"—she hesitated for a moment—"with you..."

"There were some kids playing soccer behind us." He indicated, pointing to the right and back down behind the rock.

She followed where he pointed and then looked at him in disbelief. "Yes." She didn't need to tell him the rest of the story. She sensed he already knew it. "You and Hawk—"

He interrupted her thought. "Let's just hope it's only a warning and not what really happens," he suggested. He removed his sunglasses again and looked at her for a short moment and then turned his face into the light, squinting his eyes until they adjusted.

Angel held her gaze on him. "Tell me about you and Hawkeye," she said.

Daniel met her gaze. "Didn't he tell you anything?"

"Sure he did. But I mean now. How was the journey?"

"Interesting." He chuckled. "We found out what was inside of us. We came to an understanding, and now we are true brothers," he told her.

"All in three days?" she asked.

"How long have we known each other?"

"Five days." She smiled. "Why?"

Daniel shrugged again. "And what has the Great Creator told you about us?"

Angel looked into his eyes, knowing she shouldn't have been surprised, yet she was.

"What?"

They shared a dream, and now she knew God was telling them both the same thing.

"What has the Great Creator—"

"I heard you," she confirmed.

Daniel took her hand. His golden eagle circled above, and they both looked up into the sky.

She looked up. "He is yours," she said.

"And I am his." Daniel then looked at Angel as she continued to watch the eagle above. "You are mine," he said.

Angel met his gaze. "And I am yours."

Daniel squeezed her hand. "I'm doing this without a ring, but, will you be my wife?"

"Where do you squeeze the toothpaste tube?" she joked.

Daniel was right in stride and quickly replied. "From the bottom."

"Then yes." She chuckled, resting her forehead on his shoulder. "And don't worry about the ring. For now."

He put a gentle hand on her face, guiding her to look at him.

"Silly question," he said.

"Shoot."

"Can I kiss you?"

Her smile dropped, but not out of fear, more out of nervous anticipation.

"You need to know. I've never been kissed before," she confessed.

"Don't worry. I believe in saving the passion for marriage," he assured her, putting her mind at ease. She breathed a small sigh of relief and gave a nod. Daniel then leaned in and gave her a soft kiss on the lips. When he opened his eyes, hers were still closed, and a smile slowly spread across her lips. She then opened her eyes to see him smiling back at her.

"Maybe you should tell me a little bit about yourself," he suggested.

"Of course!" Angel chuckled, rocking back and then forward again. All at once, she became quiet. She took several moments going over her life in her mind. It had been a rough one.

Hawk was sitting out at the old hiding place where he, Daniel, Sarah, and Ben hung out as children. It wasn't really a hiding place; it was only a hundred yards off one of the rez roads. He was going over the journey he'd been on with Daniel. He knew he'd been changed, transformed, all because of a simple apology. He wondered what would happen if an American president ever made an apology to his people. He knew it would only be a good thing.

Just like he had, many Native Americans carried bitterness in their hearts over something that had happened before they were born. In reality, some injustices were still happening but on a smaller scale compared to hundreds of years ago. There was something inside of him telling him that Daniel was to have a hand in bringing about an apology. He was proud to be his brother. Hawk smiled and looked heavenward. "Thanks, Great Father."

"'Scuse me."

Hawk jumped and turned. "Whoa." He slid off the rock and walked up to the stranger before him.

The Caucasian man was wearing a white shirt and blue tie with suit pants, his fancy shoes covered in several layers of desert dust. "I'm Peter Stillers. I just bought the mine in Aztec."

"Bad investment, eh?"

"Not really. I never buy without prior knowledge of profit."

Hawk rolled his eyes, hating business talk.

"Anyway, I'd like to hire some people, and, well, I thought since you folk seem to need work—"

"Meaning what, exactly?" Hawk narrowed his eyes at the man.

"I'm sorry. I don't mean anything by what I said. I just want to help your people, and I thought if any one needed a job—men only, as it's dirty, hard work—I'd like to open it up to the Navajo men first. Aztec is mostly older folk who can't work and some who already have jobs."

Hawk nodded, considering him. "So how are you going about doing this?"

"Well, if you could just hang some flyers for me and put the word out, I can compensate you for it. All the info is on the flyers." Peter Stillers handed Hawk a stack of twenty flyers.

Hawk looked over them and gave another nod. "Yeah, okay."

Peter stuck out his hand with a bright smile. "Thanks for your assistance." He then pulled out a wad of cash and handed Hawk two hundred dollars.

"You're awfully generous."

"I believe in sharing my wealth." The man then turned on his heel and trekked back to his Lexus, still parked out on the road. Hawk watched him make a three-point turn and drive away. He kissed his cash and stuffed it in his pocket.

Angel sighed and delved into her life story. "I was raised in a Christian family until my parents died when I was ten."

Daniel took her hand and gave it a soft squeeze.

"I went to live with my aunt and uncle, who were not Christians, and I suffered abuse at the hands of my uncle." She looked away as the sun made its final descent behind the horizon. "He molested me." She hesitated, afraid to look at Daniel. She continued. "He beat me and verbally abused me." When she did look at Daniel, he was studying her as a tear slipped down his cheek. She was touched by his empathy.

"I'm so sorry," he whispered.

She smiled. "I forgave them a long time ago. It doesn't hurt anymore." She took a deep breath. "Shall I continue?"

"Please," he consented.

"When I was sixteen, I ran away and found the church I'd gone to when my parents were alive. They took me in and set me up with an incredible family. They helped me through a lot of painful healing, and I had to learn to trust again. To not be afraid of men."

"Is that why you never married?"

"I believe so. Later, I really believed that God had called me to be his only."

Daniel nodded thoughtfully. "But about a year ago, he started talking to me about the husband he had for me." She shrugged. "He didn't want me to be alone anymore. He wants me to experience all he has for me." She looked into Daniel's eyes. "And that includes you."

When she had finished her story, the stars had replaced the sun as the dominant light over the desert. Daniel looked up at the beauty. "Like the star without interference from city lights. It serves to remind us that he's in the details," he finally said.

Angel looked at him curiously, not sure to what he was referring— the stars or her last comment. "Will you tell me more about your late wife?"

"We better go," he said, standing up abruptly and offering his hand.

"I didn't say anything wrong, did I?" she asked with concern.

"You could never offend me. You're a gift to me," he assured her with a smile. He then picked up the blanket, folded it, and helped her down the slope of the rock to the SUV. "It's just that it's dark, and I don't want people talking. You know, 'give no evidence of evil.'"

Angel smiled at his chivalry. She felt blessed. "You are almost too good to be true." She chuckled.

CHAPTER 16

Jeff and Johnny sat in their café meeting place again. "All right, here's the deal. We lost our dealer, and only one guy took the tourney bait, so we put the word out that there's employment at the mine. They'll all just come to us. How easy is that?" Jeff said.

"What about Patterson?"

"That's where you come in. You send a message that you know he's around and you want to talk to him. Give him a warning, and we'll do the rest."

Bill McKinley had Simon at gunpoint, seated on a bench inside his stall. "I want you to call your wife and tell her you found a job. You don't tell her where, just tell her it's an away job and you'll be home in a few weeks."

"Yeah, right," Simon mumbled.

"Just do it, or you'll be dead sooner than later. Then who'll raise those kids of yours?"

Simon took the cell phone and dialed Roberta. With that accomplished, Bill took the cell phone and crushed it under foot. He left the stall with a resounding slam of the door.

Roberta called Ben as soon as she got off the phone with Simon. She didn't want Ben to have to worry anymore, and she herself was elated that Simon had called. Yet he hadn't been himself on the phone. "Hey, Captain."

"Hi, Roberta. How are you holding up?"

"Pretty good now. Simon just called."

"He did?"

"Yep. Said he got himself an out-of-town job and has been so busy and exhausted that he just forgot to call."

"A week?"

"I guess. But ya know. He did seem kinda funny, eh?"

"How so?" Ben sat forward at his desk.

"Well, he sounded high. He don't get high. He don't even drink."

"What did he say exactly?" Ben took out a pen and paper.

Roberta paced her living room. "He said he'd struck it rich and we'd be getting our couch after all, and he kept saying that his job was *way* far out."

"Way far out?"

"Yeah, he just kept saying that. He sounded like a hippy or something." Roberta sat down, and her youngest crawled up into her lap. She kissed the side of the child's head, hoping all was as well as it seemed.

"Roberta, what do you think?"

"I'm glad he's alive. The kids still have a dad, and we'll be able to pay our bills, eh. That's good news, innit?"

"Did he say where this job was?"

"Naw."

"Okay, well I'll see if I can't find out for you. Thanks for calling me, Roberta. No worries, eh?"

Roberta hung up and looked at her children. "Dad'll be home in a few weeks!"

"Yay!" the children all yelled.

Daniel pulled into his driveway an hour later, having left Angel safe at her hogan. Daniel knew he had to keep his promise to Ben, so he got out of his SUV and walked over to Ben's house. He let himself inside, knowing everyone would be up.

"Dad! When's the wedding?" Jessica eagerly questioned.

Daniel grinned, amused at her enthusiasm. "As soon as we can get it organized."

"Lukas has already called the clanswomen," Ben said. He stood from the couch and shook Daniel's arm.

"Ben, this is all happening so fast. I'm ready to help you with finding Simon." His eyes were apologetic as he returned Ben's greeting.

"Don't worry. Simon's been found. He got a job out of town."

"Where?"

"I'll let you help me with that. Roberta was a little suspicious of the call, too."

Daniel nodded, and he followed Ben into the kitchen. "So talk to me," Daniel said, ready to get into the investigation.

They both pulled up a chair at the kitchen table. Christiana set cups of coffee in front of the two men. "Thanks, Chris." Ben smiled.

Daniel noticed the living room grow dark.

Jessica entered the kitchen. "I'm going to bed. Everyone else is, too." She kissed her dad on the cheek and squeezed Ben's shoulder.

"Good night, Jess. I won't be long. I promise." He watched her leave before giving Ben his full attention.

"Okay, Roberta got a call from Simon, said he sounded different." Ben filled Daniel in on the call, and they agreed to do some research in office the next morning.

The next morning, Daniel and Ben were in the office with Joe and Pete looking at possible jobs in New Mexico. Everyone was at a computer. Daniel was preoccupied with thoughts about a wedding and an urgency in his heart regarding the resolution in the senate.

"I don't see anyone hiring within a hundred-mile radius," Joe said.

"Same here," Pete added.

Ben sat at his desk, tapping his pen on the notes Roberta had given him. "Well, maybe his far-out expression was meant to be literal."

Daniel looked over his monitor. "So we look farther out?"

Ben gave a quick nod.

A moment later, Hawk walked in waving a flyer. "Hey, who needs some extra income?"

Daniel looked at Ben then to Hawk and took the paper from him. He read it. "Maybe not far out, after all," he said, holding the flyer up. "Says here there's job openings at the mine in Aztec."

Ben got up from his chair and stepped over to Daniel's desk. "Where'd you get this?"

"I was out by our hidie-spot, and some business guy came up to me. Paid me two hundred dollars to pass these out. This is the last one."

"What was his name?" Daniel asked.

"Peter Stillers. Wow," Hawk said. "Without the juice I can remember stuff." He pretended to shine his nails on his chest.

Daniel looked at Joe, who started typing as soon as he heard the name.

"Peter Stillers. Just some wealthy business owner from Phoenix. Not much on him. Looks clean. No shady deals and all that."

"Did I do something wrong?" Hawk said.

"I doubt it. Don't worry, Hawk. We're just making sure Simon is safe. He called Roberta and said he got a job."

"Maybe he took this one. First one on the job?"

"That's what we're gonna check," Daniel said.

The phone rang, and Joe answered it. "Criminal Investigations." Joe looked at Daniel. "For you, Daniel."

Daniel picked up the line at his desk. "Hello?" All eyes were on Daniel as his face indicated an interesting call. He also remained silent, as it seemed the caller wanted to do all the talking. "Okay. I'll be there." He hung up the phone and looked at his friends. "That was Johnny Smith. He's the kid whose sister died in Sarah's car 'accident,'" he said, his fingers in quotations.

"It didn't sound like a social call," Ben said.

"He said he found out I was on the rez and wants to talk to me. I'm supposed to meet him at the pool hall in a couple of days."

"Well then. I guess we'll have to put a bug in you," Ben said.

"*In* me? You can't do a simple wire?"

"Wait. Why do you need a wire?" Hawk asked.

"Johnny was not happy that I didn't save his sister, and he blamed me. Since I believe the McKinleys were involved, it's a safe bet they put him up to this. Bill McKinley sent me up here in the first place to look for missing clansmen. *Plural.* So far, Simon was the only one, and now he has mysteriously reappeared."

"So McKinley may have something to do with all of this?" Hawk said.

"It's possible," Daniel said.

"Better safe than sorry. I don't want to lose another man." Ben walked over to his desk and pulled out a tiny box and a very large syringe and needle. He shook a tiny object from the container and held it up between his thumb and index finger.

"What's that?" Daniel asked, concern edging his voice.

Ben placed it in the palm of Daniel's hand. Daniel studied it.

"It's a tracking device, like GPS."

"You've been busy." Daniel grinned. "I don't have to swallow it, do I?"

"Nope. It'll go under your skin. Like they do with dogs," Ben explained.

"Great," Daniel said, losing his enthusiasm.

Ben took the chip from Daniel, put it in the syringe, and looked at Daniel with a grin. "Where do you want it?"

"Ouch!" Hawk shivered, garnering another look from Daniel. Hawk just shrugged.

Daniel thought about it. "I guess under my left tricep. It shouldn't be noticed there, right?" Daniel unbuttoned his shirt and pulled his left arm out.

Ben then walked behind him and inserted the needle, injecting the chip.

"Pretty high-tech stuff for the rez, Ben," Daniel observed with a slight wince. He felt the tiny lump in his arm and then replaced his arm in his shirt.

"I've got friends in the Bureau." Ben slapped his back.

"Yeah, well, I've got to get with my girls. I've got some research of my own to do on a senate resolution."

"You're a bridge," Hawk blurted. He reached into his pocket and pulled out a familiar-looking engagement ring and slapped it into Daniel's hand.

Daniel and Ben looked at him expecting an explanation. He shrugged and then walked out of the office.

"You come with me first. Let's look into this mine to see who owns it," Ben said.

"I do owe you that," Daniel agreed.

At the Aztec courthouse, Daniel and Ben received the land deed. "W. H. McKinley," Daniel said. "I should have known!" He thumped his fist on the counter, causing the clerk to look up from her work.

Ben's cell phone rang. "Go." Daniel looked at Ben when he turned to him. "Okay, that's all right, Joe. At least it was sooner than later." He closed his phone.

"Joe missed something."

"What?"

"Peter Stillers died in 2000."

Daniel let out a low whistle. "So this is all making sense now. The McKinleys used a good business name to cover for their game."

"What's the game?"

"Maybe nothing." Daniel was silent, considering if that were indeed possible of the McKinleys.

"You believe that?" Ben said as they headed for Ben's truck.

Daniel was silent.

With paperwork in hand, they returned to the reservation.

Daniel and Angel sat in the living room with Jessica at the computer. He wanted to surprise Angel with the ring Hawk had given him.

"What type of wedding would you like?" he asked her.

"I suppose I should have thought about it. You work fast." Angel smiled.

"Not me," Daniel said.

"I know I'd like Lukas to marry us," she started, "and I'd like it to be simple, nothing fancy."

"Do you want a cake?"

"Yes, but something simple."

"Not fancy, I know." Daniel chuckled. "Angel, if you're holding back, don't. I want you to be happy. This is your first and only wedding, and I want you to have your heart's desire."

Angel smiled obviously moved by the sentiment. She touched his face. "My heart's desire has already been granted, Red Tears."

He understood. Daniel excused himself for a minute, got up, and went to Jessica.

"Jessica, I need to ask you something," he said quietly.

"Sure, Dad." Daniel snuck a glance back at Angel. "How would you feel if Angel wore your mom's wedding dress?"

"Dad, wow!" she whispered with excitement. "That would be great! With me wearing it for my wedding, too. Dad, just think about that!"

Daniel did, and it dawned on him the significance of heritage that was taking place. He kissed her cheek and returned to the couch next to Angel.

"I have a surprise for you. Two, actually."

"I love surprises." She grinned.

He pulled an engagement ring from his pocket. "This was Sarah's mother's ring. Hawk gave it to me." He tried not to choke up at the special gift from the man who used to hate him.

"Oh, Daniel!" Her response indicated to Daniel that she was deeply touched.

Daniel took Angel's hand and slipped the ring onto her finger. "Will you marry me?"

"Making it official?" Angel smiled.

"Something like that." He smiled back at her. "Where do you squeeze the toothpaste tube?" she questioned again.

"Checking to see if I'm telling the truth?" He chuckled.

"Something like that." She laughed.

Jessica just rolled her eyes. "Just say yes already!"

Angel and Daniel laughed together.

"Yes!" Angel gave in.

Daniel wiped his brow in mock relief.

"Yeah!" Jessica cheered and then turned back to the computer.

Daniel kissed Angel on the cheek, and Angel pulled her feet up on the couch and snuggled next to Daniel. The next task would be discussing Tommy's intentions with his daughter. He was hoping for another wedding in the near future.

"Hey, Dad," Jessica called to him.

He and Angel gave their full attention to her from the couch.

She read the pages she'd read to Angel. "Okay, so now that you're up to speed on what I told Angel, let me give you the rest," Jessica said, clicking on a link.

The women looked to Daniel.

"What?" he asked after a long silence.

"You will speak to the fathers," Jessica told him.

Daniel and Angel stared at her.

"How?" he asked quietly.

"That would be God's problem," Angel reminded him. "Just let him show you."

Daniel knew she was right. He also knew the Great Creator would tell him when he was ready.

"There's also some great info from John Loren and Jim and Faith Chosa," Jessica cut in. "Here's what they said. This is John Loren," she informed.

"In 2 Samuel 21, a famine was recorded. It was discovered that the famine had occurred because King Saul broke the covenant made with the Gibeonites four hundred years earlier. In America, over eight hundred solemn covenants (treaties) were made with Indian people. Not one was kept! A tremendous curse hangs over America! Not as though Indian people have not been forgiving. Many have done so, many times. But sometimes apologies and resultant forgiveness must be done by the *right* people. Never have officials of our government taken up authority to apologize officially.

"It is my hope that many will see this apology in that light, as an act that can begin to lift the curse of the law of broken covenants off this land. To me, that is the significance of this apology. But, so far, in the many discussions I have heard about it, too few seem to grasp the real significance. I believe our native community needs to see this as an official act that can touch history with redemption! Many others have repented and prayed, but this is the first opportunity for those who can truly represent our nation officially to repent and begin the official process of lifting away the curse.

"For this reason, I believe we need to call for our people to pray that the resolution will be passed and acted upon by our president. I fervently believe our American Indian people need to realize and pray about this apology's true significance, for if our faith and forgiveness is joined to this act, great good can follow, and if we do not respond appropriately, what kinds of present day 'famines' may still occur needlessly? This resolution is not merely some kind of political action that may have little practical effect. This is a spiritual event of profound importance for us and for many generations to come."

"Now for Jim and Faith Chosa," Jessica directed for them. "'There are three hundred and seventy-one treaties that have been negotiated between the federal government and Indian Nations and ratified by the Senate. All of these treaties have been broken by the federal government in a multitude of ways. The most distressing has been the removal of Indian nations from lands recognized by these treaties as belonging to these Indian nations.'" Jessica paused and sat back.

She, Daniel, and Angel knew of the removals, exterminations, and other ill treatment of their ancestors but had never heard the information on the treaties themselves.

She then continued. "'The results of violating and breaking the covenant, the constitution, the supreme law of the land, adds the defilement of bloodshed to the land, which serves to root a shroud of the spirit of death over the land, significantly manifesting in the death of those most vulnerable, the unborn in the womb.'"

Daniel could feel his heart pounding in his chest.

"'These defilements in the land are the root of spiritual causes of the many social curses now plaguing our nation, especially those resulting from dysfunctional family relationships due to the high divorce rate. In addition, the attack on the sanctity of marriage itself, drug abuse, street gangs, and epidemic lawlessness are all rooted in the breaking of these three hundred seventy-one covenants.'"

"I never realized what an impact on the spirit of this nation those actions had," Angel said, visibly dumbfounded. "Now I can see why I was drawn to the First Nations People."

"I never knew it either, but I guess that's what the Creator has been stirring in me," Daniel surmised.

"Shall I go on?" Jessica asked.

Daniel and Angel nodded.

"'In the realm of the spirit, broken covenants greatly defile the land and provide an environment for evil to work in all facets of society. The ancient testimony of the nation of Israel reveals how broken covenants weakened the nation from within and made it extremely vulnerable to external forces from without.'"

"The scriptures are given for our learning," Daniel spoke up, remembering the verse from the Bible. The girls nodded in agreement.

"We don't like to learn, do we?" Jessica asked, staring at the screen.

Angel and Daniel nodded.

"He goes on to say, 'We have, by God's Spirit, been alerted to the reality of how these broken treaties have created spiritual breaches in our borders and how terrorists will potentially recruit radical elements within the Indian nations located in the border regions of our nation. The cultural barrier, manifesting as mistrust and deep bitterness between the Native Americans and the rest of our society stems from the breaking of these treaties.'"

"Oh wow, get this." Jessica emphasized what she was about to further read. "'The most significant arena where these unresolved issues manifest is in the church where Native Americans resist the message of Christ because they view it as the white man's gospel.'"

"That's why there are so many who feel hopeless and turn to drugs and alcohol, crime, and even suicide," Angel pointed out. "We've only lied to them ourselves when we preach a God of grace and love and then show them fear and hate toward their culture and traditions." Angel stood up. "I mean, why don't we get it? Why can't we see the hypocritical thinking? We are all just Pharisees!" she said.

Daniel stood up and took her in his arms. "Shhh." He smiled at the little badger he was going to marry soon. "The Great Creator will get our attention. He'll wake the church up. He has to. His name's at stake," Daniel assured her.

"Don't you see? That's where the terrorists will find their army!" Angel said urgently.

"That's what Jim Chosa says in his next sentence," Jessica confirmed. "Pastor Chosa says, 'A vital aspect of the resolution of apology is homeland security. To undermine what the enemy is trying to do begins with an apology.'"

"Just like Israel did when God sent them prophets to warn them unless they repented," Angel said.

Daniel had released Angel to pace the room again.

"But Israel still didn't learn," Daniel pointed out.

"Dad, when they did repent, the Lord relented from allowing evil to take over and healed their land. Listen to more of what Jim Chosa says. 'The Resolution of Apology initiates this repentance action.' And I'm summarizing now, but basically he says it will enable the church to really reveal the truth of the gospel to the First Nations People so a spiritual restoration can begin in them and then 'righteously connect them to the larger fabric of society in this nation and…'" She paused, reading over the words and then continuing, "And 'once we are rightly aligned with the native indigenous people and their spiritual authority, we can spiritually remove the defilements of the broken treaties, negate the associated curses, and close the spiritual breaches of our borders.'" Jessica straightened her back for a moment. "Wow!"

Jessica had one more thing to read. "'The Resolution of Apology is not just about Native Americans. It is an issue that greatly impacts all inhabitants of America, and all its citizens will greatly benefit from its passage and declaration of the apology.' I had no idea," Jessica finished, sitting back. This was all news, even to Daniel.

"You're our prophet," Angel said, looking pointedly at Daniel.

Daniel shot her a stare. Jessica turned and looked at him as well.

Daniel then felt the weight of their gazes and spoke up. "No! Not me! How am I supposed to—"

He was struggling inside, a war between wanting to do what the Great Creator had for him, whatever it may be, and the strong doubt that this was it. Or was it hope that this wasn't what he wanted Daniel to do? "I don't know what to say!" He went to the window and stared out as the day turned to sunset. "Who am I that I should carry this message?" Suddenly he realized he'd just bumped into Moses who had asked the Great Creator the very same things. "But why me?" he finished, suddenly feeling weak.

Angel and Jessica simply smiled.

Next, Jessica clicked on a link from the Native American Resource Network page and found more information. "Look at this site. It's NativeRes.org. They have a video showing interviews with all the people involved and a presentation of the resolution." Jessica clicked on the video link, and Daniel pulled up two more chairs as the family gathered around the computer to watch.

The information was enlightening and intense, to say the least. After the twenty-minute presentation, the three were in tears. Daniel sat back in his chair in silence, his heart still pounding as it had days before when the Great Creator had begun stirring this burden in him. Now he had another piece to the picture. He got up quickly and went to the front window, letting the tears flow freely. At the moment, what he was feeling was a strong emotion that he couldn't put his finger on, but he knew it was the Great Creator's heart that was pouring into him. He hugged his stomach and dropped to his knees as if in pain, weeping deeply.

"Dad!" Jessica made a move to get up, but Angel put a gentle hand on her arm.

"He's all right, Jessica. He's experiencing God's burden. It's like being in labor but without the physical pain. The emotion runs very strong, and it is difficult to bear. Come on. Let's go for a walk. We'll pray for him."

Jessica nodded, and they grabbed their jackets and left Daniel alone with his Creator.

"So where are we walking?" Jessica asked, pulling her jacket around her as the chill of the evening crept in.

"We're walking around the hogan. Daniel will be literally circled in prayer."

Jessica nodded and took Angel's hand. Having a prophetic mom was going to be an adventure in itself. They began to ask the Great Creator to enable Daniel to understand what he was telling him and for him to be able to put it into words.

Inside, Daniel was now facedown on the floor, sobbing. He knew it was because of the video he'd seen; he knew it was because of the resolution, but such things didn't normally cause him to feel this way. He felt a sorrow and a hope all blended together with the inability to control his tears and their intensity.

"Be still and know that I am God", the Great Creator told him. *"I don't mean that you must stop this. You are my vessel, and if the mountains quake before me, how can you not?"*

Daniel nodded, understanding that he should continue to let this burden keep him on the floor. He felt he had no choice.

"This is my heart. To set my heart in yours is what I am doing. It is a birth process. Does it sound strange for a man to bear me a baby?

And yet this is my child, my baby. It has grown quickly, and now you are experiencing the labor pains, birth pains."

Another wave of deep sobs hit Daniel, and he had to be vocal about it with groans. "Oh God, oh God! Show me. I am willing!"

"I will show you. You will deliver my words to the Senate of this country, and they will hear and they will act. Wait for the word. It will come soon."

Daniel could only nod, exhausted from the ordeal. The intensity diminished enough to allow him to rest. He remained on the floor, feeling the presence of the Great Creator, unable to move. Finally, after what seemed an eternity but had only been an hour, Daniel felt able to get up off the floor. He went to the bathroom and washed his face and then sat on the couch, astonished.

"It's time," Angel told Jessica. "We can go back in now." When Jessica stepped inside, she immediately went to her dad and sat down, hugging him. The air was thick with God's peace.

"Are you okay?"

"I'm fine, sweetheart," he told her. Angel reached out her hand as she sat, Daniel taking it with a smile.

"Pretty intense, huh?" Angel observed.

"It's almost like a drug. He overwhelms you to the point that you think you're going to explode or die, and when it's over, you want more," he confirmed.

"Why?" Jessica said.

"Because you've been touched by the Great Creator, the one who made the universe. To realize that he's your father and he has chosen you to carry his heart… wow!" was Daniel's explanation. He threw up his hands in exasperation.

Angel chuckled. She'd been there before and was blessed that she would soon have a husband to share the experiences.

CHAPTER 17

The next morning, Lukas had Tommy on the Plains discussing Navajo ways and the way the Great Creator had taught him to use the traditions to glorify him. He also taught him the Great Creator's way to respect a woman and how to treat and care for a wife. Tommy had his faithful Navajo translation guide with him but was needing it less and less as the language began to take hold of him.

"So are we too young to marry?" Tommy asked his adopted great sicheii.

"Some would say yes," Lukas began in Navajo, "that you need the experience of age, but if you love the Great Creator and have surrendered your heart and life to him and allow his Spirit to always guide you, then that is enough." Lukas paused for a moment. "But now, you have been given a strong family to guide you. We carry his wisdom and will always be there for you."

Lukas could tell the wheels in Tommy's head were spinning a thousand miles an hour, but he also could see his heart, and he was proud of the young man before him. He also noted his dedication to Jessica and her family.

"So I'll ask her then," Tommy said with a quiet determination.

"You must first face a great wall," Lukas said, as if it were a great mystery.

Tommy looked at him his expression implied he was eager to hear about a wonderful journey. "You must ask her father first," he finished with a grin.

Tommy chuckled and gave a nod as Lukas patted him on the back.

It was close to true that nearly every woman of the Navajo Nation had passed through Angel's hogan, bearing wedding gifts and items for her wedding preparation. Four of her closest friends, Ben's wife, Christiana, being one of them, along with Jessica, stayed with her for two days to prepare her.

Jessica was learning quite a bit. "So this is just like being Esther."

Angel was soaking in rez mud with herbs. "Just as if I'm to marry a king."

"Dad would say so." She giggled.

"Marriage is very important to the First Nations People. They have a deep understanding of covenant that only the Great Chief could have given them, and it has been that way for thousands of years. They knew it was a gift," Angel said.

"Are you scared?" Jessica asked.

Angel thought over her feelings, taking her time to make sure she had a full understanding of how she really felt. "Here's what I am," she began. "I'm excited, expectant, and a little nervous. But scared? No." She smiled. "At least, not yet." She and Jessica laughed together at that.

Jessica became quiet. "You've never been married before, so that's why I asked. You know, your first time and everything." She looked down. "It's a little uncomfortable because Dad's in the picture."

"I know." Angel took her hand. "But I also know that God has prepared me, and I trust the man I'm about to marry." She noticed Jessica's sensitivity and switched gears to a blanket statement. "Jessica, when a man and a woman get married, the vows aren't just words. Marriage itself isn't a contract. It is a covenant. God is all about covenants."

Jessica nodded.

Angel felt her relax and so continued. "In fact, marriage is a picture of his kingdom. There are three in every marriage."

"Three?"

"Husband, wife, and God," Angel explained. "Unless he is at the center, no marriage can be all that he has called it to be. It can seem perfect, but it never is unless he is the foundation."

"The picture of his kingdom—there are three in his family: Father, Son, and Holy Spirit," Jessica said.

"Exactly. Marriage is also a partnership, and the Great Creator designed intimacy between a husband and wife. He made it to be beautiful, to be enjoyed, and as a reminder of the oneness of God. It's an act of worship, a sacrifice of the husband to the wife and the wife to the husband." Angel looked at Jessica.

Jessica was smiling. "Never thought of it that way. Of course, I never asked my mom about it, so I'm glad you're telling me. Keep going, please."

"The husband and wife give each other completely over to the other," Angel continued. "So his desire is to please his wife and the wife's desire is to please her husband, so fear shouldn't exist."

Jessica nodded. "I don't feel worried about my wedding night, however far off it might be." She giggled again. "Thanks, Angel. I never saw it that way before."

"Well, it isn't the way society sees it either for the most part."

Tommy raptly observed as Ben and Lukas were praying over Daniel with several of the clansmen. Daniel knelt in the center of a dance circle out on the Plains, and the men shook rattles and sang to the Great Creator with the others on a ceremonial drum. Four small fires burned outside their circle. Daniel could feel the deep rhythms in his chest as smoke swirled around him. It wasn't long before he had a vision.

Daniel was standing at the foot of Mt. Rushmore, clothed in buckskin breeches and moccasins and was shirtless except that he wore a warrior's breastplate, with his pouch hanging over it. His face was painted, and an eagle's feather hung from his hair and sat over his left shoulder. Red tears streamed down his face as he looked up at the monument of the four white leaders who had betrayed the First Nations People and broke treaties and covenants with them.

Daniel began to tremble violently, dropping to his knees. He bowed down for a moment, not as if paying them homage but in deep grief, soaking the earth with his tears and clutching the red dirt. Suddenly, from the core of his being, a deep groan built like pressure in a volcano. Daniel straightened upright and, with every fiber of his being, let out a roar. His golden eagle flew above and cried out with him. As the sound carried up the rock faces, Mt. Rushmore began to quake and crumble until the monument completely collapsed into nothing.

He stopped, heaving in air and blinking at the ruins of what was considered by America to be greatness. Then, standing before Daniel were Geronimo, Sitting Bull, Red Cloud, and Crazy Horse—four of the greatest chiefs of the First Nations People and the true founding fathers of America. He stared at them for a moment and then stood. He felt a smaller hand take his, and he looked to his right. There beside him stood Angel. Each chief stepped forward and put a hand on Daniel's shoulder and then walked away, disappearing as he went. The last chief, Crazy Horse, spoke to Daniel.

"The Great Spirit has given his Angel to help strengthen you." Daniel gave a nod, and then the chief turned and also disappeared.

After the vision Daniel fell onto his back and passed out. Tommy wanted to go to him, but the lack of concern from the rest of the men made him relax. He realized it was an expected occurrence.

That night, Jessica and Angel also dreamed.

Jessica stood on a plateau, staring at Mt. Rushmore and heard a roar. She felt the earth shake and watched the monument crumble but didn't know what had caused it until the dust had cleared. She looked down into the valley and saw her dad. She realized it had come from him. Then she saw him stand up, and Angel appeared next to him and four chiefs in front of him. She looked to her left and saw her uncle Hawkeye, who winked at her and then disappeared. She looked to her right and saw Ben and Lukas watching Daniel as well.

"He shall speak to the fathers," a voice told her. She knew it was the Great Creator who had said the words. She smiled and gave a nod of acknowledgment. It was a confirmation of what she'd told her dad earlier.

Angel stood beside Daniel, holding his hand. He had just let out a roar from the Great Creator, and it still reverberated in her being. She stood in awe as the four chiefs each silently thanked Daniel and as Crazy Horse gave his directive about her. She only knew his strength and hers

came from the Great Creator, so she understood that her strength for Daniel was a gift flowing through her as his wife.

Daniel awoke at five in the morning of his wedding day. The vision he'd had from the night before was still fresh in his mind. He dressed in his sweats and went for a jog. As he ran down the road, he heard the Creator's voice in the wind.

"You will speak to the fathers."

Daniel stopped and looked up. His golden eagle was flying above and gave a cry. He let the words sink in as he remembered the vision.

When Daniel returned home, the house was completely cordoned off with yellow police tape, reading "Police Line. Do Not Cross." Ben met him with a slap on the back.

"What's this?" He chuckled at Ben.

"It's off limits until tonight. We've got your clothes at my place."

"What about the wedding dress?"

"Jessica took it to Angel's last night," Ben told him. "Quit worrying. Everything's under control, bro."

"Yeah, not mine," Daniel mumbled.

"Exactly!" Ben laughed and then steered Daniel across the driveway to his house.

Daniel also was now immersed in the mud at Ben's house and staring at two flickering candles at the foot of the tub. They flanked an unlit taller one. The significance was obvious to him.

"They are you and Meda," Lukas said, startling Daniel out of his fixation.

"You're still good at sneaking up on people, Sicheii," Daniel said in Navajo. He looked back at the candles then. "Why did I ever leave here?"

"There is always a reason. Can you not see why when you see where you are now?" Lukas said.

Daniel sighed and sunk down to his chin in the mud, still studying the flickering flames. "Yeah."

"Those two flames are you and Meda," Lukas reiterated. "The center will come to life when you both feed it. That is your marriage. You will become one."

Daniel already understood all of that, but he was glad his sicheii was there to remind him. "You're working on your sermon, aren't you?"

Lukas grinned again. "You have learned to read your sicheii well." He got up and left Daniel to finish his soak.

At sunset, the clan and tribe gathered out on the plain where four separate fires were burning at the four directions, and in the center, a larger unlit fire pit waited. Daniel was led in from the east on a horse and dismounted at the north end of the circle. He wore buckskin breeches and moccasins, and a crimson plains ribbon shirt with the four colors of the four directions. His pouch was on the outside of the shirt, and a sachet was around his waist. He turned to the west to eagerly await his bride.

Angel was led in on a white horse by Ben. She smiled, honored to be wearing the beautiful white leather wedding dress Sarah Yanaba had worn before her. Ben helped her off the horse, and Lukas took her hand and led her to Daniel. He placed Angel's hand in Daniel's and then stood in front of them. Daniel could only smile at the beautiful gift before him. Lukas removed the sachet from Daniel and wrapped it around their hands and began the ceremony.

"My friends, we have come together this day to celebrate the union of two flames. These two flames will unite to become one passionate fire, a light for all to see. A light that will bring hope to those lost in darkness. The Great Creator has done this, and it is awesome indeed."

Lukas gave a nod to Ben, and he handed Daniel and Angel each a torch. They turned together and touched the torches to the center ring of wood and kindling. It caught quickly, and a large fire began to burn fervently. A cheer went up from those gathered around, and then Daniel and Angel turned back to Lukas.

"The Great Creator made the earth and all its creatures and while he was happy and pleased, he felt lonely somehow, for he could not love his creation in the way he needed."

Lukas stood regally as he related the story of the first husband and wife. "The Great Creator decided he would make a man in his image, and so he did, but he still felt something was missing. He put the man into a deep sleep and took a part of his bone and fashioned a woman for him. This made the Creator and the man very happy. The Creator had two souls he could relate to and talk to as friends and children, and the man and woman had each other."

Ben took the blanket that Daniel's grandmother had made so many years ago for his first wedding and draped it over the couple. He removed the sachet from their hands and held onto it for Daniel.

"Daniel and Angel will speak to each other of their love and commitment to one another," Lukas said, and it became very silent as Daniel and Angel got closer and spoke to each other.

"I didn't come back here expecting to get married." He smiled. "I…I never expected to fall in love."

Angel smiled at him.

"I know it's obvious as we stand here, but I am head over heels in love with you. I give you my heart, soul, and body—my life. You are a gift to me from the greatest giver in the universe, and I am so blessed," he breathed out. "I am yours until death."

Angel sighed as she looked into his deep-brown eyes. "I feel as if your eyes are leading me into your heart," she whispered. "I know you are a gift from the Great Creator. I know that he chose you specifically for me from the very beginning and in his infinite wisdom, his time was chosen for our love." She wiped tears from her eyes.

Daniel put his hand to her face.

"I love you, and I give my whole being to you until death," she finished.

Daniel leaned in and kissed her tenderly.

Lukas introduced them to the clan. "These two spirits, these two souls are the image of the Creator and were brought together to represent him on this earth. The Great Creator says, 'It is good!'"

The clan cheered and danced with an intensity that made the ground vibrate. Daniel and Angel stared into each other's eyes, the flames from the fire reflecting red on their faces. Daniel slipped a wedding band onto Angel's finger, and Angel slipped a wedding band onto his finger.

Ben slapped Daniel on the back. "It is time."

Daniel looked at Ben and realized they were being told they could go home together. He took Angel's hand, and they walked around the fire to Daniel's SUV. He helped her inside as the wedding goers celebrated.

Daniel pulled into the driveway and opened the vehicle door for his bride. She let out a chuckle.

"What's this?" she asked of the police tape.

"That is our very loud 'do not disturb' sign." He chuckled with her. They walked to the front door. Daniel had no clue what to expect. When he opened the door, he took in a breath of delight.

Angel drew in a breath as well. "Daniel, it's incredible."

"Yeah, it is," he said, staring.

The home was completely lit with white Christmas lights and candles. Small candles inside of lanterns lined the hallway to the master bedroom. They walked to the master suite. He opened the door, and they found more of the same lighting. At the foot of Daniel's bed was the wooden chest, and on it was one large, beautiful candle. Daniel closed the door, smiled, and hugged her. "You are beautiful."

CHAPTER 18

Daniel brought breakfast in bed to his new wife the next morning. "Good morning, my wife."

Angel sat up. Daniel placed the tray over her lap. "I feel so special."

"You are special. I feel like a rat leaving you today."

"Daniel, we talked about this. You and Ben need to make sure our clan isn't being railroaded. Consider it taking care of the family, eh?"

"It is family business, innit?" Daniel leaned in and gave Angel a hungry kiss. "I will make up for this."

"I know you will. I'll see to it." She pulled him in for another kiss and then released him.

Daniel stopped at the bedroom door. He stared at Angel longingly and then let out a sigh of frustration. He could hear her giggle as he closed the door behind him.

Ben and Daniel had to proceed with caution now. Johnny's message had been cryptic at best. Daniel stood at the doorway to the pool hall. "You'll be right around back, eh?"

"Nervous, are we?" Ben grinned.

"I've been set up a time or two in my life," Daniel said.

Ben understood Daniel's reference to the warehouse incident. "Right. Well, no worries, I got ya covered. Joe's got one side and Pete the other. Wherever you come out, we'll see you. If we did miss you—"

Daniel shot him a look of concern.

"Which we won't, you've got that chip. You're safe. I promise."

Daniel nodded, feeling relief wash over him. Ben stepped back, and Daniel opened the door and walked into the pool hall.

Daniel immediately removed his sunglasses and hung them in his shirt pocket. He spotted Johnny sitting at the bar.

"Johnny?" Daniel patted the nineteen-year-old on the back.

Johnny looked at Daniel with a scowl. He popped some peanuts and stared back at the bar's mirror.

"It's been awhile. How are you doing?"

"Not long enough," Johnny grumbled.

"You look good. You doing okay?" he asked him again.

"Yeah, sure," Johnny answered bitterly and took a swig of his beer.

Daniel was disturbed by Johnny's early morning breakfast. "I looked for you after the accident and wanted to help you, but everyone said you'd run—"

Johnny shot him a glare so Daniel rephrased, "Left town."

"Like you helped my little sister? Must be nice to get over someone you love so quickly," Johnny said.

Daniel sat down next to Johnny, desiring to help him get through the grief he was obviously still carrying over the death of his little sister. "I'm not completely over it. I don't think it'll ever stop hurting," Daniel told him. "The time it takes to get through grief isn't a reflection of someone's ability to love."

"Such wise words," Johnny said. "I'll tell you what! Keep your wisdom! You're gonna need it 'cause it's payback time," Johnny warned him, finishing his beer. He got off his stool and stormed over to a booth of skinheads who seemed to accept him with smiles and pats on the back. Daniel looked in the mirror at the men in the booth, studying their faces.

Daniel stepped back outside and walked to Ben's position.

"Interesting conversation?" Ben said, hand on his gun. He relaxed when he saw Daniel.

"To say the least. He gave me a warning. That's all."

Ben's eyebrow went up with interest.

"He said it's payback time."

"So watch your back, in other words," Ben said. "We need to figure out what that really means." Ben called Joe and Pete. "You guys go back to the rez. We're gonna stake the hall out for a while."

"Roger that, Ben. Keep us posted," Daniel heard Pete reply.

Ben pulled around the back of the pool hall and drove down the dirt road about one hundred fifty yards from the building to a flat, elevated rock. He parked behind it and cut the engine. He pulled two sets of binoculars from behind his seat and handed one pair to Daniel. They scurried atop the vantage point and waited.

Jessica was over at Angel's hogan helping her get packed so the men that hadn't left for a job could relocate her to her new home with Daniel and Jessica.

"This will be a fun sleepover. First, it's been a long time since I've been to one, and second, it's like a new beginning!" Jessica gushed.

"It's been a really long time for me, too." Angel paused as she placed a paper wrapped item into a box. "I noticed you were looking at my ring a lot." Angel held her hand out to Jessica. "It's okay to ask to see it. It's part of you, right?"

Jessica nodded. She held Angel's fingers and studied the ring.

"Are you and Tommy serious?"

Jessica smiled when she thought of Tommy. "Yes. We went through high school together. It's all kind of happened so fast."

Angel clapped her hands once with a chuckle. "It seems the Great Creator wants to get things done! So what is he like? I haven't really had a chance to meet him yet."

"Thank God he's nothing like his father," she began, and she told Angel about the connection of Tommy's family with Daniel.

"That's quite some history!" Angel expressed. "I'm glad Daniel and Tommy are friends, despite all of it."

"Me, too. Dad's been so good to us. Once he realized Tommy's view on things and how he treats me, he really got on board with him."

"The Great Creator has a curious way of making connections," Angel observed.

Jessica nodded in agreement.

"I think you two were made for each other."

Jessica stopped, mid sip of her water, and looked at Angel. "Is that straight from the Great Creator?" She needed verification.

Angel simply shrugged. "I can't say that it is or isn't, but it is a strong impression I'm getting," Angel said. "Why don't you ask him?"

"I've never thought of that," Jessica realized. "I guess I'll have to. Thanks!"

Just before the sun slipped behind the mesas, Daniel's and Ben's patience was rewarded when they observed Johnny with a clipboard walking out to the parking lot behind the pool hall, followed by ten Navajo men with duffel bags.

"What the—" Daniel said.

An old military bus pulled up in a cloud of dust and stopped in front of the group.

"Johnny's helping them," Daniel whispered. "Why?" He watched as the men willingly boarded the bus. He could tell some were laughing.

"Well, I can only guess what they're up to," Ben said. "But it looks legit, bro. Let's come back tomorrow."

Daniel didn't budge as he watched the bus drive away, down a dirt road away from the hall.

Ben looked at him. "Maybe the loss of his sister sent him over the edge."

"Disenfranchised?" Daniel noticed several of the Aryans exit the building and mill about the parking lot.

"There's still no evidence that there's any foul play," Ben reminded.

"Seems like it. Wait." Daniel had an epiphany. "The McKinleys are putting a small army together."

"You told me, and—"

"Do you really think McKinley will pay those guys to work for him? His family goes way back as slave owners."

Ben looked very interested in Daniel's theory. "Go on."

"The Help Wanted flyers have to be the bait."

"But our guys can't be the army. What do they want with our guys?"

"I don't know. Am I the only detective on this rock?"

"The only one getting the revelation. Keep talkin'."

"Okay, I don't think Johnny would be involved if it were about murder. He might be angry and a little messed up, but not enough to murder his own people." Then it hit him. "An army needs money."

Ben looked at Daniel. "Yep."

"Where's the money coming from?"

Ben caught on. "The mine. So, like I said, we come back tomorrow," Ben said.

It was obvious to Daniel that Ben was disappointed by the look of dismay on his face. "I'm sorry, Ben. I'll teach a class on revelation next week. How's that?"

The two men scurried down and drove home.

Angel and Jessica awoke from sleeping on her floor in sleeping bags. Jessica stretched. "Mmm. Good morning! Another day of packing."

Angel smiled. "I would think that after the big move you just had, you might be a little tired by now."

"Like I said, it's a new beginning."

"But wasn't it before, when you moved up here?"

"That was under duress."

Angel looked at Jessica. "How so?"

"Dad had been forced to move up here. I know he's glad he was forced now. I bet he'd hate it if I told him that he had the McKinleys to thank for getting you two together!" Jessica burst out laughing.

The same morning, Lukas took Tommy out on the Plains while Daniel and Ben picked up their suspect's trail from the night before. Ben took a short cut across the desert; the bumps reminded Daniel that his ribs weren't completely mended yet.

"Hey, hey!" Daniel shouted over the roar of the engine. "What's in that mud anyway?"

"Herbs!" Ben shouted back and then added, "And a little mud! It's working, eh, bro?"

"It was working until you decided to go off the beaten path!" Daniel said, annoyed. "You think you could slow down a little?"

"Sorry!" Ben chuckled, easing off the gas.

Daniel hugged his ribs and looked at Ben, offering a fake laugh that told Ben he didn't find it funny. Finally, Ben pulled onto the road about a mile north of the pool hall, and then they drove for a good hour. Eventually, Ben stopped the vehicle, and the two men got out, climbed a small rise, and halted. They scanned the horizon with their binoculars, and far in the distance, they found what they were looking for.

❖ ❖ ❖ ❖ ❖

As Angel and Jessica took a break from packing and sat down for lunch, there was a knock on Angel's door.

"I wonder who that is. The guys aren't supposed to be by until tomorrow morning."

"Maybe Hawk is being charitable?" Jessica suggested. Angel opened the front door.

"Hello, ladies!" Jeff grinned.

❖ ❖ ❖ ❖ ❖

"What do you see, bro?" Ben asked Daniel.

"I see a working mine," he answered. "Let's get closer."

Ben nodded in agreement as the two grabbed some water from the truck and took a walk toward their quarry. They stopped a mile later, finding a canyon that hadn't been visible from their previous vantage point. They low crawled to the edge. Ben frowned, seeming unfamiliar with it.

Daniel noted his expression. "What's the matter? You can't tell me you didn't know this was here." His voice was incredulous.

Ben stared across the small canyon. "We *used* to be nomadic," he said, covering for his ignorance. "We stay put these days. Besides, we're off rez, remember? This is their territory, not ours."

"There's our men," Dan observed, pointing. "Makin' us slaves again." His anger began to show.

"Wonder where they're housing them. And I don't see them being forced. If they were slaves, it would be obvious, no?"

Daniel nodded.

The two men eased back from the cliff edge and walked back to the truck. As Ben went for the driver's door, Daniel grabbed it.

"*I'm* driving."

CHAPTER 19

Tommy tapped his knees nervously, awaiting Daniel to return from work. He had gone over in his mind time and again how to ask him for Jessica's hand. Daniel walked into Ben's house and Tommy shot out of his seat. Daniel gave him a hard look. Tommy asked Daniel to speak with him outside.

Tommy considered Daniel for a moment wanting to clarify the look. Then he could gage the safety of asking the big question. "Am I in trouble, sir?" Tommy asked Daniel, "The look you gave me—well, I thought I was in trouble."

Daniel tried not to grin at Tommy's nervous behavior. "I hope not," he said. "But I'd like to know your intentions toward my daughter."

Tommy stared at the ground, biting his lip, and kicked at the dirt before answering. "That's what I wanted to talk to you about. I love her, sir. I want to marry her."

Daniel raised an eyebrow.

"But I'll wait. As long as you want me to." He held his hands up in surrender.

"You'll wait?' Daniel asked.

"Yes, sir. Lukas told me to be sure I knew the Great Creator first and that I would commit my life to him."

Daniel nodded, barely able to contain a smile.

"I have, sir. I promise to commit my heart to him and to Jessica."

Daniel patted Tommy's back. "I'd be proud to have you as my son-in-law, Tommy."

Jeff and Sam tore through Angel's home, knocking shelves off the walls and slapping her and Jessica when they tried to run for the door. Jeff grabbed Angel by the arm and flung her back. She fell over a chair and then tried to get her cell phone out. Sam had Jessica in a bear hug, cackling at her.

"Let me go!" Jessica shouted angrily.

Jeff saw Angel trying to make a call and rushed over to her, backhanding her. The force of the blow knocked her unconscious. Jeff then stormed over to Sam, his eyes red with hate.

"I'll take her, Sam. You can have that one!" he said, jerking his thumb over his shoulder at Angel's unmoving form.

Suddenly, an evil face flashed in Daniel's vision. He felt as if he were being choked and dropped to his knees. Daniel tried to get up but jerked again, feeling strikes to his body but not knowing where they were coming from. It was then he realized that Jessica and Angel were in danger. "Get Ben and Hawk!" he gasped, doubling over.

Tommy ran into the house. "Something's wrong with Mr. Patterson!"

Ben and Hawk ran outside to Daniel who was on his feet but still doubled over. He staggered away by another invisible strike. Ben grabbed him and felt the evil force.

"Daniel!"

"Angel and Jess!" Daniel groaned, catching his breath. "They're in trouble. We have to go now!" Daniel staggered to Ben's truck as he, Hawk, Tommy, and Ben got in.

Inside Ben's house, Lukas and Christiana prayed.

Jeff took Jessica roughly by the arm and shoved her into the kitchen. Sam waded though the strewn furniture to Angel with a menacing grin.

"What do you want, Jeff?" Jessica cried nervously.

"Just helpin' my little brother out, darlin'." Jeff smirked. "I'm gonna make sure his squaw is ready for him." He sneered at her as he unbuckled his belt. Jessica began to pray under her breath and backed up against the counter. She found a knife. As Jeff came at her, she raised it, but he caught her wrist with one hand and punched her in the face with the other. The blow sent her crashing against the kitchen table, striking the edge of it with her forehead. She fell unconscious onto the floor.

Jeff grinned. "That's better." He took a step toward her with evil intent but stopped short, sheer terror crossing his features.

A very tall Indian dressed in white war regalia, a spear in one hand and a shield in the other hand, stood in front of Jessica, and he did not look happy.

"Jeff!" came a scream from the other room.

Jeff quickly exited the kitchen to see what Sam was so frightened by and saw an identical warrior standing over Angel. Sam was on the ground, scrambling backward like a crab. The two skinheads climbed over each other as the "angels" advanced on them. The boys fell out of the front door and into the dirt in their haste to escape the white-clad Navajo warriors. Jeff and Sam drove away from Angel's hogan, spitting dirt from the tires in desperation to move the mass of metal.

Five minutes later, Ben skidded to a stop in front of Angel's home, and the four men piled out, making an urgent dash for the front door, which was still open. Daniel made it inside first and found Angel just regaining consciousness. He knelt beside her, helping her to a sitting position while the three others urgently looked for Jessica. Daniel put a gentle hand to her face, noting her bruised and swollen lip.

"I'm okay," she assured him. Daniel motioned for Hawk as he got her into a chair.

"In here!" Tommy's cry came from the kitchen.

"I've got her, Daniel," Hawk assured.

Daniel hurried into the kitchen where Ben knelt beside Tommy, who was cradling Jessica's unmoving form.

"I don't think she's breathing!" Tommy cried, tears streaking his face.

Daniel knelt next to Jessica's other side and pried Tommy's hold from her. He laid her down as he and Ben began CPR.

"Call nine-one-one!" Daniel ordered in between rescue breaths.

Tommy got his cell phone out.

"She can't die!" he said though gritted teeth.

"Pray, Tommy," Ben urged.

Hawk had helped Angel to the kitchen, and he took the phone from Tommy, seeing he was in no condition to make the urgent call.

Angel put an arm around Tommy and guided the shaken man out of the kitchen away from the scene.

"She'll be all right, Tommy," she assured him.

Tommy looked at the stranger, knowing who she was but not having met her until now. "Pray and she will be. Trust God."

Once again, the family found themselves at Banner Page Hospital, only this time the group included Tommy and Angel. Angel had only sustained a black eye and swollen lip, but Jessica had a severe concussion, needing twenty stitches, and was in a coma.

Daniel spoke with Angel, who was signing her own release forms after treatment. "Who did this?"

"I think they were skinheads."

"Were they dumb enough to use their names?"

. "Jeff and Sam," she confirmed.

Daniel's fist came down on the counter, startling her. "Sorry," he apologized. "Don't tell Tommy. Jeff is his brother, and he and Sam were the ones who ambushed me a couple of weeks ago," he said. "I'm going to go check on Jessica."

"I'll go with you," she said, leaving her last signature. She took Daniel's hand, bringing a sad smile to his face, and they walked to Jessica's room together.

"Where's Ben?" he asked Hawk, who was standing by Jessica's bed.

"He's down getting us some coffee," Hawk answered.

Daniel stroked his daughter's slightly swollen face. She was beautiful as ever and seemed peaceful. Daniel took her hand. "Great Creator, she's yours. You know the plans you have for her. They're not for harm, but they're for her good. You have a purpose and a hope for her," he prayed, quoting Jeremiah 29:11.

Angel smiled and gave his hand a reassuring squeeze. "I told Tommy, and I'm sure of it. She'll be okay," she said, looking into his glistening eyes.

After Daniel got the full report from the doctor, he was relieved to hear neither Jessica nor Angel had been raped. "Will you stay with Jessica?" he asked Angel.

"Of course I will. Where are you going?"

"I have some work to do." He gave her a quick kiss on the cheek and then left the room.

Hawk had noticed the expression of resolve on his face and went after him. "Where you goin', bro?"

"To leave a message for Jeff."

"I got your six," Hawk said, keeping pace with him.

Daniel and Hawk drove the two hours back to the rez border and directly to the pool hall where Daniel intended to leave a message with Johnny.

Ben returned from the hospital's food court. "Angel, where are Daniel and Hawk?"

"I don't know, Ben. Daniel just asked me to stay with Jess until he got back, and then Hawk went after him," she explained.

Ben realized he didn't have any coffee with him. "I'm sorry, Angel. Got busy on the phone with Joe." Then it all dawned on Ben. "Oh, no," Ben growled. "I have to go. When did they leave?"

"About an hour ago," she informed him.

He glanced at Jessica with a worried expression.

"Ben, what's going on?"

"Hopefully some smart investigating," he said, and then he also left.

Angel sat back in her chair with a sigh. Tommy cast a furtive glance at Jessica. Somehow he felt she would be okay. He turned and went after Ben.

"All is well," she whispered to herself.

"So what's the plan?" Hawk asked.

Daniel parked his SUV behind the hall and near the road in case they needed to leave in a hurry. "I'm just delivering a message to someone who knows where Jeff is," Daniel said, staring out onto the Plains.

"You've got a gun, right?" Hawk asked.

Daniel nodded. "Open the glove box."

Hawk opened it and found a .38 revolver inside. He clipped it to his belt and looked at Daniel. "I guess this means I'm deputized."

"Something like that," Daniel said.

They got out of the truck, and the two men entered the pool hall. They checked behind them before closing the back door. Once inside, as Daniel expected, he found Johnny sitting at the bar nursing a beer. Hawk and Daniel took note that the rest of the hall was mostly filled with skinheads playing pool. Daniel gestured toward Johnny with his head, and Hawk took a seat on Johnny's left while Daniel stood by his right side.

"What do you want?" Johnny sneered at Daniel.

"I've got a message for Jeff."

"Heard he left one for you." Johnny chortled.

Daniel suddenly grabbed Johnny by the shirtfront, yanked him off his stool, and into the rear exit hallway. He slammed him into the wall.

Hawk watched the doorway. He noticed the skinheads had taken an interest in the small display. Hawk observed as one by one, the skinheads left by the front door.

"You think raping women is funny?" Daniel snarled at the young man. "I no longer feel bad for your loss. Your little sister is in a better place. Without you!" he emphasized with an extra shove.

"You got a message, tell him yourself. He's out back!" Johnny snapped.

"Hey, bro. The white boys are leaving," Hawk announced over his shoulder.

"Come on, Hawk." Daniel roughly directed Johnny out the back door.

Hawk backed out and then turned and joined Daniel, who was following Johnny to the back of the lot. Daniel and Hawk soon became aware that they themselves had a small group following them. The hair on the back of Daniel's neck rose.

"We have company," Hawk mumbled.

Daniel gave a nod but didn't look.

Johnny led them right up to Jeff. Jeff smugly leaned on his car with Sam by his side.

"Well, Danny boy. Those girls of yours are real fine." He snickered, grabbing his crotch to make his point.

Daniel lunged for Jeff while Hawk shoved Johnny to the ground and then put Sam out of commission. Daniel slammed Jeff in the face and then hauled him to his feet and shoved him against his car.

"Don't ever go near them again!" Daniel warned. He pulled his handcuffs and restrained Jeff for arrest. He then pulled his .45 and held it to Jeff's temple. "I oughta splatter your brains all over this desert!"

Jeff suddenly lost his bravado. "Y...you can't shoot me. That's murder!"

"You're right. We'll go to the rez. Out there we have Indian justice. That means we're not governed by any white man's law. I shoot you, it's no big deal. Hawk, go get a shovel."

"Hey, man, you can't shoot him," Hawk agreed.

"Why not?" Daniel growled.

Jeff squirmed in Daniel's grip.

"Well, what about all that talk? Love your enemy and don't repay evil for evil?"

"Yeah," Jeff offered.

Daniel could feel Jeff trembling in his grip. "Shut up!" Daniel yelled at Jeff. He pressed the gun to Jeff's head a little harder. Daniel was seething. He felt the hate trying to grab a hold of his heart. He knew what he wanted to do was wrong. It would be murder, and the Great Creator was his witness. Daniel pressed the gun yet harder against the frightened man's head so that Jeff's ear was nearly touching his shoulder.

"Hey, man, we've got a slight problem," Hawk said. Hawk tapped him on the shoulder and drew his gun.

Daniel turned and saw that they were now surrounded by Jeff's cohorts. Daniel eased his gun from Jeff's head, realizing he was out of line. He took a deep breath and let it out.

Jeff's confidence quickly returned. "Guess you've got to decide who the bigger problem is."

Daniel put the safety on and slammed Jeff in the face with his elbow. Jeff slumped to the ground. "Time to go," Daniel said to Hawk.

"So this isn't part of your plan?" Hawk said.

Daniel shook his head no. "We're going to the truck."

"Got it," Hawk agreed.

Slowly, with guns aimed at the closest target, they shuffled their way to Daniel's SUV.

"It's two against ten. Where ya think you're going?" Sam said, having recovered.

"Technically, it's fourteen to ten. Who wants to take the extra rounds?" Daniel inferred.

The group exchanged worried glances.

"Now!" Daniel said. He and Hawk made a dash for Daniel's vehicle.

The skinheads charged, and one of them grabbed Daniel as he was about to get into the driver's side. Daniel struck him with the butt of his gun and made his way in as Hawk fought off two guys. Daniel threw his door open on another attacker coming at him. Hawk was finally able to get into the SUV, and Daniel floored it, the momentum slamming the door on one of the skinhead's hands.

Their attackers piled into their cars and trucks and gave chase.

"Why are we going this way?" Hawk shouted over the gunfire. A bullet hit the side mirror, causing him to throw his hands up against flying glass fragments.

"Shortcut!" Daniel shouted back, ducking as another bullet took out his rearview mirror. Daniel maneuvered the SUV as well as he could on the dirt road, going at break-neck speed, up and over dips and fishtailing. A bullet blew out the front driver's side tire. Daniel lost control. The SUV took a sharp turn and dip to the left and then rolled to its roof and skidded several yards. As the dust settled, Jeff's group had caught up.

Chapter 20

Daniel, a cut over his eye, and Hawk, with just a few scratches, were dazed as they tried to get their bearings. Slowly, each made his way out through his perspective window. The skinheads now surrounded the toppled vehicle. Jeff, still handcuffed and now highly agitated, awaited Daniel's emergence. Daniel didn't notice Jeff standing over him as he pulled himself out of the driver's side window. As he got to his hands and knees, Jeff kicked him viciously in the face. Daniel flipped to his back, stunned.

"Get the keys," Jeff hissed.

Sam rifled through Daniel's front pockets. He released Jeff's wrists. "Now what?"

"Cuff the dog!"

They rolled Daniel to his stomach and cuffed his hands behind him.

In the meantime, Hawk had three guys on him, making sure he'd remain a silent partner for Daniel. Daniel was roughly hoisted to his feet. He was held against the vehicle, head lolling while Jeff smiled through his split lip. He then slammed Daniel in the gut several times and a couple of times in the face, adding to the gash above his eyebrow. Satisfied for the moment, he stepped back and let Daniel fall to the ground. Daniel and Hawk were then loaded into the back of a pickup truck and carried away into the night.

Ben stopped at the office and filled Joe and Pete in. "Guys, we need to get to the pool hall. Get the rifles."

Joe and Pete opened the gun safe and pulled out four rifles and plenty of ammo. They followed Ben in their cruiser and headed out to Lupton.

"All right, boys, let's get our labor force relocated!" Bill bellowed at his thirty men.

Tom separated the Navajo men into groups with another of his men and directed them into the bus in groups of two armed men to five Navajo men.

"We're not goin' home in a couple a weeks, bro," Simon whispered to the nearest man in his group.

The man he spoke to nodded. "Hokahay."

"Don't worry. I left a message with the wife. She'll call the police, eh?" Simon was confident that Roberta had caught onto his call.

The bus lurched forward and headed away from the Aztec mine.

"Sure hope so."

Ben pulled behind the pool hall, Tommy in the passenger seat. Ben watched Joe and Pete pull behind him. He continued on to the stakeout rock he and Daniel had used. He pulled around the rock, motioning for his guys to do the same. He got out. "Stay here," he told Tommy. Joe and Pete joined Ben.

"Okay, I don't see Daniel's vehicle. I don't think he and Hawk are here, but I want you to just watch for a couple of hours. I'm going down the road a piece and see what I can see, eh?"

"Right-o, Boss," Joe said. He and Pete ascended the rock and lay on their bellies.

Ben got back in his truck and headed out toward the mine.

After five miles, Tommy caught sight of Daniel's wrecked SUV in a gully. "Hey, what's that?"

Ben slammed on the brakes and jumped out. "Great Creator, let them be okay." Ben scurried off the embankment, Tommy on his heels, and bent down to peer inside the vehicle. All he found was broken glass and some blood.

Ben circled the wreck and discovered a small blood trail and several footprints, which eventually disappeared with some tire tracks. He radioed. "Hey, guys, I'm five miles out, and I found Daniel's vehicle. The boys aren't here, but they're injured and they've been taken away."

"On our way," Joe answered through the crackle.

After Joe and Pete looked the crash site over, they followed Ben and Tommy to the canyon he and Daniel had found. It was getting late, and they had little daylight left. The four men lay on the ground, peering over.

"I don't see anybody, Sheriff," Tommy said.

"I don't, either," Ben said. Ben didn't know what to think. "Let's get down there."

They approached cautiously, guns drawn. Tommy remained behind the three professionals.

Ben walked up to the boarded entrance to the apparently abandoned mine. "We saw them here yesterday, working. They didn't seem under duress at all."

"Maybe they took off early, Boss."

Pete was the smallest of the three and climbed between the boards to look inside. "There's nothing in there," he told Ben and Joe as he stuck his head back out.

"Equipment?"

"Nothin', Boss. Not even a pan. The back's all blocked off too, but it looks fresh."

"Why?" Joe asked.

Ben swept his hand through his hair. "There's another entrance! Joe, can you find tracks?"

Joe started searching the dirt. "Here!"

Ben, Tommy, and Pete joined him and followed Joe on foot as he tracked his quarry. After a mile the tracks disappeared. "I lost 'em. Ground's too hard. Sorry."

"That's okay. We've got a general direction. Let's get back to the station. Maybe Stanley White Powder will roll with some persuasion."

"All right!" the dealer said, shying away from one of Ben's big, burly Indian investigators. "Just call 'em off!"

Ben chuckled with delight at just how fast the skinhead had rolled when threatened.

"Scalping's illegal!" the dealer said, eyeing the bowie knives and the scalps hanging on Joe and Pete's belts.

"Not on the rez. Standard procedure." Ben shrugged. Then he leaned in close. "Chief Investigator Patterson's out of practice. That's why you didn't lose it the first time. These guys, well, as you can see, they're pretty good at what they do. Now talk."

"We're mining some gold in a vein we found in an old mineshaft to the east."

"I know, the Aztec mine. What's the gold for?" Ben asked.

"Weapons."

"What kind?"

"You name it, we're getting it."

"Why?" Ben asked.

"To clean this country up. Why else?" the drug dealer spat.

"I should have known," Ben said with disgust. "Where are they keeping our men?"

The drug dealer re-evaluated his predicament, looking the Indian's up and down and still not finding the odds favorable. "They're about ten miles south of the mine. There's an old homestead there with a barn. And there's another entrance to the mine not far from there."

"Who's supplying your weapons?"

"If I tell you that, I'm dead," the skinhead grumbled.

"Well if you don't"—Ben leaned on the arms of the chair again—"you'll have fun in the rez prison where they don't take kindly to Indian haters." Ben smiled sweetly. "So take your pick. Die quickly or die slowly."

The man gulped at the ultimatum. "His name's Tommy James, out of Phoenix."

"And the McKinleys are runnin' the show?"

The man gave a nod.

"Thanks. Boys, he's earned a meal," Ben said.

Ben stepped over to Tommy. Tommy hated the Aryans as much as his father hated color.

"Are you ready for some hard truth?" Ben asked him.

"Yes, sir. I think I know some of it, but if there's more, then I'm ready," Tommy said.

Ben sat him down and filled Tommy in on what he didn't already know about the mine. Tommy had been stunned when he found out that his dad had ambushed Daniel and was further bewildered at his dad's treatment of him when he told his dad he was leaving. Putting all the pictures together created a panorama of truth about his family's life of hatred that would have made even the strongest of men lie down and die in defeat.

"There's one more thing, Tommy," Ben said.

Tommy nodded as he sat in a chair, staring at the floor in stunned silence. Nothing else could surprise him.

"Jeff and Sam were the ones who attacked Jessica and Angel," Ben told him as gently as possible.

Tommy wondered how he could have been so ignorant and blind to his family's activities, living in the same house with two white supremacists, and he hadn't a clue as to the secrets they carried nor their daily actions. He could blame it on a lack of communication with them. He could point his finger at them as he had before and say they never told him what they were doing. Tommy knew he was just as guilty as they were, but he was guilty of being ignorantly silent. At that point, he would have never guessed that his life would be in danger. So why hadn't he confronted them and asked what they did all day? Perhaps it was because he was afraid—afraid to find out what kind of evil he willingly lived under.

Ben patted Tommy's back. "You must forgive yourself before you can forgive your father."

Tommy looked up at him. "Forgive my father?" he asked. "How can I forgive? After what he's done? After what I've done?" he finished, and he cast a shamed look to the floor.

"Do you know what was done to the Great Creator's Son, Jesus?" Ben asked him, pulling up a chair next to Tommy.

Tommy shook his head.

"He was beaten, spit on, mocked, whipped, and then nailed to a cross." Ben stopped to observe Tommy's response and then continued. "Do you know what his Son did?" Ben didn't wait for a reply this time but forged ahead. "He asked his Father to forgive them."

Tommy looked at Ben.

"He asked them to forgive them because he loved them and all those to come after them. Us, Tommy. Because we have no clue what we're doing and we need much grace and much forgiveness." Ben brought it down to the present moment. "Your dad and Jeff don't really know any better. That's what they were taught."

"He taught it to me. Why didn't I end up like that?"

"Because once in a while"—Ben smiled—"God finds a pliable heart he can work with, and yours is one of them. You broke the pattern, and now the Great Creator can use you to ask forgiveness for them. You can be Jesus for them."

"But will it save them?"

"The decision to receive it is theirs. You can only present them with the truth."

Tommy understood but didn't know if he could find it in his heart.

"Forgiveness comes from his love inside you," Ben explained. "It is also a choice. Ask the Great Creator. He will help you."

Hawk woke up face-first in old pine shavings. He coughed, clearing the dust from his lungs, and then looked around. He saw wooden walls and then sat up as his mind slowly cleared. He realized that he was in a horse stall. He groaned, making his way to his feet, staggering a moment as his head pounded. He peered out of the bars of the stall. It was too dark to see much, but he could tell the door was a slider with a slide latch that was locked with a pad lock. He tried to reach through the bars, but they were too close together for his arms. He took in the rest of the barn. It appeared to have been refurbished. The wooden planks making up his stall were new. His watch was gone, so he didn't have a clue as to the time, but his internal clock was telling him it was early in the morning.

Then, as his eyes adjusted to the dark, he could make out a figure in the center of the aisle of the barn. It was Daniel, and he was on his knees, his wrists in handcuffs that were hooked to long ropes to either side of the aisle. He was cross-tied like a horse. His shirt was gone, and he was still unconscious, his head hung between his shoulders.

Hawk yanked and pulled on the bars, unable to even rattle them. He searched his stall desperately for a way out. At the top of the stall he noticed a hatch, but it was too high and there was no foothold to reach it.

He went back to the stall door and looked at his brother. "Hang in there, bro," he whispered.

An hour later, a generator roared to life behind the barn, and lights winked on inside. Hawk scrambled to his feet and over to the bars to check on Daniel. He was still out, but in the light Hawk could see why. He'd been badly beaten, and Hawk could see a small puddle of bloody mud gathering in front of him from a gash somewhere on his face.

Hawk watched as two men opened the stall doors. There were five stalls on either side of the barn, and each stall held at least five men, except for his. Five skinheads guarded each stall, having in hand a rifle, shotgun, handgun, or cattle prod as the prisoners were escorted out. A skinhead then came to Hawk's stall, blocking his view of Daniel. Hawk backed away as the door opened.

"Move out!"

Hawk only hesitated for a moment and then obeyed, falling into line with the rest of the Navajo men. He and the others had their hands tied tightly in front of them with cable ties and then marched to waiting trucks at the other end of the barn. Hawk stared at Daniel, relieved to see the rise and fall of his chest. All Hawk could do now was gather as much info as possible, talk to his brothers, and try to find a way of escape. He was only confident that Ben could find them because of the tracking device in Daniel's arm.

Daniel was rudely awakened by a bucket of water to his face. He gasped and sputtered as his mind slowly cleared. His vision was blurry, so he opened and closed his eyes several times, trying to focus them. He didn't have much of a chance. Someone grabbed a hand full of hair and yanked his head back. He could now see the man standing in front of him.

"Wake up, Danny boy!" Tom McKinley sneered at him.

Daniel had no choice but to look at his nemesis.

"Now, what was that message you had for my boy?" Tom McKinley paced back and forth casually in front of Daniel. "Stand him up!" he ordered Jeff and Sam.

Daniel was lifted by his arms to his feet, putting slack in the ropes that restrained him. It was only enough to lower his arms halfway to his sides. He could at least breathe a little easier.

"You weren't very nice, Daniel. You hit my son and then handcuffed him?"

"You call attempted rape nice, I s...suppose." Daniel rasped in pain.

A jolt from a cattle prod sent him back to his knees, sucking in desperate gasps of air. Jeff and Sam then stood the trembling man back to his feet.

"My son just wanted to help his little brother by breaking in his girl for him." McKinley shrugged smugly. "Guess you already took care of yours, huh?" Tom snickered.

Daniel's anger sparked. He tried to move toward McKinley but to no avail.

"You must ask their forgiveness", the Great Creator spoke in his heart.

"Save you energy there, half-breed." Bill chuckled at Daniel's futile effort. He then switched gears. "Heard you married a white girl. Good for you. You're getting' smart, although"—Bill McKinley stepped closer to Daniel with a wicked grin—"I don't think you'll be celebrating your wedding. A funeral maybe. Yours." He chuckled again. He then thrust a stick under Daniel's chin.

"I'm not afraid to die," Daniel said.

"Well, that's good to hear. We'll have to fulfill your little death wish."

Daniel pulled his head away in disgust.

"You must ask their forgiveness. And you must forgive them."

Daniel heard the disturbing command and hung his head.

"Don't worry, Dan. I'll take care of your woman for you." Tom McKinley turned from Daniel. Daniel let out a growl of frustration. He managed to kick Tom McKinley in the back, sending him sprawling into the dirt.

Daniel was punished for his actions with repeated jolts from the cattle prod. He fell to his knees, having no way to escape, and could only jerk at the painful shocks. Tom McKinley got up with Bill's help. Jeff stopped the prods and pulled Daniel by the hair again to look at his father and uncle.

"You'll soon find out the right side to be on!" Tom McKinley seethed. He backhanded Daniel into unconsciousness. Spitting on Daniel, Tom stormed away. Bill followed his younger brother.

"Have patience, little brother," he said. "You can't get answers out of him when you beat him senseless."

Tom merely waved him off and continued on to the small timber cabin to wait for his half-breed to regain consciousness. Bill turned to his nephew. "Jeff, you and Sam wait here. Call us when he comes to."

Jeff nodded, kicking dirt at Daniel.

Jessica stirred awake. Her head was throbbing, and the faint smell of pure oxygen filled her senses, but other than that, she was glad to be alive. Her vision was blurry when she opened her eyes, and it scared her.

Angel sat up and took her hand. "I'm here, Jessica," she told her, noticing the worried furrow in her brows.

"Why is everything blurry? Where am I?"

"You're in the hospital. You hit your head. That's why you're not seeing clearly."

Jessica gave her a nod, not feeling comforted yet.

Angel stood and touched Jessica's face, directing her to look at her. She prayed, "Oh Lord, Great Creator, heal Jessica's eyes. Bring her clear vision, in the natural and in the spiritual."

Jessica blinked a few times, and slowly her vision cleared. She smiled at her new mom. "Wow! He answers quickly!"

"When the time is right," Angel agreed.

Jessica looked around the room.

"Where's Dad and Tommy?"

Angel brushed a stray hair from Jessica's face with loving gentleness. "They had to go back to the reservation on business."

"Jeff and Sam! Did they hurt you? Did they? He was going to—"

Angel took Jessica's worried face in her hands and shook her head no. "They didn't rape us. There were two angels there that protected us before they could really hurt us."

Relief flooded over Jessica as tears streamed down her face. "Angels?"

"Uh huh." Angel nodded again. She wiped Jessica's tears with a smile.

"Wow," Jessica whispered in amazement. She then winced and touched her hairline where she discovered stitches. "How long have I been out?"

"About a day and a half. Now just rest, and in a couple of days, you can go home."

"When will Dad be back?"

Angel looked away, but Jessica could see her try to hide her concern. She put on another smile and looked back at Jessica. "Soon."

Somewhere in Daniel's subconscious mind, the Great Creator held counsel with him.

They sat in front of a blazing fire, Daniel across from the Creator, on his knees in respect. He couldn't see the Creator's face for the flames. But he felt the weightiness of his presence and holiness. Daniel shivered in front of the fire as he listened to the Great Creator speak reverberating words that shook his soul. "My son, you must be like me. I did not fight back. I did not revile. I forgave. It is the greatest vengeance. Vengeance is mine. You must kill the old man inside. The two wolves are fighting."

At that moment, Daniel realized that the wolf he was to fight, the bad one, was still inside, and yet he also sensed the bad wolf was the evil embodied in the McKinleys.

"I'm sorry, Great One. Forgive me."

The Great Creator smiled compassionately at Daniel. "I do. Fear not. I know your heart, and you will be victorious. The great evil will be dealt with soon. You will live. They will not."

CHAPTER 21

Hawk and his fellow Indians were brought to the cave where a vein of gold was being harvested. Once inside, he discovered that it was actually an old mine tunnel. They were set to work with picks, shovels, and pans. One team would fill wheel barrels with dirt, and another crew outside would either sift it or pan it. After the gold was cleared, another group melted it down and poured it into bar molds. It was slow arduous work. Hawk was grateful that the tunnel was cool, as they had been working much of the day. With his mind on Daniel, he shuddered to think what they had planned for his brother in the barn.

Jeff had been pacing impatiently, waiting for Daniel to return from his forced slumber. Occasionally he would jab him with the end of a broken shovel handle to see if he'd wake up. He decided that the bucket of water had been most effective, so he sent Sam to the small pond out back to refill the bucket.

Jeff eagerly threw it in Daniel's face, which brought Daniel back into awareness of his unpleasant circumstances. Jeff gestured to Sam with his head toward the cabin, and Sam ran to get the McKinley brothers.

"You see what you did?" Jeff bent over toward Daniel to show him his black-and-blue split lip.

Daniel winced at his own pain as he tried to turn his face from Jeff's ugly display.

"Please, forgive me," Daniel said quietly.

Jeff stood with a shocked expression on his face for a moment and then leaned in again. "Begging for mercy, are ya?"

Sam jogged up behind Jeff, Tom, and Bill McKinley following behind, taking their time in the heat.

Daniel slowly shook his head. "No. I forgive you. Will you forgive me?" Daniel winced as his arms jerked from a spasm caused by the position they were in.

Jeff let out a belly laugh and walked up to his dad and uncle. "He's askin' me to forgive him!" He bent over, slapping his knee.

Tom ignored his son with a scowl. "Welcome back, half-breed. I hope your mind has cleared from your little siesta," Tom drawled, looking him over.

Daniel was too exhausted to raise his head as his face dripped a slowing stream of blood from his cuts.

"Now, I have a question for you," he said, yanking Daniel's head back by his hair. "Where's my Tommy?"

Daniel only cringed but didn't answer. Tom yanked on his hair harder, so Daniel spoke in Navajo. "He is safe."

"Don't even start that, boy!" Tom snarled angrily. He shoved Daniel's head forward and nodded to Jeff, who happily applied the cattle prod to Daniel's ribs.

He cried out in pain but refused to answer in English.

"Tom, let me try," Bill told his brother. He walked up to Daniel and gave Jeff and Sam a cue to stand Daniel up.

Once on his feet, Daniel swayed and trembled, not looking at his captors. He prayed silently for strength because from that point on, he purposed to only speak Navajo. Bill grabbed hold of Daniel's shoulders to hold him steady. Daniel tried to raise his head.

"Daniel, for your own good and for the sake of Jessica, I think you ought to answer Tom's question," he said. Still no acknowledgment came from Daniel. "You don't want him to lose his patience, do you?"

Bill turned and walked around, calmly, appearing to be deep in thought. He walked back up to Daniel. "You were a good sheriff, Danny. Why'd you want to go and destroy your career?" Still only silence. Bill sighed. "I'm worried about Tommy," he said patiently. "Tom and Jeff were too rough on him. They went overboard when he told them he was leaving," he said. "They think he may have come up here to find Jessica. Am I right?"

Daniel remained silent.

Bill paced in front of Daniel, occasionally glancing at him for some indication that he was even listening. "Now, Jessica is a beautiful girl, and I'd hate to see that disappear. I'd also be concerned about your little lady." He got close to Daniel.

Daniel spoke in Navajo. "You and your family will die soon."

Bill only chuckled. "Sam, Jeff, gather 'round now."

They stepped up and gathered around Bill and Daniel.

"That was Navajo. Seems he wants to play boarding school."

Jeff made a face. "What's that?" he asked. "What's a boarding school?"

Bill flashed anger at his brother. "You're supposed to be teaching your boys to know the enemy!" he grumbled.

"Well, Bill, they don't even teach that stuff in school. Why bother?"

"This is why!" He pointed to Daniel. "Jeff, at the boarding schools, they tried to make the Indians white. Beat 'em if they even spoke their language. Get it?"

Jeff let a slow, evil grin spread across his face. "Got it."

"Now, let's try again," Bill said, turning back to Daniel. "Where's Tommy?" He grabbed Daniel's face roughly, forcing him to look at him.

"Careful. You'll get my blood on you," Daniel answered in Navajo.

Jeff jolted Daniel's back with a prod, slamming him to his knees.

The workday finally ended at sunset. Hawk had never felt so tired. Even when he had served in Desert Shield in '89, he'd never known exhaustion quite like this. Every muscle in his body ached, and because they were given little water and few breaks, he was stiff. He hoped that Ben would have by now swooped in with his war party, but it hadn't happened. His other hope was that Daniel was all right and his tracking device was still working.

As the clansmen were loaded into pickup trucks for the ride back to the barn, Hawk was able to catch a glimpse of a five-ton truck parked on the far side of the mining tunnel where ten skinheads were loading gold laden crates into the back. He realized that once the truck was full, they'd have a hefty payment for weapons.

Ben slammed the phone down in frustration, causing Tommy to jump. "They won't be here until the morning."

"Why can't *we* just go? We can get Mr. Patterson and Hawk out and then go back for the rest."

"If we only take Hawk and Daniel, we would endanger the lives of the rest of our brothers, and the Aryans would also clear out. When we go, we get them all out. That's the only way."

"Couldn't we at least go out there and make sure they're all right? We'll wait for the FBI and then strike when they show up. We'll at least have the advantage of a sneak attack as they roar in, right?"

"Maybe," Ben said. He looked at the map and the signal Daniel's chip was sending. "He's about a mile from the back side of mine, so maybe they aren't working him. I just hope he's still alive."

"Let's go find Daniel then," Tommy said eagerly, standing to his feet.

Moments later, Lukas walked in with two small cans of paint.

"Red Tears is still alive," Lukas told them in Navajo.

Tommy and Ben breathed a sigh of relief.

Lukas set the paint down, walked over to Tommy, and sat him back down in his chair. "A warrior must not go to battle without his war paint."

Ben smiled at Lukas's address. Tommy looked at Ben with wide eyes. Lukas opened the cans and painted Tommy's face and then gave a whoop when he was done. Tommy looked in a mirror, and Ben gave him a whoop along with his officers. Tommy just grinned. Ben reached into his drawer and pulled out a gun and a badge. He handed them to Tommy.

"You're one of us now."

Tommy gave his own whoop as the officers slapped him on the back. Tommy clipped the gun to the side of his belt.

Ben handed him an extra clip. "Use them wisely."

"Yes, sir," he said and smiled at Lukas.

"Hokahay!" Joe and Pete shouted.

Tommy looked to Ben, a question on his face.

"Don't ask."

The men loaded Ben's truck with water, ammo, rifles, and binoculars and headed out to get their men back.

Hawk and his Indian brothers were unloaded and marched back inside the barn and locked in their respective stalls. They all studied the man tied in the center of the aisle. Hawk spoke quietly to the Indian in front of him.

"He's my brother, and they hate him even more than us."

Hawk was jabbed with the barrel of a rifle.

"What are you sayin'?" Sam asked. "You speakin' your language, too?" Sam knocked Hawk to the ground. "You get busted up for it if you do, just like this one." He gestured toward Daniel.

"I was just saying it would be great to have a nice juicy steak right now. That's all."

"Yeah, well, bread and water is all that's on the menu. Keeps our costs down."

Hawk waited for the all-clear to get up, and when given it, he did so cautiously and then marched to his stall. His bonds were cut, and he was shoved into his cell, the door slamming loudly behind him with a finality that gave him little hope of escape. The barn finally cleared of all but the prisoners.

Hawk called to Daniel. "Hey, Red Tears."

Daniel slowly lifted his head in the direction of the familiar voice.

Hawk winced at the sight of his face soaked in sweat and blood dripping down over his shoulders and chest. "You don't look too good."

"Had a rough day, Hawk. How about you?" he answered, sarcasm and pain filling his voice.

"Ben should be here any time now. Hang—" He corrected himself, "Be tough, bro."

Daniel's head dropped again.

Jeff, Sam, and the McKinleys returned to the barn. They had with them a loaf of bread and a cooler of water. As Jeff and Sam passed out "dinner," they laughed.

"Gotta keep the work crew strong!" Sam chortled at his little joke, but only Jeff found it funny.

Tom and Bill McKinley walked back to Daniel. "You speakin' our language yet, dog?" Tom kicked Daniel on the left side of his thigh to get his attention. But Daniel's only movement came from the force of the blow. Off in the corner, Jeff watched his father at work while he braided four pieces of bailing twine together.

"Now we realize we've treated you a little roughly. We're willing to make you a little more comfortable in exchange for information on my boy's whereabouts. Does that sound fair?" Tom asked, standing over Daniel. Tom crossed his arms over his chest.

Sam yanked his head back by his hair again for Tom's benefit.

"I said, does that sound fair?" Tom seethed.

Daniel blinked the sweat and blood from his eyes and gave a slight nod. The grip on his hair was released and the cuffs around his wrists removed. Though Daniel was on his knees, the ropes had been the only thing holding him up in his weakened state. When that support was no longer there, he collapsed face-first into the dirt. Bill rolled Daniel to his back with his boot and considered him. He wondered about the pouch around Daniel's neck. He knelt with one knee beside Daniel and took hold of the pouch. Daniel's hand suddenly gripped Bill's wrist with a look of warning. This elicited a derisive grin from the sheriff, and he cut the leather strap from Daniel's neck and tossed it away haphazardly.

The pouch smacked against Hawk's stall. He was the only one to watch its flight path, so he snagged it as it hit the bars and dropped it to the ground, burying it quickly in the shavings.

"Get him up!" Bill said.

Jeff and Sam grabbed Daniel by the wrists and hauled him to his feet. They cabled tied his hands in front of him. Jeff slipped his braided twine around Daniel's neck from behind, pulling on it to let him know what fighting would feel like. Daniel coughed, turning red at the constriction.

"We're going to let you sit down over here for a while," Bill said as Jeff roughly directed Daniel over to a support beam near Hawk's stall. "Let you get your mental energies back. This would be a real good time to think about speaking our language," Bill hinted.

Jeff slipped another loop of braided twine through the "collar" around Daniel's neck and began to tie it around the beam. He shoved Daniel roughly to a sitting position, measuring how much room

Daniel needed to breathe. Jeff gave him just enough. Daniel coughed when he tied it off.

Bill inspected his nephew's work, making sure his dog wouldn't strangle, and then gave him a nod of approval. Bill squatted in front of Daniel. "Now, that's better, isn't it?"

Daniel couldn't answer. He pulled on the twine around his neck, struggling to put slack in his bindings.

"When we get back from dinner, I expect to have an answer about where Tommy is. I love that boy, and I just need to know that he's safe," Bill said. "You do understand love, don't you?" He snickered, slapping the side of Daniel's arm. The group left the barn again.

Hawk hurried to the stall door near the support beam. "Daniel, I'm here," he told his brother.

Daniel managed to look up and to his right to see Hawk.

"I can just touch the rope. Do you have a knife?"

"In my boot," he said, his voice raspy from the twine pressing on his vocal chords.

"Can you reach it?"

"I'll try." Daniel turned and started to get to one knee but lost his balance, almost hanging himself. After struggling, he righted himself and then gasped for air and tried again. "Are you praying?" he asked with slight annoyance.

"Right! Good idea! Great Creator, we could really use some help. Please get us out of here. Amen!" Hawk said.

Daniel's next attempt was successful, and he was able to reach the inside of his boot and retrieve the knife he kept hidden there. He'd had his boots specially made with a leather sheath sewn on the inside of the boot neck so he could always have a back-up weapon. His other knife and gun were dislodged from their holsters when the SUV rolled.

The knife was only six inches long from end to end, but it was sharp. He held it up to Hawk, who managed to grasp it with his fingers. Hawk repositioned the knife in his fingers and could just reach the rope with the blade and began to saw away at the plastic coated twine.

CHAPTER 22

It was dark outside and the hour promised to Daniel had long since passed to the point that the sun had set two hours earlier. Hawk had made some progress with the twine, but having only the tip of the knife to cut with had made the process more daunting.

"Try it now," Hawk said. He craned his neck and checked the ends of the barn for intruders.

Daniel tugged on the rope, trying not to strangle himself in the process. The twine finally broke, and he fell forward to the ground with a thud. After Daniel caught his breath, he got to his feet and held his wrists up for Hawk to now focus on the cable tie.

Hawk worked furiously. "Next time, get a knife with a saw blade on it," he grunted.

"I'll put it on my shopping list," Daniel answered. He looked from one end of the barn to the other, pain wracking his body. "Hurry. They're already late."

"Maybe they forgot," Hawk offered hopefully.

"Somehow I doubt that," Daniel growled back. Finally he was free. He caught his breath, and staggered to a nearby stall. "Where do they keep the keys?"

"They keep 'em with 'em all the time," one of the Indians inside said. The rest gathered at the stall bars. "You're Lukas's grandson, eh?"

"Yeah," Daniel answered, studying the lock on the stall door. "Have you seen any bolt cutters or a crowbar?"

"Naw, man, but every stall's got a ceiling hatch. If you move the hay, maybe we can climb out," Simon said.

Daniel gave a nod. "The ladder's over der," he told him, pointing a finger through the bars in the direction he should go.

Daniel turned, hugged his ribs, and moved as fast as he could toward the end of the barn. He found an attached wooden ladder that led up to the hayloft. Daniel slowly began to climb.

"Daniel, look out!" Hawk warned, but it was too late.

Daniel had only made three rungs when Jeff jolted him with the cattle prod. Daniel lost his grip. He fell in a heap on the ground.

Sam ran to inspect the leash dangling from the post. "He cut it somehow!"

Jeff grabbed the remainder of the choker still around Daniel's neck and used it to drag Daniel to the center of the barn.

Daniel struggled to get to his feet, but Jeff was moving too fast for him. He couldn't get a foothold in the hay and dirt.

"Easy there, Jeff. We need his voice intact," Bill said. He casually sauntered up to the sputtering man on the ground.

Jeff hit Daniel again with the prod, its muted electrical tone coursing through his body as he writhed on the ground. Sam ran up to Jeff to see how he could help punish his attempted getaway.

"Where'd you get the knife, dog?" Jeff demanded.

Daniel gasped in Navajo, "I had it in my boot,"

"Speak English, you stinkin' half-breed!" Jeff kicked him.

"Let's stick to the more important question right now, shall we?" Tom stepped in. "Like where's my son?"

Again, Daniel answered in Navajo. "I already told you. Are you deaf?"

Some of the other Indians laughed in their stalls. Sam raked a shovel across the bars to shut them up. Daniel knew he was only frustrating the fire out of the men and making them even angrier.

"You know what makes you worse than a full blood?" Tom grabbed the choker around Daniel's neck and forced him to his feet. He twisted it, making sure Daniel was very uncomfortable.

Daniel's face turned red as he tried to get air into his lungs, clawing at the twine around his neck. "The fact that you mixed our blood with theirs and polluted it!" he seethed into Daniel's ear.

He shoved Daniel back to the ground where Daniel rubbed his throat, coughing and gagging, chest heaving.

"Put him back on the ropes, boys. Looks like we're gonna have us a hangin' in the mornin'!" Tom announced.

Jeff and Sam whooped with anticipation. They positioned Daniel on his knees, put his wrists in the cuffs, and then tied the ropes off.

"Let's get the lights on," Bill ordered. "I think if he wants to be an Indian, he ought to look like one."

Tom looked at his brother curiously for a moment and then smiled, slowly. "I think we've got some paint in one of the trucks," Tom offered. "Jeff, would you mind getting it for us?"

"Not at all!"

Hawk sank down in the shavings and sat against the wall, now having no hope for Daniel's rescue.

❖ ❖ ❖ ❖

Daniel didn't raise his head but managed to sneak a glance at Jeff, who was carrying in three small cans of paint. Daniel sighed as much as his expanded ribs would allow.

"What's wrong, dog? Having second thoughts about the Indian thing?" Bill McKinley asked. "Look me in the eye, boy!"

When Daniel didn't, Bill raised his head for him by grabbing his hair and yanking his head back. Every nerve in Daniel's body was raw from the repeated electric jolts, and any kind of touch now made him want to scream. But all he could do was push out a breath of pain through gritted teeth.

"Hurry up, Jeff. I want the paint dry by morning," Bill ordered.

Jeff and his dad walked up to Daniel, and Tom gave him some instructions for his canvas. Bill released his grip on Daniel.

Daniel put himself in the Spirit and began to sing a Navajo prayer song. It was weak and halting at first, but the Great Creator gave him breath, and the song became a little stronger.

At first, no one paid attention to Daniel's song, but as he continued, Bill stepped in.

"Shut up!" Bill yelled, striking Daniel across the back with a thin stick.

Daniel's song only momentarily stopped with a yelp of pain. A moment of silence passed, but as Daniel envisioned Jessica and Angel standing on the rock, he took the song up again.

Bill and Tom looked at each other and shook their heads. "You done, Jeff?" Bill asked him.

"Done!" Jeff announced. He stepped back from his masterpiece. He'd painted two black lines down across Daniel's cheeks with red and white stripes across his chest and along his ribs. With that, Bill walked around to face Daniel.

226

Daniel now had the strength to lift his head and face his foes in defiance. "Now that you have put my war paint on, you will surely die tomorrow," Daniel promised in Navajo. "And you will meet the Great Creator and answer to him."

A vicious fist connected with Daniel's face, and he was sent into a dark and painful sleep.

"Now stay quiet!" Tom growled at Daniel. The men left the barn. The generator shut down, and the lights went off.

After a few minutes, a new song began to rise from the barn. Hawk sat up and listened. It was the other Navajo men. He listened as the song of solidarity hung in the air, seemingly intended to breathe life into their brother, Red Tears.

Daniel dreamed about Hawk again. It repeated several times in his unconscious mind. Hawk stepped in front of Daniel as Lukas's spear pierced his heart. Hawk's heart was then lifted up to the Great Creator and then blew away like dust up into the sky. Daniel remained unconscious until he was awakened by a jolt from the cattle prod. He sucked in a painful breath and then let a shaky breath out.

"Stand him up!" Tom ordered.

The other prisoners with Hawk were being led off to work. Hawk caught Daniel's eye for a brief moment and gave him a nod and wink of reassurance. Daniel gave an almost imperceptible nod and dropped his head again as Jeff and Sam lifted him to his feet.

Early that morning, on the plateau above the original mine, Ben, Tommy, Joe, and Pete scanned the area. "According to the dealer, the other entrance is to the south about ten miles," Ben said. Through his binoculars to the south, he found reasonable cover for them. "We need to find Daniel," Ben said, checking the coordinates on the GPS. "Joe, you and Pete head to the south entrance. I'll take Tommy."

They nodded. Ben and Tommy then hustled back to the truck and drove toward Daniel's signal.

Ben stopped near an outcropping of rocks and spied an old homestead through his binoculars about a quarter of a mile out. He looked at Tommy. "We walk in from here."

They grabbed some water and an extra rifle and then started their trek. The sun hadn't given enough light yet, so they had about a half hour of cover. They stopped again and took a position behind a large boulder. They could just make out the barn about seventy-five yards away. There was the sound of a generator, obviously fueling the lights in the barn. From what Ben could tell, there were four white men and a shirtless Indian tied in the center of the barn.

"That has to be Daniel, based on my signal. Find your way into the loft, and don't get caught," Ben instructed Tommy.

Tommy nodded and snuck away, going around the barn to find a way in without being detected.

From what Tommy could see, there was no way to the loft from outside the barn. He searched further and found a door at the back of the barn. He peeked inside to see where it would put him. He found it to be an entrance to the tack room, built off the side of the barn, and it faced out to the side of the first stall. There on the ground was an old axe, so he took it and hung it in his belt. To Tommy's delight and relief, there was a ladder directly in front of him leading up to the hayloft.

The barn was old, so he checked the rungs and prayed they wouldn't squeak or break as he climbed. He scaled the ladder quickly and quietly. Once in the loft, he remained close to the far wall so he wouldn't be seen, in case someone looked up. Suddenly, he ducked out of reflex when he saw a rope spring into the air and over a crossbeam. Cautiously, he belly crawled to the edge of the stall and peered over. He saw Jeff fashioning a noose out of the end of a rope he was holding. By his skill at it, Tommy could tell it wasn't Jeff's first time doing it.

Tommy watched and said a silent prayer as they untied Daniel from the bonds that stretched his arms across the aisle and then cuffed his hands behind him. Tommy could tell that Daniel was badly injured as he swayed on his feet. He could only see his back but could see the welts and bruises there from obvious beatings.

Once again, Daniel took up his prayer song.

"Defiant bugger, ain't ya?" Tom said. He backhanded Daniel in an effort to quiet him.

As the sting of the strike slowly subsided, Daniel started in again. Jeff put the noose around Daniel's neck and synched it down. Bill walked up to Daniel, thrusting a stick under his chin, and made Daniel look at him. Sam and Jeff checked with Bill and at his nod, forced him onto a crate, and then tied the rope off on a hitching rail.

"One last chance, half-breed. Where's Tommy?" Bill asked him.

Daniel looked at Bill. The Indian's face held a look of complete peace. Daniel didn't answer, but a slow smile crept across his split lips

Ben had snuck up to the barn from the other end and searched the loft. He saw Tommy peering over the side watching and waiting for the right moment.

Bill gave a nod, and Jeff kicked the crate out from under Daniel. At that same moment, Tommy let out a war cry and flung himself at the beam. He slammed the axe blade into the hanging rope on the wood. It didn't severe completely until Daniel's weight hit it. Daniel hit the ground hard, along with Tommy. Tommy had the strength to drop and roll, coming up with his gun drawn. Ben joined him from the other end of the barn and shot Sam as he reached for a gun, killing him.

"I'm right here, Dad!" Tommy shouted.

Tom turned in surprise. "What in hell are you doin', boy, taking their side?"

"Move away from Mr. Patterson, Dad!" Tommy warned, ignoring the question.

Tom grabbed Daniel by the arm and yanked him to his feet, not about to take orders from his Indian-loving son.

Ben watched, gun drawn on Jeff and Bill for what might happen next.

"Dad, please. It doesn't have to be like this," Tommy tried to reason.

"You made it like this!" Jeff yelled.

"Shut up, Jeff!" Tom ordered.

"No! You chose to hate!" Tommy shouted back through tears.

Tom hadn't yet pulled his gun but still held Daniel by the arm. Daniel struggled just to stay on his feet.

"Dad, I forgive you. Please, just stop this," Tommy pleaded.

"You forgive me, but you'll still shoot me?" Tom guffawed.

"If I have to."

"Or I could shoot ya," Ben offered.

Tom then shoved Daniel away from him against a stall. Daniel hit the stall wall hard and landed on his right side. Tom then began kicking Daniel. His hands cuffed behind him, Daniel had no way to defend himself.

"Dad, stop!" Tommy yelled.

Ben could do nothing as he kept his gun trained on Jeff and Bill, who stood snickering in amusement at Tom's display of defiance.

"Or you'll what?" Tom dared, kicking Daniel with each word for emphasis. "You'll...shoot...me?"

Tommy fired a warning shot, surprising his family members and Ben. Tom stopped, looking at the bullet hole next to his head in the support beam and decided to back up a step from Daniel's limp form.

"I don't want to shoot you, Dad. I want you back."

Tom looked at his son with an ice-cold stare and then looked at Jeff and Bill. Suddenly he pulled a knife and lunged for Daniel. A deafening crack echoed through the barn.

CHAPTER 23

Hawk was out of the cruiser and running to the barn. The FBI had descended on the mine and freed him and the others who were close behind. Hawk took his place beside Ben, who had just lowered his rifle. His shot put Tom McKinley dead on the ground next to Daniel.

Tommy lowered his gun, his hands shaking from the adrenaline. He slowly walked over to Daniel. He was in shock at what had just transpired and knelt beside the Navajo he'd quickly grown to love and respect. He helped Daniel into a sitting position. Joe and Pete finally arrived and confiscated Jeff and Bill's weapons. Ben and Hawk joined Tommy and Daniel.

"I'm sorry," Ben told Tommy.

"I didn't want to. I couldn't pull the trigger."

"I know," Ben assured him. "One should never have to kill his own father. You forgave him. That's the important thing."

Tommy nodded numbly and went over to his dad's body and sat down next to him. Hawk and Ben helped Daniel up. They removed the noose and handcuffs. Hawk put Daniel's arm over his shoulder and helped him out of the barn.

While Joe was cuffing Jeff's hands behind him, he spoke a snarling warning to Daniel. "You're gonna die, half-breed!"

"Not today," Daniel replied in Navajo.

Jeff released a demonic howl.

Hawk helped Daniel to a nearby truck where he gripped the bed to hold himself up.

"I'll be right back," Hawk told him. Hawk hustled across the barnyard to the vehicle he'd been loaned to get back to the barn from the mine. He had some much-needed water in the cab for his brother. Ben walked up to Daniel to check on him while Joe and Pete escorted

Jeff and Bill out of the barn to a waiting FBI van. Ben handed Daniel his gun. Out of habit Daniel checked the chamber and rounds and clipped it to his jeans.

Ben stood facing the truck bed with Daniel. "You look pretty good in war paint, bro," he said.

"Yeah, I was thinking about making it permanent," he joked back. He wiped some of the paint from his face with his fingers, rubbing them together.

Tommy was just emerging from the barn when he noticed Jeff making a bold move. Jeff had freed himself, using the key he'd taken from Daniel. He grabbed Joe's gun from his holster and in one quick motion slammed the butt of it across his forehead and then took aim at Daniel. Hawk also noticed the move as he headed back for Daniel.

"Daniel!" Both Hawk and Tommy yelled.

Hawk broke into a run. Jeff fired the gun. Hawk took a flying leap through the air and crossed Daniel's path, the bullet penetrating Hawk's heart. Daniel and Ben turned, and both fired, killing Bill and Jeff, not knowing who had actually shot at Daniel. Daniel crashed to his knees, trembling from the exertion and dropped his gun on the ground.

Hawk didn't get up.

Daniel clamored on his hands and knees to his brother's unmoving body. "No," Daniel said desperately. He watched the bloodstain in the center of Hawk's chest soak through his shirt. He took his brother in his arms and sat down, cradling him.

"Gotta watch your back, bro," Hawk breathed out with great effort. He held a smile.

Daniel heard a distant roar as he looked up and saw the rest of the cavalry arriving, their vans loaded with liberated Navajo and their captors.

"You stupid half-breed," Daniel said, trying to hide his concern.

"Thought I was, apple," Hawk sputtered, slowly losing his ability to talk.

"No. You're a warrior," Daniel assured. Hawk's smile was fading. "Need paint."

Daniel took paint from his own face and marked Hawk's.

Hawk's smile grew. "Had a dream." He coughed and swallowed hard, determined to get the words out. "We...gave...our...hearts."

Daniel nodded, knowing the dream well. Now he knew what Hawk's part in it had meant. Hawk reached for Daniel's hand, which he had resting on his wound, and placed his medicine pouch into it. "Build the bridge, Red Tears."

Hawk's eyes closed with a shaky breath, and his hand fell from Daniel's.

Daniel squeezed his medicine bag, staining it with Hawk's blood, and then hugged the dead man to him, rocking him. After a moment, he took up another prayer song. Tommy, Ben, and the now liberated clansmen had gathered around and witnessed the exchange, and now they formed a half circle around Daniel and his fallen brother and joined in his song.

Daniel was back at the hospital.

After the doctor had examined his X-ray, he looked at Daniel, puzzled. "I can see what they did on the outside, but the films aren't reflecting it. I see our repair"—he pointed to the small pins in Daniel's ribs—"but there should be more damage."

"Trust me, Doc, it felt like there should be more damage, but I also know the Great Creator was protecting me."

The doctor frowned slightly, not used to hearing such a testimony.

"I'm mostly healed, right?"

"Right."

"Can you explain that?"

"No, no, I can't." The doctor shook his head, removed the X-rays, and put them away. "I guess miracle comes to mind."

"That's exactly right." Daniel put his shirt on and shook the doctor's hand.

The doctor shook his head again, bewildered, and opened the door.

"Thanks," Daniel said.

Daniel's next order of business was to locate the two women he loved. After finding out where Jessica's room was, he hurried there.

"Dad!" Jessica cried. She threw her arms out toward him as he walked into her room. Angel smiled and stood from her chair, her heart pounding. He gave her a warm smile and a kiss on the cheek and then hugged Jessica and carefully kissed her on the cheek.

"Yanaba. As beautiful as ever," he said.

After a moment's embrace, she released her dad, knowing he was eager to hold Angel. Jessica indicated as much with her expression.

Daniel turned to Angel with a joyful sigh. "My Angel, my wife," he said quietly. He hugged her tightly and then pulled back and looked into her eyes. They sparkled with joy and relief. He kissed her softly and then looked back at Jessica.

"I understand you're going home today?"

"Yes! Angel will help me, if you wait outside."

Daniel gave her a wink and exited the room.

As they drove home, Daniel filled them in on Tommy's experience and Hawk's death.

"Tommy's going to need some time," he told Jessica.

"I understand." She became pensive. "Do you think he blames us?"

Daniel and Angel looked at her.

"Sweetheart, why would you say that?" Daniel said.

Jessica was quiet for a moment. "Because loving us separated him from his family. He had to watch his dad die because of it."

Daniel waited a moment before answering, glancing at Angel whose eyes were closed and lips moving ever so slightly, obviously in prayer.

"Tommy chose God's way of love over the enemy's ways of hate. He chose well. It doesn't mean those decisions are easy and pain free," Daniel explained.

"All decisions come with consequences," Angel added gently, giving Jessica's hand a squeeze.

Daniel could tell that Jessica was contemplating what had been said. The rest of the drive home was silent.

When the trio arrived home, Tommy was waiting for his beloved Jessica. She rushed into Ben's house, and they greeted each other with a long embrace. Angel and Daniel followed and greeted Ben and his wife, Lukas, and Tommy. It was a happy reunion for the most part, though Tommy's and Daniel's losses hung in the air, muting the joy.

Lukas walked up to Daniel and placed his hands on his grandson's shoulders. "You and Tommy must cleanse from the pain," he said in Navajo. "Tomorrow you will go to the sweat for the day to fast and pray to the Great Creator."

Daniel nodded his consent.

"I am proud of you, and so is he."

Daniel told Tommy over dinner what Lukas had said, and Tommy was eager to experience it.

Early in the morning, Ben and Lukas, with Tommy in tow, collected Daniel, and then the men continued on to the sweat where Daniel and Hawk had begun their journey.

"Learn well, heal completely, and return free." Lukas dropped them at the lodge and then drove away.

Daniel, Tommy, and Ben entered the sweat lodge and removed their shirts. Ben started the fire while Daniel grabbed a bucket and went out to the pond for some water.

Tommy watched silently as Ben prepared the fire and took a bunch of white sage hanging on one wall, lit it, and then blew it out so its essence could be released. Daniel returned and slowly poured water on the hot rocks, causing them to sizzle and steam to fill the small building. Daniel and Ben sat on the ground, and Tommy followed suit.

"Tommy, you and Daniel are here to gain back what you have lost. You both lost someone you loved but only recently discovered. That can harden a heart. You must surrender and quiet your heart completely and let the Great Creator heal it. Learn from the bad, and remember the good," Ben said.

Tommy looked at Daniel, who gave him a nod.

"Why aren't we eating?" Tommy said.

"Food kills our desire to hunger. When we aren't hungry, we are lulled into satisfaction and so we do not seek," Ben explained.

"We lose our dependency on our Creator," Daniel added. "But hunger reminds us of who it is that feeds us."

Tommy nodded thoughtfully. "What do I do?"

"Wait. Pray," Ben said.

"How?"

"What is in your heart?" Ben asked.

Tommy remained silent. He didn't like what was in his heart at that moment.

"He's not angry with you. He loves you, son," Daniel assured him.

Tommy looked at Daniel, deeply touched that he had called him "son." He gave a tentative smile.

Daniel and Ben sang the welcome song to the Great Creator, and Ben spent a few more hours with the men in prayer. Afterward, he returned home with the promise of watching over Angel and Jessica.

While Tommy struggled with the issues inside his heart, Daniel opened his medicine bag and spread the symbols out before him. As he looked at them, he asked the Great Creator to show him what they meant. He picked up the stone that had a spiral hand carved into it. He knew it meant healing, but exactly how it applied to him aside from the current healing he needed, he was uncertain. He prayed and asked the Holy Spirit to bring him revelation.

It wasn't long before the Great Creator spoke to him. "*This healing hand is my healing in you. You understand a broken heart. You understand a bitter heart, and you have allowed me to heal those issues. Now I will use you to bring healing to two nations. These two nations are brothers."*

As Daniel heard these words, the burden in his heart, the thing that had been stirring there, became clear, and he began to weep silently. The tears of his people and of his Creator were crying through him.

"Yes, my son Red Tears, I will use you to build a bridge between the First Nations People and what is now America. You are half white and half red by my design. You are a picture of that unity I long to see between the brothers. Stay close. Listen and trust. Remember my resolution."

Daniel picked up the tiny scroll and nodded and then picked up the other stones, now understanding them all. They were all connected to what the Great Creator had just told him.

The white stone with the eagle represented his oneness with the Great Creator and his Spirit. The stone with the red tear, of course, represented his name and the broken heart, the heart of the First Nations People. Daniel shook his head slowly in amazement that the Great Creator of the universe would speak so clearly and lovingly to him. He was overwhelmed as he collected the symbols, replaced them in the pouch, and put it back on. He then sat back and closed his eyes to soak in the revelation of God, who was so personal.

Tommy had been sitting with his knees to his chest, resting his forehead on his arms, crying deeply. He felt safe there with Daniel and so let all the emotions out that had been hammering against the wall of denial he'd built.

"Tommy. I am your Father."

Tommy was surprised at the voice and looked up, wiping his tears. He thought Daniel had said it. "W…what?" he asked.

Daniel opened his eyes. "I didn't say anything."

"Someone said, 'I am your Father.'"

"That would be God."

"God, as in the Great Creator God?" Tommy said incredulously.

"Uh huh."

"He talks to people?"

"Why wouldn't he?" Daniel said, wiping sweat from his eyes.

"Because he's so…" Tommy didn't know what to say.

"Untouchable? Far away?" Daniel offered.

"Yeah."

"He's not. He's here." Daniel tapped his own chest. "Just relax and listen to him. He won't lie to you. Ever," Daniel assured.

Tommy smiled uncertainly, and Daniel leaned back, closing his eyes again. Tommy watched Daniel. He seemed to have such peace, even though tears streamed down his face, in deep communion with the Great Creator's Spirit.

"Your heart has a deep wound in it. If you allow me to heal it, my peace will grow out of that wound. It seems a difficult thing, but nothing is too hard for me. I have given you a new family who loves you. They will help you heal."

"Thank you, God. I want your peace," Tommy cried, covering his face.

Both men left the sweat lodge with stronger hearts and were ready to move on—Tommy to study in the life of the Great Creator in order to prepare himself for a life with Jessica. Daniel knew he was to speak before the Senate; he just didn't know how that was to transpire.

CHAPTER 24

At breakfast one morning, Jessica finally told Daniel of the dream she'd had the night before their wedding. "Dad, you're supposed to speak to the fathers," she told him after describing the dream to him.

Angel looked at Daniel.

He froze in the middle of bringing a spoon to his mouth. He looked at her.

"I believe the Great Creator wants you to speak to the Senate," Jessica clarified.

Angel sat back. "I have to agree," Angel said.

Daniel now looked at her.

"I had the same dream, but I was standing beside you." She took his hand and squeezed it. "I'll venture to guess you also had this dream."

Daniel slowly nodded. He was always amazed at God's incredible ways of communication. Once again, Daniel began to weep. Jessica and Angel took their cue and left him alone with the Great Creator.

"My son, why are you afraid? Have I not made you a warrior? Is it me you doubt or yourself?"

Daniel was sprawled out on the kitchen floor, listening, trying to be the brave he was. "I don't know, Father. But you do. Forgive me for doubting. I don't want to be afraid, and I don't want to doubt."

"Have I ever abandoned you?"

"No, sir."

"Have I ever broken a promise?"

"No, sir."

"Do you have faith in me, and do you trust me?"

"Yes, sir." Daniel felt the heaviness lift from him as if the Creator himself was in the room, helping him off the floor. Daniel got up and stood there in surrender.

"You are willing then?"

Daniel let out a chuckle at the Creator's kindness and grace. "Yes, I am. Thank you for trusting me."

"*I know your heart, Red Tears. Don't worry. Trust me, and you will see it happen.*"

"Thank you," he whispered to the air and sat down again.

The girls returned, and he marveled at their timing.

Angel knew what Daniel was thinking. "We know when he's done with you." Angel smiled.

"Are you okay, Dad?"

Daniel smiled. "I'm not only okay. I'm great because I have two women who can hear God speaking. How much more blessed could I be?"

The phone rang then, and Jessica answered. "Hello? Oh hi, Maria, just a minute. He's right here." Jessica handed the phone to Daniel.

"Hi, Maria. That's great. Okay, I'll be there in a couple of hours. Thanks." He hung up the phone and looked at Jessica. "The house sold."

Jessica nodded with a less than enthusiastic smile. "It's final, I guess. All that I've ever known is gone, except for you, Dad."

Daniel stood and embraced her tightly. "It's a good thing, Jess. We can't live on past memories."

"I know," she agreed.

"I don't suppose you want to come along?"

"No, you and Angel go. I want to spend some time with Tommy."

Daniel kissed the top of her head. "All right."

Daniel and Angel pulled in front of the real estate office and walked in.

Shortly, Doctor Thompson walked in. "Sorry I'm late, folks!" he said, removing his hat.

"Hey, Doc, what are you doing here?" Daniel grinned, shaking his hand. "This is Angel, my new bride."

"And what a beautiful bride she is!" he said, giving her a gentle hug and then kissing the back of her hand. "Well, let's get this done, shall we?"

"Get what done?" Daniel said, quite confused.

"Daniel, Doc Thompson bought your house," Maria informed him.

Daniel stared at the doctor in dumbfounded silence.

Thompson slapped him on the back. "That's just what I thought you'd say." He laughed. "The house is all yours, Daniel."

"But the house was already paid off. I don't understand."

Angel gave an amused smile.

"It's simple, my boy! I bought your house, and now I'm giving it to you as a gift, and you get the money from it, too!"

"But why?" he had to ask.

Angel nudged him. "Don't look a gift horse in the mouth, dear."

"I can't take it with me. In case you haven't noticed, I'm getting up there in age. You're my only family left, and if you must, call it a wedding gift."

"Doctor Thompson, thank you for such a wonderful gift!" Angel gushed, and she hugged him tightly.

Daniel still stood flabbergasted at what he'd just heard.

"Snap out of it, son. We need to sign these papers and get your check."

Daniel finally nodded and closed his mouth. Angel steered him to the desk where he and Thompson signed all the necessary papers, and then Maria handed the deed and the check over to Daniel. His hands were shaking with excitement and awe. This he suspected was another gift from the Great Creator. Daniel smiled at Angel. They embraced in laughter.

"Wow," was all he could manage.

Daniel took Angel to meet Marge and treated her to lunch there, and then they drove home to the rez, eager to share the news with Jessica.

"I think this would be a great gift for Jess and Tommy when they get married," Daniel beamed. "She loved that house and to have it as her own and to have a place she and Tommy could settle into worry free. It does my heart good."

"Love always does," Angel agreed. She looked at Daniel, curiously. "Are you expecting Tommy to propose to Jessica?"

"He better!" Daniel looked at Angel as they both began to laugh.

At home, Jessica did all she could to stop herself from screaming, but as she looked at her dad and Angel, who both held grins plastered on their faces, she could hold back no longer. She jumped into her dad's arms, and he spun her around as she laughed.

"Shall I talk to Tommy?" he asked her as he set her down. "You know, give him the green light?"

"I don't want to push him, Dad," she said.

Angel hugged her and pushed the hair out of her face. "You're ready," she affirmed.

"And he's ready," her dad assured her.

Daniel was outside later that afternoon trying to create a garden for Angel. He wanted so badly to take his bride to Hawaii, but he felt he had to wait to hear from the Great Creator about going to the senate.

Ben pulled up and walked over to him. "She's got you working hard, eh, bro?"

Daniel straightened up and looked at Ben. "It's the least I can do since we haven't taken our honeymoon. Anyone else out there missing lately?"

Ben shook his head. He reached into his back pocket, pulled out an envelope, and handed it to Daniel.

Daniel let the hoe drop and wiped his hands on his jeans. "What's this?" he said, opening the envelope. He pulled out two round trip tickets to Washington, DC. "Wait, how did you—? Never mind." He shook his head in amazement. "I'll never get used to this."

"Good, because if you do, then pride has gotten in. Better to stay amazed."

Daniel smiled at Ben and nodded. "Guess I better get us packed, eh?"

Daniel and Angel settled into the hotel room in DC that Ben's friend had arranged for them. He had also arranged a meeting with a key senator involved with Resolution 14. After that point, Daniel had no idea what was to take place. All he knew was what the Great Creator had told him that he would speak to the fathers.

There was a knock on their door, and Daniel answered it.

"You must be Daniel Patterson," the man said. "I'm Frank Wilson. I'm your guide, so to speak. If you're ready, we'll get started."

Daniel wanted to ask where they were going but stifled the desire, opting to practice being delightfully surprised. "Sure, come in. I'll get my bride," Daniel said, stepping aside and offering his hand to Frank.

Daniel walked through the suite to the bedroom where Angel was just putting on a pair of earrings.

"Beautiful as ever." Daniel grinned. "Our tour guide is here."

Daniel introduced Angel, and then the three left the hotel.

Frank drove through DC, causing Daniel and Angel both to realize they had been born for wide-open spaces and beautiful landscapes.

"Beautiful, isn't it?" Frank glanced at Angel in the front seat.

"Beauty is in the eye of the beholder," Angel said with a polite smile.

"I know. It's got to be in your blood to live in a place like this. But this is where I'm supposed to be, and I can feel God's hope for this city—and his grief."

Daniel looked out his window at the humanity screaming by. He wanted to feel the Great Creator's hope as well, but at the moment, the grief part was consuming him. "Yeah," Daniel agreed quietly.

Frank looked in the rearview mirror and saw Daniel's expression.

Daniel changed the subject. "So how do you know Ben? You two are worlds apart."

"Has he ever told you about his friend in the Bureau?"

"So you're that guy?"

"That would be correct."

"Tell me, how do I get this chip out of me?"

"You don't."

"Great."

"Don't worry. It stays put for the most part. No ill effects."

"No one's going to pick up my signal accidentally and ambush me, right?"

"Each chip has its own signal for a specific mission. Once the mission is over, it's deactivated."

"Oh, here we are! The Lincoln Memorial. Let me drop you here, and I'll go park."

Daniel and Angel got out and stood in front of the gargantuan statue of Abraham Lincoln. After Daniel's vision, he and Angel had researched Mt. Rushmore and found out a few unpleasant things about the one president who seemed to have a heart. But, as is the history of America, history books only told the good side of the president in order to create for themselves yet another idol to fit their ideals.

Daniel pulled in halting breaths, trying to keep the emotions of his Creator from overtaking him. At least he wasn't crumpling to the ground, and for that he was thankful. Angel squeezed his hand, knowing what was tugging at his heart. "I can't do this," he said, turning from the monument and looking out across the capital mall.

"You can, Daniel."

"No, I mean stand here and take this in," he gestured behind him. "I just want to go back to the hotel room and pray."

Frank rounded the corner, and Angel went up to him to explain the situation. Daniel watched as he nodded in understanding and went back for the car.

Daniel was silent for the return to the hotel until he got out of the car. "Frank, I appreciate the tour, but I wasn't expecting this reaction."

"I understand. I was overwhelmed when I first got here, too. Just let me know the timing of the meeting, and I'll come and get you. I'm at your service."

"Thanks," Daniel said, offering his hand. They shook, and then he and Angel went to their room.

Daniel unpacked his white sage and an abalone shell, and then he set it up at the foot of the bed and removed his shirt and boots. Angel sat beside him and prayed.

Daniel lit the white sage, blew it out, set it in the shell, and waved the smoke over him. "Come, Holy Spirit. I need you," he said quietly. He then inhaled deeply and waited with his eyes closed.

Daniel was standing in a long white hallway. On either side of the hallway were white pedestals with blood dripping from them. Each pedestal held the bust of a president of the United States. As Daniel walked slowly down the hall, he could see the progression of each president until he reached the last. The last pedestal was empty. He looked back down the hall as it seemed to stretch to eternity. He turned back and found himself face-to-face with the current president. The president had tears in his eyes, and then he dropped to his knees before Daniel.

Daniel reached down and lifted him to his feet. "I am just a man like you," he said.

The president nodded, and the two men grasped each other's arms in a greeting.

"I am sorry for all that has been done to your people," the president began. "I see that my pride was taking me down the same path as those who have gone before me."

Daniel remained silent, feeling compassion in his heart for this man who needed the Great Creator.

"The position of power is intoxicating, and when the position has an historical bent to it, like my color, then one feels invincible. To rule a nation and own the land, to pass laws to control people…" The president stopped there and looked down.

"It is only for the Great Creator," Daniel said.

The president nodded. "Can you forgive us?"

"For the healing of this nation, we must. Forgiveness has a power all its own. We do forgive and ask that you be guided by his Spirit and not that of power," Daniel told him.

The president then stepped aside, and a giant white buffalo appeared before Daniel. For a flash of an instant, Daniel was afraid, just because of the sheer size of the animal. But the fear faded quickly, and the animal took a step toward Daniel. Daniel looked up into his eyes, and the buffalo breathed on Daniel. He inhaled, smelling an unusual scent of sweet incense, the force of the breath seemed to penetrate his being. As Daniel opened his eyes, the buffalo kicked open a door behind him and then turned and walked through. Daniel followed and the animal disappeared.

Daniel opened his eyes and found himself still kneeling on the floor at the foot of the bed. Angel was singing a quiet song beside him. He smiled at her and touched her knee.

She opened her eyes and sighed. "All is well," she said.

"Yes," he agreed. Daniel stood, put his shirt on, and then walked to the large sliding glass window of their balcony. He stepped out and watched as people, oblivious to the spiritual climate, went about their busy day. "How long was I gone?" he asked after a few moments.

Angel joined him on balcony. "About two hours."

The phone rang, and Daniel returned to the room to answer.

"Daniel, this is Frank. You're not going to believe this!"

"I might." Daniel smiled to himself.

"Great, because I had trouble believing it. I went back to the capital, and I was having dinner with some friends. They all work with senators and congressmen. Anyway, they were talking about the buzz going through the capital. Everyone's been having these dreams," he explained.

"Dreams?" Daniel was indeed surprised, if only for a moment. He knew the Creator was at work. "Go on," he urged.

"Well, it seems the dreams are the same. Something about a buffalo, a hallway, and two Native Americans."

Daniel sat down on a chair nearby. He would have fallen down otherwise. The point about two Native Americans stumped him. "I just had that one a couple of hours ago. Actually, it was a vision. I was in it, but the president was the only one with me."

"Whoa!" was all Frank could come up with.

There was a long silence as Angel went up to Daniel and rubbed his back, noticing the befuddled look on his face.

"Do you have a time frame?" Frank asked.

"Not yet."

"I think it'll be soon."

"Yeah, that's the feeling I'm getting, too," Daniel confirmed. "So I guess we just wait.

"Right. I'll be in touch."

"Thanks, Frank." The two men hung up. Daniel took Angel's hand as she moved around to face him.

She knelt in front of him. "Good news?"

"The Great Creator is talking to people at the capitol," he told her with a shrug. "I thought I could expect what he'd do, but for everyone to have the same dream as my vision—" He just shook his head.

Angel smiled. "Come on. Let's get some rest," she suggested, rising and pulling him with her.

As they settled into bed for the night, Daniel needed reassurance. "You're going to be right there with me, aren't you?"

"As far as the Great Creator will allow," she said, snuggled against his side.

He regarded her with concern, so she looked up at him. "I don't think I'm actually supposed to be in the room with you. That's what I mean."

Daniel nodded slowly. He relaxed with his new bride in his arms and fell asleep.

Daniel was once again walking down the long white hallway lined with the presidents. This time, they were all lying face down on their pedestals, still bleeding. Daniel felt a strong presence close to him, yet he was the only one there in the hallway.

"I am with you. I will be with you in the room. Do not fear," the Great Creator told him. Daniel turned to his left, and there standing before him was the Great Chief, wearing white Indian celebration regalia. Daniel

immediately dropped to his face before him in reverence and honor. The Great Chief bent and took hold of his arms and stood Daniel to his feet. Daniel was trembling in his presence, and he touched him again. Daniel could feel strength return to his body. "They will be astounded." He smiled.

Daniel nodded. "What do I do?"

"Trust me and listen. Say what you hear," the Great Chief instructed. "Do you know what the number fourteen represents?"

"No, sir."

"It represents a double measure of divine perfection."

Daniel blinked, and then Jesus disappeared. Suddenly, Daniel understood the significance of the resolution's number. It had been number fifteen in the beginning, meaning "acts shaped by the energy of divine grace." It also represented government, unity, and grace itself. Now that it had been renumbered for the 111th Congress, to fourteen, God was sending a message. It was time for this resolution, God's resolution, to be enacted.

Daniel sat up in the bed, breathing quickly at the revelation he'd just had.

Angel sat up beside him. "Are you okay?"

"Yeah," he said, slowly getting his bearings. "It was a dream."

"A good one?"

He looked at her, and a slow smile spread across his lips. "Yeah."

The next morning, Daniel awoke to the sound of a ringing telephone. He carefully climbed out of bed and hurried to the next room. "Hello?"

"Daniel, this is Frank. Senator Brownback just called me and wants to talk to you. It's time, buddy."

"Yeah, the Great Creator told me last night in a dream," Daniel informed him. "Today is the day."

"He works fast, doesn't he?"

"That's for sure."

"Let me tell you something," Frank added. "This is unprecedented. Things don't happen this fast in Washington."

"Should I laugh?" Daniel chuckled.

He heard Frank chuckle back, but then he got quiet. "I don't know."

Daniel felt the Creator's Spirit tugging at him to prepare. "I need to get ready."

"Yeah, okay. I'll be there in an hour."

Once he was dressed, he woke Angel. He sat on the bed beside her. She was always an early riser, but he figured she needed the rest, or perhaps the Great Creator was honing him to be less dependent on her for his spiritual strength. He was called to be the warrior, after all, and he could feel the Creator working that in him and building his confidence.

He looked at her beautiful features and gently brushed the hair out of her face with a smile. "Angel," he called softly to her.

Before her eyes opened, there was a smile on her face. She turned her head in his direction and looked at him. "Good morning," she said, sounding completely awake.

"How do you do that?" he asked her with amusement.

She leaned up on her elbow. "Do what?"

"Wake up without sounding like you just woke up?"

She moved to get out of bed, and he stood to get out of her way. She put her arms around his neck and gave him a quick kiss. "It must be a gift." She shrugged with a smile. "You have an appointment," she then said, looking into his eyes.

He nodded, still feeling the tug from earlier. He released her. While she showered, he met with his Creator.

Frank drove them to the Senate office building, a rectangular fortress; trees dotted the landscape. There was no parking anywhere near the building, making the long approach an even heavier task for

Daniel. It gave him more time to ponder what was about to take place inside.

"You have my authority and my power to carry this out. I am with you", the Great Creator whispered to him.

Frank ushered Daniel and Angel to the Senate hall to Senator Sam Brownback's office. Again, Daniel and Angel were struck by the size and grandeur of even his office. Frank spoke to the secretary.

She stood. "Mr. Patterson, welcome to Sam Brownback's office. He's eager to meet you." She smiled, shaking his hand.

"Thank you," was all Daniel could muster at the moment. *Come on, Red Tears. Pull it together*, he told himself as she ushered the three inside.

The door closed, and Senator Brownback stood from behind his desk. He stepped from around it and strode up to Daniel. He offered his hand, remaining silent for a moment, but Daniel and Angel could see a hint of moisture in his eyes.

"Sir," Daniel said.

"Mr. Patterson, I had a dream about you."

Daniel needed to settle his nerves and so opted for a lighthearted response. "There seems to be a lot of that going around lately." He grinned.

The senator slapped Daniel on the back and grinned. "Please, sit down. Is this your wife?"

Daniel blushed for not remembering to introduce her. "Yes, this is Angel. We were just married a week ago."

"Congratulations!" Senator Brownback took her hand and shook it gently.

As they got comfortable, he began his questions. "What is your heart, Daniel?"

Daniel sat back to gather his thoughts. "I know that the Great Creator has sent me with a word from him regarding Resolution 14," he began. "I don't know what that word is yet, but I know, when it is spoken, Resolution 14 will not be denied." Daniel paused. "I was an unwilling participant at first, but God has shown me that it is his will to use me."

"We'll never know why, will we?" Brownback offered. "All we can surmise is that he knows our hearts."

Daniel nodded in agreement.

"You do understand that this is something that's never happened before—a civilian on the floor of the Senate?"

Daniel looked at him, needing clarification. "What exactly do you mean by that?"

"I believe you are to present this to everyone in the Senate, meaning all of the senators in America. I've already set it up. I think it's obvious that God has sent you, and we cannot deny you getting on the floor. In fact, there are ten others who are backing you as you go in, and they also back the resolution. Some of them don't know the truth behind the resolution. What's your take on it?"

"All I know is what the Creator has told me. He said that the resolution is his word and his word is his resolution, meaning his Word resolves all conflicts and heals all wounds and brings repentance, forgiveness, and reconciliation," Daniel espoused.

"This land is in great need of that. I had a group of First Nations People come and meet with me in 2003. They spoke of the spiritual significance of this apology that has gone so long ignored," Brownback said. He stood and walked to the window, gazing out over the lawn. He had seen some of the documentary films, and now scenes from them flashed in his memory. "It took me a while to understand what they were saying, but I finally got it and felt that God wanted me to write this resolution and present it to the Senate. What I never understood was how important it is to God," he said, turning and wiping his eyes with his handkerchief. "This is it, Daniel. He wants his word to stand, and we are called to stand beside this word, this resolution." Brownback returned to his seat.

"Thank you, sir," Daniel said. "I must tell you that I had a vision of Mt. Rushmore crumbling down," he said. "I didn't know what it could mean until just now." Daniel sat forward, feeling the intensity return to his heart, pushing all the fear way. "It is God's people invading the spiritual realm of the present systems in place and breaking the bondages created by those who are now manipulating the system. It is a picture of their system being destroyed by the word of the Lord."

Senator Brownback, Frank, and Angel all pondered this new revelation.

The senator then looked at the clock on the wall. "Daniel, I expect that what he said will happen, *will* happen. Let's go watch, shall we?" He stood up.

Frank, Daniel, and Angel followed the senator out of his office to an elevator. The four stood in silence as the elevator eased downward. The doors opened, and they boarded a tram that took them underground to the Capital Building. Another elevator took them to the ground floor. Daniel's heart pounded in his chest when the doors opened, and he slowly followed the senator, Angel, and Frank out to the lobby. The senator led them down a hallway. As they walked, other senators gathered there stopped to stare at Daniel. Daniel began to feel uneasy with all the eyes on him, but he remembered the dream and knew this was the hall in his dream, even though it wasn't white and lined with the presidents.

"Why are they staring at me like they know me?" Daniel leaned in to Frank.

"They had your dream. They must recognize you," he offered.

The sea of people in the hall split, allowing Daniel, Angel, Frank, and Senator Brownback through.

Daniel looked to his left, and there was the Great Chief beside him. Like in his second dream, he was completely in white Native regalia, very tall and glowing with an almost blinding light. "*Your brothers have plowed this ground, and now you will plant.*" He smiled at Daniel and urged him forward.

Daniel puffed his chest out slightly and lifted his head, sensing the authority now coursing through his heart and body.

Daniel stood by the door to the senate room, feeling his heart crash against his chest as the hallway emptied.

Angel rubbed his arm with a sweet smile. "I'll be right here," she said, and she touched his heart. "And he will be right here," she told him, touching his heart again and then his lips. "And here."

CHAPTER 25

As Senator Brownback ushered Daniel through the massive doors of the Senate Chamber and they stepped inside the filled to capacity room, there was an immediate silence as everyone turned to look at Daniel Red Tears Patterson. Daniel froze for a moment until he saw huge white-clad warriors stationed at every door of the chamber and flanking him. As he stepped forward, the two flanking him moved with him. If God hadn't yet gotten through to him of the authority and power he had been given for this moment, he understood it now and walked with humble confidence beside Senator Brownback to the senator's desk.

"Your supporters have a red flag on their desks," Senator Brownback told him.

Whispers went around the room, indicating that most, if not all, of the three hundred-plus in attendance somehow recognized the Native American man standing with the senator.

The Senate session commenced with the recognition of the majority leader and the acting president pro tempore. The senate majority leader then asked for the Pledge of Allegiance to be recited, and afterward he introduced Senator Brownback. Daniel bristled slightly at the rigid dialog of the Senate but then remembered that God was about to break through.

Senator Sam Brownback stood and addressed the Senate floor. "Mr. Reid, Madam President, I ask unanimous consent that Daniel Red Tears Patterson be allowed ten minutes or so to offer one last word regarding Senate Joint Resolution 14 and that when he is done we, the Senate, proceed to immediate consideration of the resolution."

There was a vote, and then Daniel was given a nod by Senator Brownback.

Daniel stood, trembling as the Creator's power coursed through him. "Th...thank you, sir," Daniel said to Brownback. He cleared his throat as the people on the raised bench looked at him from their power perches.

"Mr. Patterson, I understand it seems a daunting thing to speak to us, but I assure you, we are just everyday people. There is nothing to be afraid of," the president pro tempore told him.

"Thank you, Madam President," Daniel said. He slowly continued as the Creator spoke through him. "As I'm sure you all must understand, this resolution does not ask for recompense for damages done throughout the years, but rather it is an issue dealing with the heart of the nation. This nation's heart is sick and diseased and cannot function as it was designed by the Great Creator. The host people of this nation reached out in peace, and the government, set up without their permission, returned their offer, not with peace but death."

There was a slight mumble that waved through the chamber until a loud crash of a gavel reverberated. Everyone looked around, understanding that the sound had not come from Madam President, and saw the sentries at the doors, standing at attention. The attendees were shocked at what they beheld, some blinking to clear their eyes, some wiping their eyes with their fingers, and then the room became still and silent.

Daniel felt the Great Chief next to him and his touch on his shoulder as a signal to continue. "The crime, hate, abortion, moral decay, and economic struggle we are facing daily is not a coincidence or a temporary downturn. It is a signal that should be loud and clear that this nation has arrogantly turned from its true leader, the Great Creator." He paused, awaiting backlash, but the room remained transfixed on him. "If you truly care about America, you must turn your eyes to heaven and cry out to God in repentance on behalf of our cruelty toward the First Nations People. We speak of the rights of all people, the equality of all people, but when those thoughts are called upon to be acted out, it is pride that stops us."

"Excuse me, Mr. Patterson, but why do you address us to include you?" the president pro tempore asked.

"In delivering this message, I am not above you. I am not full-blooded Native American, but I am half white and half Navajo. I speak as one responsible, and I cast no blame nor pass judgment," Daniel answered.

She nodded and indicated that he continue.

"I am a picture of what America was and is to be. Two brothers unified as one. Our white pride must die, and we must cry out to the Great Creator for falsely claiming his name as the First Nations People were treated with disrespect. What fools and liars we have been to kill our brothers, our hosts, our allies and break treaties and our word because we see ourselves as better due to the color of our skin. We must cry out to him who gave us all breath and admit our sins and ask for forgiveness and help," Daniel said as tears streamed down his face and his body visibly shook.

The whole row of senators beside him was now weeping as the sound of muffled nose blowing moved around the enormous room.

"This is the only way America can rise up and live and give life to other nations. Otherwise, we remain vulnerable to outside attack and America's heart will be crushed." Daniel paused for a moment. He felt there was just a little more as his breaths came haltingly, and he tried to contain the emotion building inside. "Pride comes before the fall, and so it seems that we desire to fall, for we refuse to repent. May the Great Creator have mercy on us all!"

The chamber remained silent as some of the senators looked from Daniel to the sentries at the doors and slowly came to the realization that to speak out against this man before them would be detrimental.

A holy fear seemed to hold the people in its grip as Daniel sobbed before them in humility. His emotions became contagious, and the senators in his row one by one fell to their knees with their faces to the floor. Again, this too was contagious, and others in the chamber felt compelled to follow suit. There was a low mumbling and the sound of women audibly crying. The president pro tempore and the majority leader sat back in dismay, feeling the weight of "something" in the room but not knowing what or who that something was.

They tried to discreetly wipe tears from their eyes. Daniel eased himself into his chair, still trembling and awaiting the verdict from the appointed powers in front of him.

After several uncomfortable moments, Senator Brownback was able to rise from his prone position and shakily stand. "Madam President, I expect you understand something of what has just taken place here, and so I ask unanimous consent of immediate consideration of Senate Joint Resolution 14 and that, when passed, it be flagged as historic and hand delivered to the President of the United States for his signature," Brownback announced.

Mr. Reid, the senate majority leader, then stood and confirmed Senator Brownback's motion.

"Without objection, it is so ordered," Madam President answered, slamming the gavel down on her podium. "All in favor of passing and enacting Senate Joint Resolution 14, say 'Aye.'"

The chamber resounded with a booming consent—at least that's what it sounded like to Madam President. "All opposed, say no." There was then a booming silence. "It is unanimously agreed to," she declared.

Daniel and Senator Brownback both wept for joy. Daniel stood up, shook hands with Brownback, and then they hugged.

"He did it, Daniel!" Brownback said as Daniel grinned with a nod.

Daniel slipped out of the chamber and met Angel and Frank.

"How'd it go?" Frank asked excitedly.

Angel had a feeling from seeing the tears in his eyes and smile on his face.

"It passed unanimously and is being hand delivered to the president as we speak," Daniel said.

Angel hugged him tightly, and Frank slapped him on the back. "Okay! Now what?"

"I think we ought to thank the Great Creator," Angel suggested.

The two men nodded, and they started down the hall.

A man in a black suit, escorted by two Secret Service agents, walked with purpose toward the Oval Office inside the White House. The president was standing on the balcony facing west, taking in the landscape of DC as he contemplated the dream he'd had the night before. It seemed a strange dream, so he hadn't told anyone.

The three men entered the office of the president's secretary. When he looked up, he knew what it was about, having received a call from the vice president only twenty minutes earlier.

❖ ❖ ❖ ❖ ❖

He stood with urgency and walked into the Oval Office. "Mr. President, it's here," he informed him.

The president turned from the balcony and considered what was about to happen. He realized then that the dream he'd had had everything to do with this document. "Send them in," he said, and he stood in front of his desk.

The man in the black suit was ushered in, and he handed the sealed 8x10 envelope to the president. Holding the document felt strange somehow. It felt heavy in his hands, and he felt weightiness in his very being. He sucked in a staggered breath and then looked up. The vice president then stepped inside the office. The president relaxed slightly and walked around to his chair and sat down. The press would be invited in later when the senate had adjourned and the president could get a briefing on what exactly had prompted this urgent signing.

He pulled a pen from the drawer and opened the envelope. Slowly he pulled the document from its covering and read it slowly while the vice president and the messenger stood by reverently. He stifled the building emotions inside him as he finished reading the document. He cleared his throat and signed it. He replaced the document into the envelope and handed it back to the messenger, who made a hasty retreat from the office.

"I had a dream about this," the president said.

The vice president nodded. "Sir, I think all of Capitol Hill has had the same dream," he replied.

The president looked at him in shock. "How does something like that happen?"

"There are reports that God sent the dream," the vice president informed him carefully.

The president just blinked. He'd never really considered God before. He'd grown up without him, but now a slow fear began to grip his soul, a fear that God was not to be ignored or mocked. "I need some time. Cancel my appointments until the Senate gets out, and then let me know. I want to speak to all of them, and then we'll let the press in for the signing ceremony," he informed the vice president.

"Yes, sir," he said, turning to go, but he stopped at the door. "Do you really want to know what happened? What if it was God?"

"If it was, we have a lot to get in order, don't we?" the president inferred.

The vice president gave a nod and left the Oval Office bewildered.

Frank stood on the curb at the airport as Daniel picked up his and Angel's suitcase.

"You certainly pack light," Frank quipped.

"If you can believe it, it's Angel who did the packing." He grinned.

"Years of missionary travel," Angel informed Frank.

Frank nodded. He looked at Daniel and felt a strong bond with his brother in the Lord.

"Daniel, I'm glad to have met you," he said, shaking his hand.

"We do it this way on the rez," Daniel said, and he showed him the arm grasp used by the Native Americans. "It creates a stronger and closer bond. Thank you, my brother."

Frank smiled and then turned to Angel. "Angel, it was nice to meet you. I'm honored."

"Thank you for being our scout, Frank, and many blessings to you and your wife."

"Hey, if you ever need to get out of this flurry, come on out to the rez. You're always welcome," Daniel said.

"We just might do that. Thanks. Safe trip," he said, and then Daniel and Angel made their way inside the airport terminal.

Back on the reservation, Daniel and Angel were taking in the sunset of their Sunday, sitting on their rock. "How do you feel?" she asked her husband.

He gave a slight chuckle and then looked at her. "I'm blessed because I have you."

"No, silly, I mean about what happened in Washington."

"I am in awe that the Creator chose me to deliver his message. I feel honored and in a dangerous place," he expressed.

"Why dangerous?"

"Well, think of it. Here I am, this little nobody in Arizona—"

"A son of the King," Angel corrected.

He smiled at her. He knew that was true, but that wasn't the point. "A son of the King," he repeated. "But a son made of the dust of the earth, who can make mistakes very easily."

"That's true, but you have to remember grace and that the Creator knows your heart better than you do. As long as you keep it open to him and the guidance of his Spirit, he will look past your mistakes and continue to cover them in the blood of his Son. But you already know that." She smirked at him.

He had to smile sheepishly. "Yeah, I do."

"Daniel, he's not going to let you fall."

"I know, but the responsibility is frightening, to say the least."

Angel rubbed his back and kissed his cheek.

"It feels good to be home, doesn't it?"

"Yes, it does, and I was hoping we could celebrate that tonight," she hinted.

He turned and looked into her eyes with a bright smile. He leaned in and kissed her hungrily. "Let's get home then, eh?"

The phone rang early the next morning. It was Ben. Shortly, there was a knock on Daniel and Angel's bedroom door.

"Sorry to disturb you guys, but Ben says there's a news report on all the channels about the resolution," Jessica told them through the door.

Angel answered the door in her bathrobe. "Hi, Jessica," she greeted cheerily.

"Hi, Angel." Jessica smiled, offering a hug.

"What are you so excited about?"

"I'll tell you both later," she said firmly but still barely able to contain the surprise she had in store.

"Can you ask him to record it?" Angel said. "We'll be over later, after breakfast."

"Okay. Breakfast will be ready in a half an hour," Jessica warned her with a wink.

Angel grinned.

Jessica stood there about to burst and finally broke down. "Oh, okay!" she said, and she then lowered her voice.

"Trying to sleep in here!" Daniel said from inside the bedroom.

"Liar!" Angel threw back.

Jessica laughed.

Angel then looked at her adopted daughter again. "What?" she said conspiratorially.

Jessica grabbed her hand and squeezed it. "Tommy asked me to marry him," she squealed quietly.

Angel joined her as they both made small bunny hops and hugged.

"Don't make me come out there!" Daniel called.

"I better get back in there," Angel said. "Congratulations!" she whispered.

"Don't tell Dad. I want to do it."

"Okay," Angel promised, and then she disappeared back into the bedroom.

Daniel, Angel, and Jessica walked over to Ben's house after they ate and joined him and his wife, Lukas, and Tommy in front of the television. Ben started the recorder, and everyone settled in to watch the news reports.

"Friday was an historic day for the United States Senate when they allowed a civilian, Daniel Red Tears Patterson, a Navajo man from Arizona, to present a message to the floor, a message he said was from the Great Creator," the news reporter said.

Ben nudged Daniel.

"I didn't say that!" Daniel retorted to the TV, pointing with his hand.

"Relax, bro, just listen," Ben said.

Lukas grinned, and Daniel noticed that Jessica and Tommy were holding hands and sitting very close. He twisted his mouth for a second and then looked back at the TV.

"The Senate unanimously passed Resolution 14, an apology to the Native Americans that Senator Sam Brownback authored and has been presenting to the Senate since 2005," the reporter spoke confidently. "This day the resolution became a law. In fact, what adds to the unprecedented move is that it was immediately hand delivered to the president for his signature," she said as she walked toward the rotunda of the Senate building. "Normally, there is video from the Senate meetings, but we're told that the equipment malfunctioned when they tried to create a copy of the actual speech that was delivered by Daniel Patterson."

Ben nudged Daniel again.

"The Great Creator is holy, and that was a holy meeting," Lukas explained in Navajo.

Daniel nodded.

"We have Senator Brownback with us now. Senator, tell us what happened here today?"

"This is an apology to the Native Americans from the United States. It's an apology that attempts to start the reconciliation process. It doesn't end the wrongs, but it does acknowledge them," he said cordially. "It doesn't fix everything, but it starts the dialog. There is a deep root of bitterness for all that we, as a nation under government rule, have created in our Native American brothers and sisters from all the broken promises we've made over the years," he finished.

"Sir, what can you tell us about what actually transpired inside the Senate Chamber when Daniel Patterson spoke?"

"I really don't feel at liberty to give details, but what was delivered inside was something unusual, and it got the attention of the full Senate. I don't think they will forget their experience," he offered.

"Anything about what he said, even a hint?" she pressed.

"I'm sorry," the senator said. "That's all I can give you. Thank you," he said, and then he stepped back and walked away.

The reporter turned to the camera. "Well, there you have it, folks, some interesting secrecy happening here. I've heard from some of our affiliates and other reporters and news agencies that when they asked the same question of several different senators about what happened inside the chamber, none of them were able to speak. There were reports that when a few of them did try to give an answer, they seemed to be silenced by fits of coughing or dry mouth," she told her audience. "We'll go now to footage of the president signing this historic resolution."

The scene cut away to the president signing the resolution with Sam Brownback and the other ten senators who backed the resolution standing by his side. The president stood and shook his hand and both smiled for the camera.

Everyone in the room at Ben's house whooped except for Daniel, who sat quietly, looking at the screen. He received pats on the back from the guys and kisses on the cheek from his girls, but he didn't seem to notice.

Angel sat on her knees in front of him, hands on his knees. "Daniel, what's the matter?"

"He's been heard." He gave a small smile.

"That's a good thing," she assured.

"Red Tears, it is time to celebrate!" Ben said.

Daniel looked at him. "Will they walk it out?" he asked with concern.

"He is merciful. If they falter, he will speak again," Lukas assured him, and then he pulled him to his feet. "Come, we must worship the Great Creator for all he has done!"

"Can I add something to that reason for celebration?" Jessica with Tommy interrupted.

"Sure!" Ben said, and then he looked to Daniel.

"Of course," he said.

She and Tommy were still holding hands, and Angel held a grin that gave away that she was privy to this announcement.

"Dad, you better sit down," she told Daniel.

He narrowed his eyes at the two young people, having a pretty good idea about what they were going to say. He finally did, and Tommy stepped up to the plate.

He cleared his throat. "I asked Jessica to marry me, and she said yes!" he said excitedly.

Daniel stood and stepped up to Tommy. Daniel shook his hand and hugged him. "Congratulations! Well done." He grinned.

Daniel then turned to his daughter who was hugging Angel. She broke the hug and jumped at her dad. He twirled her around happily and then set her down and kissed her forehead. "You're not my little girl anymore. You've become a beautiful and noble woman," he said through tears.

Jessica wiped her tears and his away, smiling brightly. "Dad, I'll always be your little girl, but I'll keep the noble woman status, too," she told him.

Daniel released Jessica and turned to Angel, hugging and kissing her with a passion he was unashamed of. When he broke the kiss, he looked at her. "I owe you a trip to Hawaii."

Angel grinned. "That you do."

They hugged again, and the family went outside to call the clans together for a celebration of the Great Creator and his faithfulness.

EPILOGUE

2010

Senator Sam Brownback presented Senate Joint Resolution (SJR) 15 to Congress in 2005. It was politely sidelined, due to fear. The Government thought the Native Americans wanted recompense in the form of monetary compensation. While within the First Nations People there are individuals and groups who did want compensation, and rightly so, that was not what this resolution, requesting a national, public apology was about. Healing the heart of the nation must come first. The Government was still blind to the idea.

Every two years, the Congress changes "hands" and was numbered as such. A resolution was thus renumbered. In September 2009, the 111th Congress finally passed the Apology to the Native Americans: Senate Joint Resolution (SJR) 14. It had to be tacked onto another larger bill whose importance the Senate deemed greater. It was attached to the Defense Appropriations Bill. On December 15, 2009, it was then signed into law by the President of the United States. It was strongly suggested in the summary and language of SJR 14 that the president make a national, public apology. He had, after all, been made an honorary member of the Crow Nation. Would it then not be honorable to humble oneself and offer a confession and apology? So far, we see that apparently, it is not.

It is interesting to note the meanings of the numbers assigned to the resolution of Apology to the Native Americans. The number fifteen involves two numbers, one and five. One is unity, and five means grace. When added together, one plus five, we get the number six, which is the number for man. The whole number fifteen means divine acts wrought by God.

The number fourteen is two sevens. The number seven is the number of divine perfection and completion. Therefore, fourteen is a double portion of divine perfection and completion. Again, the one is unity and the number four stands for Jesus. The Great Creator is obviously behind this apology, and his heart's cry is that it is made with a true heart of repentance.

Some Native Americans have said that no words (as their experience with words have been that of lies) could fix what was done to them and to their ancestors. They say they want money to help with the pain they feel. They will never be healed unless they allow the bitterness to be removed by the Great Creator. It requires a humble heart and a desire to see reconciliation.

Yet, there are many more who want repentance, forgiveness, and reconciliation. There are *so* many more! This remnant of cultures and ethnic people groups will be the catalyst to keep the request before the Great Creator and before the president. It is a law he signed, after all. It is a spiritual law from God. It is our duty to stand on the wall, watching, praying, and standing ready to make the call, "One approaches with a white flag that is bathed in the blood of the Lamb. It is a message of repentance, forgiveness, and reconciliation! Open the gates and let him enter!"